Blessings

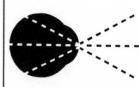

This Large Print Book carries the
Seal of Approval of N.A.V.H.

SOMMERFELD TRILOGY, BOOK 3

BLESSINGS

KIM VOGEL SAWYER

THORNDIKE PRESS

A part of Gale, Cengage Learning

GALE
CENGAGE Learning

Detroit • New York • San Francisco • New Haven, Conn • Waterville, Maine • London

GALE
CENGAGE Learning⁻

LIBRARY OF CONGRESS CATALOGING-IN-PUBLICATION DATA

Sawyer, Kim Vogel.
  Blessings / by Kim Vogel Sawyer.
    p. cm. — (Sommerfeld trilogy ; bk. 3)
  "Thorndike Press large print Christian romance."
  ISBN-13: 978-1-4104-1857-9 (hardcover : alk. paper)
  ISBN-10: 1-4104-1857-X (hardcover : alk. paper)
  1. Women college students—Fiction. 2. Mennonites—Fiction.
3. Family—Fiction. 4. Veterinarians—Fiction. 5. Large type books. I. Title.
PS3619.A97B54 2008
813'.6—dc22
                                       2009017230

Published in 2009 by arrangement with Barbour Publishing, Inc.

For Jacob Dean,
the unexpected blessing added to our
family. I know God has something
special planned for you, little one —
seek His face and heed His voice.
Joy will surely follow.

ACKNOWLEDGMENTS

When I count the blessings in my life, family tops the list: Mom, Daddy, Don, my dear daughters and precious grandsons. . . . Walking this pathway with your encouragement is a joy beyond description. Thanks, too, to my wonderful parents-in-law and the whole Sawyer clan — I'm so blessed to be a part of your family.

They say old friends are gold, and I am rich in the decades-long blessing of friendship with Kathy Henson, Phil Zielke, and Vicki Johansen. Thank you for your steadfast presence in my life.

Prayer support is crucial in any ministry, and so many lift my writing to the Father: Connie, Rose, Carla, Cynthia, Ramona, Kathy A., Don and Ann, Ernie, Ginny, Brother Ray, my "posse" members. . . . May God bless you as abundantly as you have blessed me.

Becky and the staff at Barbour: Thank you for the opportunity to bring Sommerfeld and its citizens to life. What a pleasure it has been!

Finally, and most importantly, thanks be to God, who blesses me beyond my deserving and uses me even in my failings. May any praise or glory be reflected directly back to You.

The blessing of the LORD,
it maketh rich,
and he addeth no sorrow with it.
PROVERBS 10:22

ONE

Trina Muller set the plates of hamburgers, grilled onions, and french fries in front of the booth's occupants. Straightening, she flipped the white ribbons of her cap behind her shoulders and formed an automatic smile. "Can I get you anything else?"

Even though she used her cheerful, attentive, I'm-here-to-meet-your-needs tone, her gaze drifted out the window. A row of cars drove by the café, headed south toward the highway. She stifled the sigh that rose in her chest.

"Ketchup and mustard, please," the man said.

With a nod, Trina turned from the table. Her tennis shoes squeaked against the tile floor — a familiar sound. She retrieved red and yellow squirt bottles from a small refrigerator in the corner of the dining room then carried them to the table. A glance out the window confirmed the last car had departed for Newton. The sigh escaped.

Forcing herself to look at the couple seated in the window booth, she said, "Enjoy your meal."

Trina made the rounds, coffeepot in hand. She carried on her normal banter, smiling, meeting the needs of the café's patrons, treating Mennonites and non-Mennonites with equal affability. But her feet felt leaden and her smile stiff. Her heart simply was not in the task.

Right now her friends — including Graham — were on their way to the skating rink for an evening of fun and relaxation. But as usual, Trina was stuck in the café. Waiting tables. Washing dishes. Honoring Mama and Dad like the good girl she'd always been — the good girl she had always wanted to be. When had this uncomfortable resentment started? And how could she set it aside and go back to being the cheerful, obedient Trina?

Or did she really want to be that Trina anymore?

She wrung out a soapy cloth and used it to scrub a table clean, pocketing the single bill and coins left behind to thank her for her service. She fingered the coins in her apron pocket, thinking about the growing savings account at the bank in McPherson.

In the six years she'd worked at the café — first for the original owner, Lisbeth Koeppler, then for Lisbeth's heirs, and now for her own mother — she had rarely spent the money she earned.

Since she and Graham began openly courting, he paid for the occasional dinners out and their skating expeditions. According to Mama, a girl needed only so many dresses — an overstuffed wardrobe was prideful. Books, her main source of amusement, were reasonable when purchased from the used-books shelf at the bookstore she and her friends patronized in Newton. Of course, her parents might disapprove of a few of the titles she'd chosen, but she had reasons for buying what she did. And even with the number of book purchases, the account steadily grew.

Her hand paused on the table's glossy surface; her lips sucked in. Surely, she had enough for one year. Maybe a year and a half. A good start, certainly. If only —

"Trina?"

Her mother's voice jarred her out of her thoughts. She trotted to the doorway between the kitchen and dining room where Mama stood. "Yes?"

"I see some empty plates on tables. Have you asked if people want their checks?"

Although Mama kept her voice low, disapproval came through the tone.

Trina felt heat fill her cheeks. "I'll do it now."

"Good." Mama pursed her lips, her brows low. "This daydreaming must stop, Trina. Stay focused on your work."

Trina nodded. A shoddy workman displeased the Lord — Trina knew this well. Guilt propelled her across the tiled floor to a table Mama had pointed out. "I'm sorry for the delay. Did you save room for pie this evening? We have a lovely lemon meringue made from scratch."

She went through the normal routine of slipping the check onto the table and clearing the dishes, but despite her efforts to remain on task, her thoughts drifted again. Maybe she knew these tasks too well. The familiar routine offered no challenge, no true problem-solving. Not like —

The door to the café burst open, bringing in a flow of warm evening air. Her cousin Andrew Braun rushed toward her. He left his bill cap in place over his dark hair, a clue that something was amiss. The fine hairs on the back of Trina's neck prickled.

"Trina, can you come out to the house? It's Regen — his leg. I tried calling Dr. Groening, but his wife said he's out. She'll

14

give him the message, but I don't know how long he'll be."

Trina untied her apron and slipped it over her head, careful to avoid dislodging her cap. "Of course I'll come." Regen, the sorrel quarter horse Andrew had purchased for his wife's wedding gift, was more pet than working animal, since Andrew didn't farm. But they relied on him to pull the vintage carriage Livvy's grandparents had bequeathed to her, giving rides to visitors to Sommerfeld every Saturday afternoon and many summer evenings. "Livvy must be beside herself."

"She's worried," Andrew confirmed, his expression grim. He lowered his voice. "Trina, it doesn't look good."

Trina's heart pounded. Throwing the apron behind the counter that held the cash register, she darted into the kitchen. "Mama, Andrew is here. He needs me to go with him — Livvy's horse was hurt."

Trina watched her mother's gaze lift to the clock on the wall before giving a nod of approval. "Go ahead. It's only an hour to closing time. I'll call Tony and have him come help me clean up."

Even before her mother had finished speaking, Trina caught Andrew's arm and hurried him out of the café. They climbed into his pickup, which waited at the curb with its engine rumbling. Andrew pulled into the street and headed east.

"What happened?" Trina asked. Wind coursed through the open window, tossing the string ties of her cap. She caught the ribbons and held them beneath her chin.

He snatched off his cap, threw it onto the seat between them, and ran his hand over his short hair. "Livvy went into the corral to throw Regen some hay. She leaned the pitchfork against the fence while she went to drag the hose out to the corral and fill the water tank, and somehow the horse caught his foot between the tines of the fork. She heard a pop, and he wouldn't put his weight on the leg." He grimaced. "She stayed out with him until I came home rather than calling the vet, and by the time I got there, the cannon on the injured leg had swelled up like a balloon. It looks bad."

A pop could mean tendon or ligament damage or a misplaced knee. Trina immediately began running through a list of possible treatments. "How long ago did he injure himself?"

"At least two hours." He shot her a brief, grateful glance. "I'm glad you were there. I was afraid you might have gone skating."

Her mother had insisted Trina stay at the

café and work rather than going to the skating rink with the other community young people. Sometimes on skating nights, a teenage member of the fellowship, Kelly Dick, came in to help so Trina could have the evening off, but this time Mama had said no. Although both Graham and Trina had experienced frustration at her refusal to let Trina go, now relief washed over Trina. *Thank You, Lord, that I was here. . . .*

Andrew barely slowed to make the final turn into his long driveway. Trina grabbed the dash to keep from tipping sideways. Dust swirled alongside the truck and wafted through the window, making her sneeze. He pulled up beside the barn and killed the engine.

Trina hopped out, ducked between the crossbars of the fence, and ran to where Livvy stood, petting the length of Regen's nose. Tears of grief and worry rained down Livvy's pale cheeks. Her work dress and apron looked sodden and soiled, giving evidence of her long vigil in the summer sun and gusting wind. The horse tapped the shoe of his injured leg in the dirt and released soft snorts of distress, but he made no effort to move away from his mistress. Trina dropped to her knees in front of the powerful animal and ran her hands down

17

his leg. She didn't need to feel the swelling to know it was there. The horse's leg bulged midway between his knee and pastern on his right foreleg.

"Must've torn a ligament," she muttered. Rising, she glanced at Livvy's frantic face and turned to Andrew. "Get me some burlap, two or three bags of frozen corn, and about three yards of elastic."

Without a question, Andrew spun on his boot heel and jogged toward the house.

"Livvy, can you lead Regen to the barn?" Trina gentled her voice when speaking to her cousin's wife. "He'll be more comfortable in there."

"Are you sure we should let him walk on it?"

Trina drew in a slow breath and held it. She wasn't sure putting pressure on it was a good idea, but she knew they couldn't leave the poor animal outside. The summer heat was sweltering during the day — he'd be better off in the barn, where he'd have shade and protection. Her breath whooshed out with her emphatic nod. "I think it's best."

Livvy nodded. Her arm curled around the underside of Regen's jaw, she crooned, "C'mon, pretty boy. Come with me. . . ." Slowly, she led the limping animal into the

18

barn. Trina trailed behind, watching Regen's legs.

Inside the barn, Livvy led Regen to his stall. "Should I let him lie down?"

"No. I need him up to —"

Andrew trotted in, his arms full. He plopped two clear plastic bags of home-grown frozen corn and a snarl of one-inch-wide elastic at Trina's feet. "Here you go, Trina — corn and elastic." Pressing a soft bundle of worn cloth into her hands, he added, "And one of Livvy's aprons so you don't get your dress all dirty. I've got burlap in the storeroom. Hang on." He dashed toward the back of the barn.

Trina tied the apron in place while Livvy sent her a puzzled look. "What are you going to do with the corn?"

Trina knelt and began to untangle the elastic. "It'll stay cold, which makes it a good compress. But I need to protect his leg with the burlap first so it isn't too cold against his skin. The elastic will hold it in place, and as the swelling goes down, it will continue to hold the compress against his leg."

Livvy shook her head, stroking Regen's neck and forehead. "I hope it works."

"Me, too."

Andrew trotted to Trina's side, a bulky,

19

rolled burlap bag in his hands. She squinted up at him. "Can you help me?"

Andrew crouched on the other side of Regen's leg. "What do you want me to do?"

"Wrap the burlap around his leg first, to provide some protection from the cold corn, but don't make it too tight." Andrew held the coarse fabric in place while Trina grabbed the bags of corn. Although Regen nosed the back of Trina's head, blowing air down the back of her neck, he remained still under their ministrations. She placed one bag on either side of Regen's leg. "Okay, wrap the burlap around the corn now." As Andrew followed her directions, she slipped her hands free. "Hold it." Andrew kept the burlap and corn from slipping. Trina wrapped the elastic around several times and then tied it in place.

Andrew moved out of the way as she felt around the bulky compress, frowning. It needed to be tight enough to hold but not so tight it cut off circulation. Satisfied the compress would hold without hurting the animal, she sank back in the hay and looked up at Livvy. "You've been standing in the corral for quite a while. Why don't you go in and get a drink?"

Livvy's arms crept around the horse's neck. "I don't want to leave him."

"I'll stay right here, and so will Andrew," Trina promised. "If you'd call the café and let Mama know I'll be out here the rest of the evening, I'd appreciate it, too."

Livvy pursed her lips, her brow furrowing, but she nodded. "All right. But I'll be back soon." She gave Regen another loving stroke from his forehead to his nose before turning away.

Andrew watched his wife until she exited the barn. Then he faced Trina. "Do you think the horse will be all right? I don't know how she'd take it if we had to —"

"You won't have to put him down." Trina squeezed her cousin's arm. "It isn't bad enough for that. But . . ." She paused, swallowing. "It'll be a long time before he can do any work, Andrew. If he's torn a ligament, it'll take months of healing."

"Well, even though we'll miss the income those carriage rides bring in, I won't complain. Not as long as he'll be okay again." A slight smile curved his lips. "I'll never forget when I brought him home. It was raining cats and dogs, and Livvy got drenched to the skin, but she stood outside in the downpour and kept stroking his nose and talking to him. That's why she chose *Regensturm* for his name, you know — in honor of the rainstorm." Andrew sighed. "Liv

21

looks at this horse like a child."

Trina smiled, smoothing her skirt over her knees to protect her bare skin from the scratchy hay. "She'll quit that once you have children to spoil." She knew Livvy was seeing a special doctor in Wichita for the purpose of having a baby.

"I suppose . . ."

"In the meantime, we'll take good care of Regen so there won't be permanent damage." She pushed to her feet. "While we wait for Dr. Groening, let's get some rigging set up to get the weight off Regen's leg."

Andrew rose. "What do you suggest? Rope would cut into his skin, I would think."

After a brief discussion, they decided a loop of sturdy gabardine, which Livvy had purchased for quilt backing, slung beneath the horse's belly and over the crossbeam, would provide enough support without chafing his skin. When Andrew returned with the fabric, Livvy trailed him back to the barn. Trina gave her the task of talking to Regen and rubbing his nose to keep him calm.

After a half hour of trial and error, experimenting with fabric, rope, and pulleys, they finally managed to provide a means of support for Regen. They stood back, hands on hips, looking at the animal to see if he'd be okay. He whickered softly, but he stopped tapping the sore leg against the ground.

Trina smiled. "I think that's done the trick." She pointed. "He's not trying to stamp, so it must not be bothering him as much."

"Good." Andrew wiped his brow, whistling through his teeth. "That was a chore!"

"But worth it," Livvy said, stepping forward to caress the horse's jaw. "I can tell it's helped him." The woman and horse rubbed noses.

Trina, watching Livvy with Regen, felt a rush of satisfaction. Her hour with Regen had given her more pleasure than her years of waitress work. If only she could spend all of her days helping animals.

The sound of a vehicle pulling into the yard captured their attention. Andrew headed for the barn's wide door. "That's probably Dr. Groening. I'll bring him in."

Trina linked her fingers together and waited anxiously as Dr. Groening examined Regen's leg and ran his hand under the cloth loop. Finally, he turned and put his hand on Trina's shoulder. "You've done everything exactly right here. Bringing the swelling down and getting the pressure off the leg is just what I would have prescribed."

Trina nearly wilted with relief. "Oh, thank

you! I'd never want to do anything harmful to an animal."

His fingers squeezed gently before slipping away. "I know." The older man's thick gray brows lowered. "You have an innate ability, young lady."

"Well . . ." Trina crunched her lips into a grimace. "I got the idea from a book I bought on horse care." It had been one of the pricier of her purchases, but the book, with its veterinary guide, was a wealth of information.

"So you're still studying," the doctor said, lowering his tone to a near whisper.

Trina nodded. The string ties of her cap tickled her chin, reminding her of the futility of her study. Never, never, never would Mama and Dad allow her to get the schooling she'd need to be a veterinarian. Not as long as she wore her Mennonite cap.

Two

The sympathy in Dr. Groening's eyes communicated his understanding of Trina's dilemma. Three years ago, she had confided her interest in animal care to the kindly veterinarian from Lehigh and asked how she could become an animal doctor. His brief explanation — a college degree — had crushed her.

Attending college was out of the question. She knew that. But she had finally decided she could study on her own, learn for her own interest, and maybe do some good in her community. What she'd just done for Regen proved to her that all her reading hadn't been a waste of time.

Offering the doctor a weak smile, she nodded. "I buy as many books as I can find at the store in Newton."

"And study on your own . . ." Dr. Groening shook his head, his eyes sad.

"It's better than nothing." Trina forced a

light tone, but resentment pressed at her breast. Why couldn't she go to college and become a veterinarian? It wasn't fair!

"Well," Dr. Groening said, clapping his palms together and turning to Andrew and Livvy, "the work you started here won't end soon. You'll have to keep applying cold compresses to the leg — probably through the night — and then each time the swelling comes up again." He stepped forward and patted the horse's neck. "This big boy won't be doing any work for a while, either. You'll need to keep him still for at least two weeks, then only gentle exercise — walking, no trotting or running — for another two to three months."

"It's that bad?" Livvy clasped Andrew's hand. Her wide eyes brimmed with tears.

"It could be worse," the doctor said. "But the treatment you started here helped a lot. Be grateful." He gave the horse's broad neck one more pat and turned to Trina. "Will you be staying?"

Trina nodded. Her parents would have to understand.

"Then he's in good hands," Dr. Groening said to Andrew and Livvy. "I'll be back tomorrow afternoon to check on him. Call if something changes. In the meantime, Trina, I'll leave you some reusable cold packs you can use in place of the corn." He grinned. "You'll clear out the freezer in no time using corn, but it was a perfect choice in a pinch."

Trina followed the doctor to his pickup.

He opened a metal box in the truck's bed and pulled out four rectangular, plastic-covered cold packs. "Alternate these between the freezer and Regen's leg. They're good for three hours before they need to be traded out."

"I will. And thanks again, Dr. Groening."

"You're welcome, Trina." He opened his truck door then paused and sent her a speculative look. "You still work in your mother's café?"

"Yes, sir."

"Do you ever think about doing something else?"

All the time. She lifted her shoulders in a shrug.

He smiled, seeming to understand her silence. "Well, if you ever decide on a change, I could use an assistant at the clinic. My helper heads off to college this fall, and he's decided to take the summer off to play. I need to replace him. You'd learn a lot."

Trina's heart pounded. She licked her lips. "Thanks, Dr. Groening. I'll — I'll give it some thought."

"Good." He hopped into his pickup and closed the door. With a wave of his hand out the open window, he pulled away.

Trina watched the truck head down the driveway, her heart thudding with desire to run, jump into the bed of that truck, and learn everything she could from the aging doctor.

Graham Ortmann slammed the car's back door closed and leaned against his friend's blue sedan. Laughter floated across the calm, late-evening breeze as the other young people from Sommerfeld stepped out of their vehicles to say good-bye to the group before heading to their respective homes.

"You want me to drop you off at your place, Graham?" Walt asked.

Graham shook his head, gesturing with his thumb toward the café, where lights still glowed behind the windows even though it was past closing time. "Looks to me like Mrs. Muller and Trina are still cleaning up. I'll head over there and see if Mrs. Muller will let me walk Trina home."

Walt snorted. "Good luck. The Mullers keep Trina tied to her mother's apron strings."

"I know." Most of the Old Order Mennonite parents were protective, but Troy and

Deborah Muller carried it to the extreme.

"Might be easier to walk Susan or Darcy home instead," Walt suggested, a grin creasing his face. "They'd be willing, I'm sure."

Graham glanced across the car's hood. The two young women Walt referenced stood on the sidewalk in front of Koeppler's Feed and Seed, their capped heads close together. Even with the evening shadows limiting his sight, he knew they were watching him. He sighed and turned back to Walt.

"It might be easier to court another girl, but I don't want another girl. Trina's the only one for me." He'd spent more than a year getting up his nerve to ask Trina's parents for permission to spend time with her. Their six months of visits, walks, singings at local homes, and skating parties convinced him that he and Trina were a perfect match. As soon as she turned twenty — only six more months — they would publish their relationship and plan a wedding. Or maybe they could be published now. Nineteen wasn't too young. His heart picked up its tempo at the thought.

"Well, good luck to you." Walt gave Graham's shoulder a hearty smack. He chuckled softly. "I think you'll need it."

Graham pushed off from the car and headed down the sidewalk toward the café.

He frowned as he thought of Walt's words. He didn't need luck. Luck was for worldly people — people who lacked faith. Graham had prayed about seeking a wife, and he knew Trina was the right choice.

Easily the cutest girl in the fellowship with her spattering of freckles and sweetly up-turned nose, she exuded an innocence and spark for life that made a person happy just to be near her. He'd never met anyone with a more positive attitude. His feet sped up of their own volition as eagerness to see her, talk to her, steal a few minutes of her time urged him forward.

The café door was locked, but when he tapped on the glass, Trina's younger brother, Tony, trotted from the kitchen and unlocked it. "Hi, Graham. How was the skating?"

"Fun." Graham limited his reply. Tony, at fifteen, was too young for the skating par-ties, but in another couple of years, he'd be able to join the group. No sense in getting the boy stirred up at what he was missing. He followed Tony to the kitchen. "I came to see if I could walk Trina home."

Mrs. Muller turned from the stove, a drip-ping cloth in her hand. "Trina isn't here, Graham. Andrew stopped by a couple of hours ago and took her to the farm. Livvy's horse was injured somehow. Livvy called again about an hour ago and said Trina would be staying all night."

Even though disappointment struck, Graham's heart swelled with pride. Of course, Trina would go if an animal needed her. Trina's compassionate concern for all creatures was just another reason he loved her so much. "I hope the horse will be all right."

Mrs. Muller turned back to the stove. "I don't know. Livvy said it was a bad injury, but they were doing what they could."

Graham scratched his chin, wondering if he should drive out and check on Trina. Her cousin would be there to provide chaperonage, so it wouldn't be indecent. He lifted his gaze and found Mrs. Muller watching him with narrowed eyes. He felt a blush building, certain she read his thoughts.

He backed toward the kitchen door. "Well, I'll let you finish up, then. Tell Trina I stopped by, please."

"I will." Mrs. Muller put the scrub rag to work.

Graham waved to Tony then headed out of the café. Outside, he stood for a moment, looking at the glittering stars and debating with himself. He'd had very little time with Trina this week, and he missed her. At the other end of the block, two cars remained

in front of Koeppler's Feed and Seed —
Walt was still there. Walt could drive Graham home, where he could get his own car
and head out to Andrew and Livvy's place.
Just to say hi and make sure the horse was
doing okay.

Decision made, he broke into a jog. "Walt!
Hey — I need a ride!"

The slam of a car door jolted Trina from
dozing. She blinked, looking around the
dusky barn. The lantern Andrew had hung
from a nail on the stall post glowed softly,
but outside the window, stars twinkled in a
velvety sky. It was much too late for visitors.
Maybe she'd imagined the car door —
maybe she'd been dreaming.

Regen bounced his head, snorting softly.
Livvy sat up from her nest in the hay and
nudged Andrew. "Somebody's here." He
yawned and pushed to his feet.

While Andrew went to check, Trina tossed
aside the light blanket she'd used to cover
herself. She crawled forward a few feet and
pressed the compress on Regen's leg. The
horse blew, but he didn't try to move his
foot. "Good boy, Regen," she praised, gently
pressing the compress. Certain it was still
cold enough and well secured, she straightened to her feet and nuzzled the horse.

"Trina?" Andrew stood at the edge of the stall. Someone stood behind him — a man, judging by his attire — but he stood in Andrew's shadow, making it impossible to identify him.

"Dr. Groening?" she asked.

"No, it's me, Trina."

Trina's heart did a little somersault. She stumbled forward a few steps, squinting until she made out Graham's crooked smile. "How did you know I was out here?" She longed to reach for him, take his hands, but instead she tangled her hands in the folds of her borrowed apron.

"I stopped by the café. Your mom said you were here."

"Why did you come out?"

"I wanted to make sure the horse was okay."

Andrew took a sideways step away from the couple and held his hand to Livvy. "Let's go in and see if there's any more coffee in the pot."

Livvy flicked a quick glance at Trina and Graham. An understanding smile curved her lips, and she nodded.

Trina watched her cousin and his wife stride from the barn, gratitude filling her. Rarely did she and Graham have an uninterrupted minute alone. Andrew and Livvy had just given them a gift. She skipped forward, closing the distance between her and Graham. She was close enough for him to touch her if he wanted to.

His hands remained appropriately in his pants pockets, but his smile caressed her. "So is the horse going to be okay?" The question was completely impersonal, yet his tone managed to convey deep feeling.

"I hope so." Her words came out on a breathy sigh. "It'll be a long time before he's able to work, but we're praying the damage will heal."

Graham's swallow sounded loud in the peaceful barn. "But you need to stay all night?"

"Yes. The cold compresses must be changed every three hours. So Andrew and I are taking turns."

Graham nodded. For long moments neither spoke. Then Graham cleared his throat. "I missed you at the skating tonight."

Trina's heart twisted. "I know. I'm sorry. Mama insisted I work. But it's probably best since Regen needed me." She moved to the horse and stroked his neck, her gaze on Graham. "Dr. Groening said I did everything right for him." Although she knew pride was a sin, she couldn't stop the swell of satisfaction that filled her when she remembered the doctor's praise for her ministrations to the animal. She blurted, "He said I could work for him, if I wanted to."

Graham stepped forward and cupped the horse's nose. "Instead of the café?"

Trina nodded. "I could learn so much, spending time with him! And maybe —" She lowered her gaze. There was no sense in getting her hopes up. "Of course, Mama probably wouldn't let me."

Graham spoke, his breath brushing her cheek. "Talk to your folks. Maybe they'd say yes. You won't know until you try."

Raising her head slowly, she met Graham's tender gaze. She wished she possessed hope, but she knew her parents too well. They'd never approve it. Lehigh, although less than ten miles down the road, was too far away. "They'd say no. Mama would say she needs me in the café. And Dad would have to drive me to Lehigh every day since I haven't got my license."

"Well, maybe it's time for you to learn to drive," Graham said, "and for your mom to think about getting some other help. Because you won't be available to her at the café forever."

Her heart lurched. Although Graham had never uttered the word *marriage,* she knew

35

his attentiveness indicated his interest. She also knew she wasn't averse to the idea. No other boy in the fellowship made her heart clop harder than the hooves of a runaway horse. She jerked her gaze downward and watched Graham's hands gently stroke Regen's soft nose. Her throat felt dry, and she swallowed hard. She chose an innocuous subject. "But Dad says he doesn't have time to teach me to drive."

"I can teach you."

"And Mama . . . she depends on me."

"There are other dependable girls in town."

His soft rebuttals to her arguments made something flutter through her middle. She peeked at him out of the corner of her eye. "You'd really teach me to drive?" *Dad would never approve it.*

He shrugged, grinning. "Sure. And I'll take you to Lehigh myself until you learn, if you start working for the vet."

Mama will never let me leave the café. "But I don't have a car." She waited for his response.

He opened his mouth, but Andrew and Livvy came in. Andrew carried a thermos jug, and Livvy held up four mugs. Andrew said, "Livvy fixed a fresh pot, so we can all have some."

Graham stepped well away from the horse, and Trina took the mug Livvy offered. Trina locked gazes with Graham, offering a smile she hoped communicated her regret for their interruption. His slow wink let her know he felt the same way. Trina experienced a prick of conscience — desiring to be alone with Graham was sinful. It could lead to trouble. Just as pursuing her desire to gain a license to treat animals would create problems.

She stifled a groan that pressed at the back of her throat. *God, why does everything I want seem to be wrong?*

THREE

Bright, early morning sun streaming through the barn's window wakened Trina. She stretched and yawned, opening her eyes by increments. When she could focus, her first sight was Regen, staring at her with wide, unblinking brown eyes.

She laughed. "Good morning, pretty boy." Crawling across the hay, she removed the compress and checked his leg. A smile grew on her face. "The swelling's way down." She stood and gave the horse a pat. "You'll be okay, big fella. It will just take time."

The barn door opened, and Andrew strode in with a cup of coffee in his hand. "Oh, you're awake. I was just going to get you up and take you into town." His gaze dropped to Regen's leg. "It looks a lot better, doesn't it?"

"Better, yes, but there's still some swelling. Dr. Groening said to keep the compresses on there until it was completely gone." She leaned over and scooped up the compress she'd removed. "I'll get a fresh one for him and put this one in the freezer."

Andrew caught her arm as she went to pass him. "Trina, your mom called. She needs you in the café."

Trina resisted rolling her eyes, knowing it was a disrespectful response, but it took great control. "I'll call her and tell her to get Kelly."

"She said Kelly is already there, helping her open up, but she needs you, too. With the farmers' market opening this weekend, she's overrun with customers."

Trina thrust out her jaw. "I need to take care of Regen."

Andrew's fingers pressed gently on her arm. "Livvy and I can put compresses on Regen's leg as well as you can, and I promise to call the café if something changes." Although his tone carried no reprimand, Trina knew he wanted her to obey Mama's direction.

She sighed. Her night with little sleep had left her droopy and out of sorts. Working in the café — especially on Saturday, the busiest day of the week even without the additional customers brought in by the farmers' market — would be less than pleasant. But she didn't have a choice. She must honor her parents. "All right. But take me home, not to the café — I've got to clean up."

He grinned. "I agree with that. You smell like the barn."

While he drove her back to town, she slurped the coffee he'd brought out. The hot, strong brew helped bring her to life. The drive was short — Andrew and Livvy lived little more than a mile outside of Sommerfeld on a small, four-acre plot surrounded by corn and alfalfa fields. In no time, Andrew pulled up in front of her parents' home. She set the empty coffee cup on the seat and leaned over to bestow a hug.

"Thanks for coming to get me when Regen got hurt." Her throat felt tight, and she swallowed. "It meant a lot to me, that you trusted me with him."

Andrew gave her back a pat before setting her aside. "There's no one I'd trust more."

Trina ducked her head, a huge sigh lifting her shoulders.

"Go get cleaned up," Andrew ordered in a gruff, big-brother tone, a mock scowl creasing his face. "Then march yourself down to that café and let your mother know you want to make a job change."

Trina stared at him.

His scowl turned into an impish grin. "I

40

heard Dr. Groening mention the job at his clinic. You want to do it, don't you?"

Trina blew out a long breath. "More than anything. I wish —"

Andrew pinched her chin, his familiar gesture of affection. "Don't wish. Pray. If it's God's will, your parents will come around."

Trina knew Andrew spoke from experience. Although his father and brothers were farmers, Andrew spent his days working in the stained-glass art studio owned by Beth Quinn McCauley. At first, his father had opposed Andrew's desire to be an artist, but over time, he had released his antagonism and instead offered his blessing.

If only Mama and Dad would give in, like Uncle Al.

Andrew interrupted her thoughts. "Talk to your mother, Trina, and *pray.*" He gave her chin one more gentle pinch. "God can work things out."

"Thanks, Andrew." Trina bounded out of the truck and headed inside. After a bath and change of clothes, she felt more prepared to face the day. But by the time she reached the café, things were bustling, and she had no opportunity to talk to her mother. As the day dragged on, with an abundance of out-of-town patrons as well as the usual Sommerfeld residents taking advantage of Deborah Muller's Saturday specials, Trina's energy lagged, and her frustration grew. Even with her brother, Tony, and Kelly Dick helping, there was never a minute to sit and relax, let alone tell her mother about Dr. Groening's job opening.

She thought the last customers would never leave, but when they finally did, she still faced a mountain of work. Heaving a sigh, she filled the mop bucket and grabbed the mop, but then she stood, leaning on it, her eyes closed. Someone tapped her shoulder. Opening her eyes, she found Kelly grinning at her.

"Do you want me to mop?"

Trina chuckled, keeping her hands wrapped around the handle and her cheek pressed to her fist. "If you take the mop, I'll probably fall down."

Kelly laughed. "You've been dragging all day."

From the stove, Mama snorted. "Because she was out all night instead of sleeping."

Kelly's eyebrows shot up.

"My cousin's horse got hurt. I spent the night putting cold compresses on his leg." Trina maintained an even tone, although she wanted to snap at her mother. "So I didn't get much sleep, but the horse was much better this morning."

"That's good." Kelly glanced back and forth between the two Muller women, who glared across the floor at each other. She took a hesitant step toward the dishwasher. "Well, if you're going to mop, I guess I'll . . ." She waved her hand, indicating the stack of dishes.

"That's fine, Kelly. You've put in a good day already," Mama said. "You go ahead and go home." She turned toward the dining-room doorway and called, "Tony?"

Tony immediately appeared in the opening between the dining room and kitchen.

"Are you finished out there?"

"The money is in the bank envelope, the menus are stacked, the tables are clean," Tony listed, holding up his fingers and ticking off the accomplished tasks, "and the salt and pepper shakers are full. I haven't checked the napkin dispensers, though."

Mama nodded. "I'll take care of that. You walk Kelly home; then you can go home, too."

Trina nearly wilted, tiredness bringing the sting of tears behind her nose. How she wished to be released of the duties! But of course Mama would let the youngsters go. Since Trina was considered an adult, more was expected of her than of Tony and Kelly.

The moment the two younger teenagers headed out the back door, Mama pointed at the mop. "Let's finish up so we can leave, too." She began transferring dirty dishes from the cart to a washing tray.

With a sigh, Trina pushed the mop across the floor. Normally she took pleasure in watching the mop strings bunch and straighten with each push and pull, seeing the grime replaced by a shiny clean surface. But today, she just wanted to finish and be done. For good.

Her mind drifted to the edge of town, to Andrew's barn, where Regen rested his injured leg. She wondered what Dr. Groening had said when he visited as he'd promised. She hoped he was pleased with the decrease in swelling and had given Livvy encouraging words concerning Regen's future ability to pull the carriage. She'd heard a few café patrons mention their disappointment that no rides were available today. Andrew might need to borrow a horse from one of his brothers so they could still offer the carriage rides.

With the thought of Andrew came the reminder of his advice to talk to her mother about her desire to work for Dr. Groening. She glanced across the kitchen at her mother, whose hands moved steadily between the cart and tray. Busy hands. Mama had always had busy hands. Idle hands were the devil's workshop, she always said, which is why Trina and Tony had been encouraged to find jobs when their school years were complete.

Trina stifled a snort of frustration. As soon as Tony had finished the ninth grade, he chose to work for an Amish farmer who lived a few miles outside of Sommerfeld, and he drove himself there each day in an old pickup truck their Uncle Henry had fixed up. But Trina hadn't been given a choice. The day after her thirteenth birthday, Mama had marched her into the café and asked Miss Lisbeth Koeppler if she could use Trina's help after school and on weekends. Then when she finished her schooling, she automatically began working full-time at the café. Trina had grown to love Miss Koeppler, and she didn't regret the time she'd spent with the dear old woman, but now that Mama owned the café, Trina's help seemed to be expected.

Giving the mop bucket a firm push with the mop head, she propelled it across the floor to the utility sink. She watched the dirty water go down the drain, feeling as though her dreams went with it. She was nineteen already. Her folks — and Graham — would expect her to become a wife and a mother before too long. When would she be allowed to do what she wanted to do rather than what everyone else wanted her to do? The unfulfilled desires rose up strong enough to choke her.

Spinning from the sink, she raised her voice and called, "Mama? Can we talk?"

Mama shoved the last tray into the dishwasher, closed the door, and flipped the switch. The roar of running water echoed throughout the kitchen. "At home, Trina. Let's finish up here without delays, please."

Trina clamped her lips together and nodded. Might be better to wait until she was home and could talk to both parents at once, anyway. Even though Dad was strict, he was usually more reasonable than Mama. She headed to the dining room to refill the napkin dispensers.

When Trina and her mother reached their home, the sky was fully dark. Dad sat in the living room in an overstuffed chair shaped like his bulky form, a newspaper in his hands. He set the paper aside when they entered. "Ah, you're home."

Trina glanced at the ticking clock on the wall. With worship service in the morning, normally the family went to bed early on

Saturday nights. Trina fully expected her mother to give her customary order — "Off to bed now. Service tomorrow." But she surprised Trina by sinking onto the sofa and patting the seat beside her. "All right. What did you want to talk about?"

Encouraged by her mother's apparent openness, Trina scurried to the sofa and sat, turning her body slightly to face both parents. They looked at her expectantly, and Trina offered a quick, silent prayer. *Let them say yes, Lord, please. . . .*

"Yesterday when I went out to Andrew's to help with Regen —"

"Oh, Trina," Mama cut in, sighing, "if it's about the horse, can it wait until tomorrow? I'm tired."

Trina released a little grunt of displeasure. "Mama, please, let me finish. It isn't about the horse."

Mama's eyebrows came together briefly, but she remained silent.

Turning her gaze to her father, Trina continued. "When I was helping with Regen, Dr. Groening came out. He said I did a good job getting the horse stabilized. He said I have an innate ability with animal care, and" — she took a deep breath, her gaze flitting briefly to her mother's stern face — "he offered me a job at his clinic."

47

Mama said, "You already have a job." She started to rise.

Dad leaned forward, putting out his hand. "Wait, Deborah." He looked at his daughter. "What kind of job?"

Trina faced Dad, ignoring Mama's pursed lips. "He didn't exactly say, but I would imagine I'd be helping with the animals — cleaning up after surgery and assisting during exams. Really learning how to help them when they're hurt."

Dad frowned at her. "And you'd like that?"

To her embarrassment, tears sprang into her eyes. The desire to follow her childhood dream of caring for animals welled up and filled her, and it was all she could do to keep from begging her parents for this chance. But she swallowed hard and nodded.

Dad's stern countenance softened with a gentle smile. "Ever since you were a little girl, you've brought home hurt animals and nursed them. I understand why you want to work with Dr. Groening." He propped his elbow on the chair arm, cupping his chin. "But Lehigh is too far to walk, Trina, and you don't drive."

"I could learn. Graham said he'd teach me."

Mama and Dad exchanged quick glances.

"You've asked Graham to teach you to drive?" Mama's voice was sharp.

Trina felt heat rush to her cheeks. "I didn't ask. He just offered."

"A kind gesture, but it isn't his responsibility," Dad said.

Mama cut in. "I've never learned to drive, and I do just fine."

"But you work right here in town, Mama — just blocks from home. If I —"

"I depend on you to help in the café." Mama glared at Trina, daring her to contradict her.

Trina clasped her hands together in her lap. "I know you depend on me to help in the café, Mama, but now that it's summer, there are other girls who could work there. Some, like Kelly Dick, are finished with school now for good, so maybe they'd like an every-day job. Someone else could wait tables and mop the floors. It doesn't have to be me."

Mama opened her mouth, but Dad put his hand on her knee, silencing her. He looked at Trina. "Your mother and I will discuss this, Trina. I've known Josiah Groening most of my life, and I trust him as an employer for one of my children. But there are several things that would need to be worked out for you to work in Lehigh."

"But, Troy — ," Mama started.

Dad hushed her with a look. "The girl is nineteen already, Deborah. She'll be on her own before long. She might as well explore a little bit before becoming responsible for her own home. And better she explore under the supervision of someone we approve."

Mama's lips nearly disappeared, she pinched them so tightly together.

Trina gave her father a brief hug. "Thank you, Dad."

"We'll talk more tomorrow. To bed now. We have service in the morning."

Trina hurried off, but sleep didn't come quickly. Through the bedroom wall, the mumble of her parents' voices — Mama's angry, Dad's frustrated — kept her from drifting off. Two emotions warred within Trina's heart — guilt for creating conflict between her parents and hope that they would say yes to her request.

FOUR

After Sunday morning service, the members of the fellowship mingled in the churchyard beneath the summer sun, visiting. Graham scanned the grounds, seeking Trina. When he spotted her with Andrew and Livvy, he jogged over and joined them.

Trina's smile of welcome lit her eyes. The tawny specks of gold in her brown irises picked up a hint of lavender from her dress of bold purple — a royal color that suited her somehow. Graham wished he could slip his arm around her waist and draw her near, the way Andrew did with Livvy. But that would certainly start the tongues wagging! Instead, he greeted Andrew and Livvy first then turned to Trina. "Do you have plans for lunch?"

Trina raised her hand to shield her eyes from the sun. Her squint wrinkled her nose. "Mama invited Uncle Henry and Aunt Marie and their twins for lunch."

Graham stifled a groan. Trina would probably be expected to help serve at her own table. Henry and Marie Braun had twins a little over two years old, so Marie would be taking care of the toddlers and wouldn't be much help.

"Why do you ask?"

Graham quirked his lips into a grin. "Mom said you could join us, if you were free."

Trina's mouth formed a perfect O. "I'd like that! Let me ask Mama." She scampered off.

Graham visited with Andrew while he waited for Trina to return, but he didn't hold out much hope for a positive answer. In all his months of courting Trina, she had only been allowed to come to his home without her parents one time, and that was on his twenty-first birthday. When Trina returned, however, she wore a huge smile that sent his heart to thumping.

"Mama says that's fine. Thank you for the invitation."

"She said *yes?*"

Trina's grin turned impish. "She probably wants me out of the way so she and Dad can talk freely." She turned to look at Andrew. "I talked to Mama and Dad last night, and Dad said they'd discuss it."

Andrew reached out and squeezed Trina's shoulder. "Good. I'll be praying for God's will."

"Thank you."

Graham watched the exchange with interest. "Something important going on?"

Trina peeked at him, her smile secretive. "I hope so."

"Will you tell me about it?"

"Later." She slipped her hand through his elbow, creating a mighty caroming in his chest. "We'd better go before your mother thinks we're not coming."

Graham escorted Trina across the grassy yard to his vehicle, opened the door for her, then ran around to his side. He sighed with satisfaction. Just having her in his car, sitting primly on the opposite side of the bench seat, felt wonderful. How much better it would be when they were published and she could slide into the middle of the seat.

Lunch seemed to drag on forever. Graham enjoyed every bite of the baked ham, scalloped potatoes, last year's canned beans, and gooey chocolate cake, but when the meal was over, he and Trina would be able to sit on the front porch and talk. The handmade swing was visible to his family through the large picture window in the living room, so they would be properly chaperoned without having to be around the others. Graham relished his moments alone with Trina. Those scarce snatches of time made him eager for the day when she would be his wife, when they would share their own little house and he would have hours of time every day with her.

When the meal was finished, Trina rose and began clearing dishes.

"Now you stop that," Graham's mother scolded. "You're a guest."

"Nonsense." Trina sent a smile across the table that softened the word. "If I were home, I'd be helping with cleanup. I want to help."

"No, no. You do enough cleaning up at your mother's café." To Graham's relief, his mother shooed Trina away from the table. "I'm accustomed to doing my dishes. You young people go enjoy your time."

Before Trina could launch another argument, Graham caught her elbow and ushered her through the living room and out the front door. The early June sunshine raised the temperature, but the porch was shaded by thick spirea bushes, and a slight breeze pushed from the west, making it bearable. He pointed to the swing, and they seated themselves on opposite sides of the wood-slatted hanging bench. At least a foot and a half of distance separated them. That would be considered acceptable.

All through lunch, Graham had held his curiosity about Trina and Andrew's brief conversation in the churchyard, but now that he had her alone, he let the question come out. "So what's this important topic your parents are covering while you're over here sitting on my porch swing?"

Trina's eyes danced, and she pushed her feet against the porch floor, setting the swing in motion. The white ribbons of her cap swayed beneath her chin. A silken strand of deep brown hair slipped along her cheek. Graham wondered what she'd look like with her hair down. He focused on her sweet face as she finally answered his question.

"They're considering allowing me to work for Dr. Groening."

Ah, he should have known. The look on her face Friday night had clearly indicated her interest. "I'm surprised your mom is even thinking about it."

For a moment, Trina's expression dimmed. But then her smile returned. "I know, but Dad can be persuasive. Of course" — she shrugged, bunching the ribbon on her left shoulder — "he said there would be a lot to work out for it to happen, but . . ."

"But you're still hopeful," he completed.

She nodded. "Oh yes. Working with Dr. Groening, learning how to doctor animals, would be so wonderful!"

He smiled, enjoying her animated voice and face.

"Spending the night out at Andrew's with Regen, I had such a feeling of contentment when the swelling in the horse's leg went down. I love animals, and I want so much to help them." She closed her eyes, tipping her head back and drawing in a deep breath. "There's so much I don't know, Graham, and I want to learn it. I want to learn *everything*." She threw her arms wide and giggled, peeking at him.

Graham resisted taking her hand. Her enthusiasm toward life always lifted his spirits. He could imagine coming home to her after a long day at the lumberyard, letting her smile and cheerful chatter lift him from tiredness. His chest tightened with desire to make her his as soon as possible.

Suddenly an impish grin creased her cheeks. "I told them you offered to teach me to drive."

Graham chuckled to cover his embarrassment. He fiddled with the buttons on his shirt. "Oh? And what did they say?"

Trina sighed. "Dad said it wasn't your responsibility."

Graham nodded. "No, probably not. But in a few months . . . it could be."

She turned a puzzled look in his direction. "What do you mean?"

Graham glanced through the window. His father dozed in his chair, and his mother was nowhere in sight — probably still in the kitchen. His younger brother — usually the one to spy — appeared caught up in the *Mennonite Weekly*. Graham looked at Trina and shifted a few inches closer to her. He lowered his voice, just in case it might carry through the window's screened opening into the house.

"If we were published, no one would think it wrong for me to teach you to drive."

Her eyes widened. "Published?" She licked her lips. "But — but it's summer."

"The wedding would have to wait until the winter months, when the harvest is over." He substantiated her unspoken thought. "But we could publish our engagement now."

She fell silent, only the creaking of the swing's chains intruding. He waited, nearly holding his breath. He knew they couldn't be published without her parents' permission, but he wanted to know what she thought — if she were as agreeable to the idea as he hoped she would be. When the silence lengthened, he released his breath in a noisy rush.

"Would you be opposed to that?" He feared her reply. Maybe he had misread their relationship.

But she shook her head firmly. "No, I'm not opposed. I — I like you a lot." She looked straight ahead, her cheeks flooding with pink. The color gave her an innocent appearance that sent Graham's heart thudding in the top of his head. "But . . ."

Graham leaned closer. "Then what?" His whisper stirred the ribbon hanging from the left side of her cap.

Still facing ahead, she whispered in reply. "I'm not sure I'm ready for it . . . now."

He frowned, sitting upright. "Not ready? But you're nineteen — that's old enough. You know how to keep a house. You've been baptized, so the bishop would have no reason to decline our request to be published. So what's wrong, Trina?"

Slowly she shifted her head to meet his gaze. "After I'm married, I won't work anymore."

He laughed lightly. "Of course not. You'll be taking care of a house, raising children."

Warmth filled his face at his statement. He cleared his throat and rushed on. "There won't be any reason for you to work. I'll take care of you."

Trina lowered her gaze, toying with a loose thread in the waistband of her purple dress. "But I *want* to work . . . with Dr. Groening."

Graham planted his feet, stopping the swing's gentle motion. He waited for Trina to look up at him again. He deliberately kept a frown from forming. "Trina, you realize that your job will be caring for the home once you're a wife."

"But why can't I work, too?" Her tone turned pleading. "Mama runs a café, and she's married."

"Yes, but she waited until you and your brother finished school before she bought the café. If she had tried working when you and Tony were younger, your dad would have said no."

Trina scowled. "Beth McCauley works at the art studio every day, and her husband doesn't mind."

Graham harrumphed. "Beth McCauley is worldly. She isn't Mennonite. She doesn't understand our ways." He stared at her, appalled. "You surely don't want to be like her!"

Trina turned her gaze sharply away, worrying her lower lip between her teeth.

Graham clamped his jaw and brought his racing thoughts under control. The last thing he wanted to do was push Trina away. She was young, easily influenced. He knew Trina had befriended the young woman whose mother had abandoned the Mennonite faith when still a teenager. Beth's mother — Marie — was now an accepted member of the fellowship, having returned to her faith as an adult, but Beth remained separate.

He gentled his voice and touched her arm. "Trina."

She looked at him, her expression wary.

"I admire your tender heart, wanting to be friends with everyone. But Beth — she can lead you astray. When the Bible speaks of not being unequally yoked, it mostly means marriage, but we need to be cautious in all of our relationships."

"This isn't about Beth." Tears winked in her dark eyes. "This is about me and what I feel . . . called to do."

Graham frowned. What calling would a woman have beyond being a wife and mother? Fear fluttered through his chest. "Exactly what do you want to do, Trina?"

At that moment, a pickup pulled up to

the curb. Graham slid back to the corner of the swing as Trina's younger brother, Tony, bounded up the porch steps two at a time. He started for the front door, but when he spotted them in the corner of the porch, he turned toward his sister.

"Trina, Mom and Dad want you to come home now." Tony shrugged, his face pulled into an apologetic grimace. "Mom says you've been here long enough."

When Trina pushed from the swing, Graham felt certain she looked relieved to be leaving their topic behind. He rose, as well, a feeling of dread settling in his middle.

Trina followed Tony to the edge of the porch; then she turned and looked at Graham. "Please tell your parents thank you for the invitation to lunch. Everything was very good." Such a prim, impersonal statement.

Graham forced a smile. "Sure. I'll see you Wednesday for the singing, right? It's at Walt's this time."

Trina nodded, her ribbons bouncing. "Yes. I want to go."

Graham nearly wilted with relief. He hadn't scared her away if she was still willing to go to the singing with him. "I'll pick you up at six thirty."

She flashed a quick smile then grabbed Tony's arm, hurrying him off the porch.

"Did Mama and Dad say anything about . . ." Her voice drifted away as she slammed herself into the pickup.

Graham watched Tony drive down the street. Even though he knew it was selfish, he hoped her parents wouldn't allow her to work at Dr. Groening's. He feared too many changes would take place if they did.

"So if your mother can find two dependable young people to work in the café and your brother agrees to drive you to Lehigh, then we will allow you to work for Dr. Groening."

Trina grabbed the couch cushion with both hands to keep herself in the seat. She smiled at her father and nodded. "Okay. Good. Thank you."

"But" — Dad scowled, pointing his finger at her — "we will expect you to conduct yourself appropriately. Limit your communication with the non-Mennonites who bring animals to the clinic, and be respectful at all times of your employer."

"Of course!" Trina looked back and forth between her parents, meeting their stern gazes with her most convincing look.

"But I must replace you first, Trina," Mama said in a firm voice. "And I'll expect you to help the new employees learn the routine before I allow you to go to your new job."

Trina stifled a frustrated sigh. It might be weeks before Mama was satisfied with the new employees. But she knew better than to argue. She gave another quick nod.

Dad released a sigh and leaned back in his chair. "I'll drive over to Lehigh tomorrow and talk with Dr. Groening about this job, just to be certain we are clear on his expectations and the hours."

"May I go, too?"

Mama shook her head. "No. Let your father do it."

"But the café is closed on Mondays — I won't be working." Trina used a reasonable rather than argumentative tone.

"No, Trina," Dad said, a scowl marring his forehead. "I will let you know everything Dr. Groening says."

Trina stood. "All right." Although she would have preferred to go along — see the clinic, talk to Dr. Groening herself — she knew neither Dad nor Mama would budge once their minds were made up. She also realized they had made a huge concession, allowing her to work for the veterinarian. It took no effort to offer a smile of thanks. "Mom and Dad, thank you. I appreciate your permission."

Mama sighed. "You're welcome, Trina. I just hope we don't regret it."

Trina didn't explore Mama's meaning. She gave each of her parents a hug then headed to her bedroom. After closing the door, she threw herself facedown across the bed, propped her chin in her hands, and closed her eyes, imagining the glorious days to come.

Working with Dr. Groening, caring for animals. No more cleaning floors, washing dishes, and placing plates of food in front of customers. She focused on every positive aspect of the change and carefully avoided reflecting on the worry in her mother's eyes or recalling Graham's statement about her "calling."

FIVE

Monday morning, Trina rose early, prepared breakfast for the family, waited impatiently for everyone to finish eating, then cleaned the table and washed the dishes without a word of complaint. When the final dish was placed in the cabinet, she interrupted her mother at her sewing machine.

"Mama? May I go to town?"

Mama looked up from pinning the zipper into a pair of brown twill trousers. "Where are you going?"

Trina battled the frustration that wiggled in her stomach. When would she be allowed to simply do what she desired without having to ask permission of her parents? She knew the answer — when she married and moved out from under their roof. But then she'd answer to her husband. The frustration grew.

She took a breath and released it, bringing her rambling emotions under control. "I want to go by the art studio and ask Andrew about Regen's leg."

Mama nodded. "Go ahead."

Trina spun to leave.

"Trina, wait."

Stifling a sigh, Trina turned back.

"Take some money out of my purse, stop by the grocer, and buy two pounds of link sausage. We'll fry it for supper tonight."

"Okay." She slipped away before her mother could give her any more directions. The summer sun beat down, warming her head and shoulders. She walked the familiar streets toward town, just as she had every day for the past six years on her way to the café and her parent-chosen job. Her heart skipped a beat, a smile growing on her face without effort. But soon her routine would change. She'd be climbing into Tony's pickup, riding down the highway the few miles to Lehigh and Dr. Groening's clinic to the Trina-chosen job.

Oh, please hurry and hire those workers, Mama! her heart begged. She could hardly wait to start a new routine — a routine she'd dreamed of since she was a little girl. She hurried her steps, eager to move into the future.

Even though it was still morning — not even nine o'clock yet — by the time she reached the studio on the west end of Main Street, her hair felt sweaty, and perspiration dampened her skin. Stepping into the air-conditioned interior of the studio was a welcome relief. The smells of the studio were so different from the café's — burnt metal and something that left an acidic taste on the back of her tongue as opposed to grease and baking bread. She wondered briefly what the animal clinic would smell like.

The moment she closed the door, Andrew looked up from the worktable in the middle of the floor and broke into a smile. "Good morning, Trina."

Beth Quinn McCauley, Andrew's employer, turned from the large platform on the floor where she and her cousin Catherine Koeppler arranged cut pieces of colored glass into a rose pattern. "Well, good morning, Miss Katrinka."

Trina grinned at the silly nickname her grandfather had chosen. No one used it except Grandpa Muller and Beth.

Beth asked, "What brings you here? Checking up on Winky?"

At the cat's name, he sprang from beneath the worktable and attacked the laces on Trina's tennis shoes.

Andrew muttered, "The cat's the same as

always — ornery."

With a giggle, Trina leaned over and scooped the furry critter into her arms. She always enjoyed playing with Winky. She had nursed his injured eye when he was a lanky kitten. The cat still bore a small scar below his left eye, but he was beautiful with thick gray fur and white markings. He set up a loud *purr* as she scratched his chin, and she laughed again.

"As much as I enjoy seeing Winky, I actually came to see Andrew." Still holding the cat, she turned toward her cousin. "How is Regen?"

"Still in the sling," Andrew reported, scraping a small stone over the edge of a piece of blue glass. "Dr. Groening said we need to keep him from putting his full weight on the leg for at least another five days. Then we'll let him stand in the stall. But the leg's looking good. Livvy keeps a close eye on it."

"Good." She filed Andrew's comments away for future reference, in case she ever needed to treat another horse with a torn ligament. She skipped forward, lowering her voice to avoid disturbing Beth and Catherine. "Guess what? Mama and Dad said I can go to work for Dr. Groening."

Andrew's eyebrows shot upward, and a

smile broke across his face. "Wonderful!"

Trina nodded happily then grimaced. "Of course, Mama has to find some workers to replace me in the café, and I have to work out transportation with Tony, but when that's all done, I get to be an assistant in a veterinary clinic!"

Andrew put down his stone and glass long enough to throw his arm around her shoulder for a quick hug. "Congratulations! I'm sure you'll enjoy it."

"I know I will, too." Winky wriggled in Trina's arms, so she set the cat down and leaned her elbows on the worktable. She frowned slightly. "I wish I knew more about veterinary science. I read every book I can find on animal care, but most of the books I buy are used, so they don't have the most recent information."

"Hmm." Andrew pursed his lips. "You'll learn a lot from watching Dr. Groening, won't you?"

"Yes, but I'd still like to know things in advance. I can be more help that way." Her hunger for knowledge ate at her, creating a hollow ache in her chest.

"Trina?" At Beth's voice, Trina turned and faced the young woman. "You're welcome to use the computer in here to search the Internet for articles on veterinary science."

Trina's mouth went dry. Would Mama approve? She licked her lips. "The Internet?"

"Sure." Beth slid a slice of pink glass next to one of deeper rose. "The Internet is a great source of information. You can do a Google search for veterinary science or animal care. All kinds of Web sites and articles will come up."

"Google?" Trina laughed. "That's a silly name."

Beth grinned. "I suppose, but it's a very useful search engine."

Trina shook her head, awareness of her limited education smacking hard.

Beth continued in a thoughtful tone. "You know, there is very little that can't be accomplished online these days. I conduct three-fourths of my stained-glass business over the Internet — and Sean and I can communicate with each other through e-mail no matter where he's traveling."

For a moment, Beth's brow pinched, and Trina's heart turned over. She knew Beth missed her husband when he was away on his travels, meeting with church committees about building projects. They had been married less than a year, and Beth often bemoaned how much of that year had been spent apart. Trina wondered if Beth would ever hand the operation of the studio over to Andrew and travel with Sean instead of staying behind.

"Not only that," Beth continued, "but I took an online course through an art institute in Maryland to learn how to color my own glass." She raised one brow and sent Trina a speculative look. "The Internet is a handy tool." Then she shrugged. "Like I said, you're welcome to do some searching for articles on animal care, if you want to."

"I want to." Trina clasped her hands beneath her chin. "Could I do it right now?"

"Sure." Beth got up and crossed the floor, linking her hand through Trina's elbow and guiding her to the desk in the corner where a computer waited. "I'll get you online and show you how to use Google; then you can search as long as you want to."

Trina caught on much more quickly than she had expected, which gave her a rush of self-satisfaction. She chose to explore "veterinary science," and she released a surprised "Whew!" when she spotted the number of hits on the topic. "Three million four hundred and thirty thousand sites!" She stared at Beth. "I'll never get through all of those!"

Beth laughed. "You don't have to. Look at the descriptions. A lot of those are Web sites for different veterinary clinics. You can avoid those and just find the sites that offer information about veterinary science itself. Choose ones that seem the most interesting." She patted Trina's shoulder. "Have fun, Katrinka."

While Andrew, Beth, and Catherine worked on the stained-glass projects, Trina scanned articles on everything from animal reproduction to the latest techniques in animal surgery. The vocabulary used frustrated her from time to time, but she plowed through, absorbing as much as she could. She wished she'd brought paper and pencil to make notes.

She was amazed at the number of educational institutions that specialized in training people for the field of veterinary medicine. At first, she avoided those sites, focusing instead on information concerning the care of animals, but eventually, curiosity drove her to click on a site titled "To Be a Vet."

The Web site was geared toward children, she realized, but a quick glance showed a variety of interesting topics. She leaned forward, propped her chin in her hand, and began to read. *"Getting into veterinary school is harder than getting into medical school. . . . High school subjects you must have mastered include English, biology, chemistry, physics, and several math classes. You need to pass the ACT in those subjects, as well."*

Trina's chest constricted. She hadn't even attended high school beyond grade nine! She didn't know what physics was or what ACT stood for. Tears pricked her eyes. She blinked rapidly, clearing her vision, and forced herself to continue.

"To earn your Bachelor of Veterinary Science degree takes five years of full-time study in an approved university."

Five years! Full-time? Trina jerked upright in the chair. Although she had harbored a glimmer of hope that perhaps one day her parents would relent and allow her to seek a degree, that hope now plummeted. College cost money, and she couldn't possibly have enough saved for five years. That was if she could get into a college. Tears stung again. She rubbed her eyes, erasing the tears, and leaned closer to the screen to reread the information. Maybe she'd missed something — some other way to become a veterinarian.

The telephone blared, and Trina jumped.

"Trina," Beth called from the platform, "would you mind answering that?"

Reluctantly, Trina moved away from the computer and picked up the telephone. "Quinn's Stained-Glass Art Studio. May I help you?"

"Trina?" Mama's voice.

Trina glanced at the clock on the wall. It was nearly noon! Her hands began to tremble. "Yes, Mama?"

"What are you still doing there? I've been waiting for you to come home."

"I'm sorry, Mama. I —" But she didn't want to tell her mother what she'd been doing. "I'll get that sausage and come straight home."

"No, just go to the café." Mama sounded completely exasperated. "I made a couple of calls this morning, and Janina Ensz is interested in working in the café. I want you to show her how to run the dishwasher and to figure tabs for customers."

"Yes, ma'am! I'll be right there."

The phone line went dead. Trina faced Beth. "It was for me. Mama needs me at the café." Spinning to include Andrew, she said, "Janina Ensz wants to work at the café. If Kelly Dick will work full-time, too, then I'll be free to go to Dr. Groening's."

Andrew winked. "Sounds like it's working out well, Trina."

Catherine pushed to her feet, her hands on the small of her back. "Trina, if Kelly doesn't want to work full-time, have your mother call my house. My sister Audra

74

finished school this past term, and she's looking for a job, too. Maybe she and Kelly could split the time."

Trina squealed. "Oh! I'll tell her! Thank you!"

Beth waved at her. "I'll shut down the computer for you, but anytime you want to use it, just come by."

Trina bit down on her lower lip, sending a pleading look in Beth's direction. "Anytime? Even an evening?" If she worked days at Dr. Groening's, her only free time would be after supper.

Beth shrugged. "I don't know why not. When Sean isn't home, the evenings get long. I'd enjoy the company, even if you are so wrapped up in reading that you don't talk to me." The teasing note in her voice made Trina laugh.

"I'll read out loud to you," she suggested.

Beth grinned. "Deal. See you later."

Yes, Trina would certainly see Beth later. She needed to finish reading the information on the Web site. Surely there was a way to see her dreams come true without going through five years of college.

At supper, Trina wanted to ask her father how his meeting with Dr. Groening had gone. But Mama, still upset about her spending the entire morning at Beth's studio, glared across the table, and Trina decided it was better to wait until she could talk to Dad alone.

Not until the dishes were cleared, washed, and put away did she find a minute to join her father in the yard, where he tinkered under the hood of his car. When she spoke his name, he jumped, nearly banging the back of his head on the metal hood. "Trina." The single word held a hint of exasperation.

She leaned sideways, peeking beneath the hood. "What are you doing?"

"Adjusting the carburetor."

"Why don't you let Uncle Henry do it? That's his job."

He sent her an impatient look. "Because I'm capable of doing it myself. What do you need? I'm busy."

Trina clasped her hands at her apron waist. "I wondered . . . what Dr. Groening said. About me taking a job at his clinic. But if you'd rather wait . . ." She held her breath, hoping he wouldn't send her away.

He heaved a mighty sigh and rested his elbows on the car's fender, angling his head to look at her from beneath the hood. "Well, the job doesn't sound all that good to me, Trina. You'll be cleaning up: cleaning up cages and kennels, cleaning up the exam room, cleaning up after surgery. Are you sure that's what you want to do?"

Trina met her father's steady gaze. "Yes, sir. I know I don't have an education" — her thoughts added the word *yet* — "but I can learn a lot from watching. And maybe I'll be able to help people around town if their animals get sick or hurt."

He shook his head. "You are determined to see this through, aren't you?"

"Yes, sir."

His gaze narrowed, a hint of sympathy showing around the edges of his unsmiling face. "Is it really that bad, working at the café?"

"Oh, Daddy . . ." Trina paused, gathering her thoughts. "It isn't that I dislike my work at the café. It's fun to be around the people, and I know it serves a purpose. But it isn't . . ." She furrowed her brow, seeking an appropriate word. "Fulfilling."

"And cleaning up after animals would be?"

Her father's incredulous expression made Trina want to giggle. But she kept a serious face and nodded. "Yes, sir." Cleaning up after animals was just the start. She'd do more. Someday.

He shook his head, slapped the fender, and leaned back over the engine. "Well, all right, then, daughter. The job will be from nine in the morning until five o'clock each evening. With the distance, you won't be able to come home for lunch, so you'll need to pack yourself a sandwich each day." He glanced at her. "I hope you know what you're doing."

Trina gave him a bright, beaming smile. "I know what I'm doing, Dad. Don't worry."

Six

Trina stuck her arm out the open window of Tony's truck, her hand angled to catch the warm, coursing wind. The pressure against her palm and cupped fingers created a tickling sensation, and she laughed.

From behind the steering wheel, Tony sent her a grin. "You're really happy to be out of the café, aren't you?"

The wind threatened to pull her cap loose, so she shifted a little closer to her brother and caught the dancing strings of her cap, holding them together beneath her chin. "I'm happy to be on my way to the vet clinic," she said. After two weeks of training, Mama had finally deemed Janina Ensz and Kelly Dick capable of handling the tasks of taking orders, serving, and cleaning up at the café. Trina wished Tony would drive faster so she could get to Dr. Groening's as quickly as possible.

The Groening Animal Clinic, located off

Highway 56 between Sommerfeld and Lehigh, was housed in a red brick building that had previously served as a country school. Trina had visited it once before when she rode along with Beth McCauley to get Winky's vaccinations. She admired the way Dr. Groening had divided the one-room classroom into a small reception area, two examination rooms, and an operating room. Most of his supplies were stored in the storm shelter beneath the clinic. Although small and unpretentious, the clinic met the needs of those who brought their pets to him. And now Trina would be learning to meet those needs, as well, through firsthand experience. Her heart twanged crazily at the thought.

"I hope taking you doesn't make me late to my job." A hint of worry underscored her brother's comment.

Trina shot him a concerned look. "Will Mr. Bruner be terribly upset if you're a few minutes late?"

Tony hunched his shoulders, his eyes on the road. "He's pretty particular. Suzanna" — he glanced briefly in Trina's direction, his cheeks splotching with pink — "that's his daughter — she warned me to follow his directions carefully if I wanted to keep my job. He's older and set in his ways, and he expects things to go just so. Suzanna can't wait until she's old enough to have her own family so she doesn't have to live with him anymore."

"Where's her mother?"

"Remember? Mrs. Bruner died several years ago."

Trina nodded. "Oh, now I remember." She patted his arm. "We left plenty early. You should be okay." Then she grinned. "Or are you more worried about missing time with Suzanna than you are about being late for your job?"

"Trina!" Tony jerked his arm free of her hand. "She's Amish."

Trina shrugged. "Stranger things have happened."

Tony gritted his teeth. "Her dad would never allow it."

Trina considered pursuing the subject a little further, but then she spotted the clinic up ahead. "There it is!" She pointed out the window, leaning forward to grab the dash. "Oh, look! He's added kennels in the back. Those weren't there when I came over with Beth. I wonder if he keeps dogs overnight." Maybe she could help with their care, too.

Tony slowed down to pull into the graveled driveway. "I don't know. I don't see any dogs out there now."

She craned her neck, disappointment striking. "Neither do I." Then she brightened. "But I'm sure there will be animals inside. Oh! Hurry, Tony!"

He laughed as he brought the truck to a stop in front of the building. "We're here. Get out so I can go to my job."

She flashed him a grin, snatched up her lunch bag, and jumped out of the pickup. Giving the door a slam, she called, "See you at five!"

"Or a little after," he replied. "It'll take me awhile to get over here from the Bruners'."

"I'll wait outside for you. See you later!"

"Have a good day, sis."

She waved as he pulled away; then she turned and dashed up the three steps leading to the clinic's door. She stepped into the room, stopped, and drew in a lengthy, lingering breath, processing the smell. Clean, a little bit like a hospital, but with an underlying essence of wet dog. She laughed out loud. At the sound, Dr. Groening stepped from the far examination room.

He grinned, his gray eyebrows high. "You find my clinic amusing?"

Trina tangled her hands in her apron and gasped. "Oh no! Not at all! That was a happy laugh, that's all."

His grin grew, twitching his mustache. "Well, we'll see how happy you are by the end of the day. It gets pretty messy around here."

Trina swung her lunch bag. "Don't worry. I'm used to messy."

She discovered by the end of the day, however, that messy in the café couldn't compare to messy in the vet clinic. Nervous dogs often emptied their bladders — or worse — on the floor before they made it to an examination table. One poor dog, a golden retriever named Mo, threw up three times in the reception room and twice on the exam table. While Trina's sympathy was roused, it was the least pleasant scrub job she'd ever encountered. And cats shed terribly, their hair clinging to everything.

By lunchtime, she was ready for a break, but when she lifted her sandwich, she suddenly thought about all the other things her hands had touched during the morning. Even though she'd worn latex gloves for the cleanup tasks and washed her hands with an antiseptic soap afterward, she couldn't make herself take a bite of the sandwich. Instead, she drank the milk from her little thermos and put the sandwich back in the bag.

Dr. Groening made visits to local farms

during the afternoon. Trina would have loved to ride along with him, but he left her behind to hose out the kennels and wash all the dog dishes — even though they weren't being used at the moment — and dust the shelves in the storm shelter. It was hardly the day of animal treatment she'd been anticipating, and her spirits flagged as the day wore on.

At five o'clock, she wrote her time on a little card Dr. Groening had given her in the morning and went to sit on the front stoop to wait for Tony. Chin in hands, she contemplated the day of cleaning, cleaning, cleaning, and she realized it was exactly what her father had told her to expect. Still, considering her conversation with Dr. Groening, she had hoped for something . . . more.

A vehicle approached, and Trina shielded her eyes from the late-afternoon sun, squinting. When she recognized Graham's sedan, she trotted to the driver's window.

"What are you doing here?" She bent forward and peered into the backseat. "You don't have an animal with you."

Graham grinned. "I came for you."

Trina stood upright. "But Tony is supposed to pick me up."

Graham's grin turned impish, and he

raised one eyebrow higher than the other. "I talked to Tony about an hour ago when he came into the lumberyard to pick up some nails. I told him I'd get you instead."

"And Mama cleared it?" Despite the disappointing day, Trina didn't want to do anything to jeopardize this opportunity. Getting Mama riled was the best way to lose her new job.

Graham shrugged. "I don't know why she would protest. I've driven you places before."

"With other people along, too," Trina pointed out. Boys and girls spending time alone together was discouraged in their fellowship. Others who had disregarded the dictate of group activities had received reprimands from the minister. Trina had no desire to be disciplined — not by the minister or by her parents.

Graham tipped his head to the side and fixed her with a steady look. "Well, Tony isn't coming, so unless you want to walk, you'd better hop in."

Trina bit down on her lower lip for a moment, but finally she sighed and slid into the passenger side of the front seat. "All right. But I'll need to check with Mama and make sure it's okay for you to do this another time."

Graham turned the car around and aimed it toward the highway. "How about I come in and ask your parents if I can pick you up each day? And while I'm talking to them, I'll make another request."

Trina stared at his honed profile and waited.

"I'd like to ask if they'd allow us to be published, Trina."

She jerked her gaze to the ribbon of highway. The white dashes zipped by, one after another, as mixed emotions zipped back and forth in her chest.

Graham's hand started to reach toward her, but then he wrapped his fingers around the steering wheel again. Eyes ahead, he asked, "Is that all right with you?"

A part of Trina wanted to exult, "Yes!" But another part of her wanted to exclaim, "Not yet!" She examined her heart, trying to understand the confusion. She cared a great deal about Graham. Of all the young men in Sommerfeld, he was the only one she could imagine spending her life with. She did hope to marry him . . . someday. But now? Was she ready for it now?

She had to say something. "I — I —"

The car began to slow, and Graham eased it onto the shoulder of the road. Leaving the engine on, he put the vehicle in PARK and turned to face her. "Trina, I love you. I've loved you for over a year now. I want you to be my wife. But I need to know: Do you love me?"

Trina stared into his dear, stricken face. Something inside of her melted. A feeling of longing rose up, putting a mighty lump in her throat. She swallowed and formed a sincere answer. "I do love you, Graham."

"Then what's wrong? Why won't you let us be published?"

"I want to be published, too! It's just —" How would Graham feel, knowing she was putting the opportunity to work with animals ahead of him? Yet if he truly loved her, wouldn't he support her desire to be more than a wife and mother? Wouldn't he encourage her to fulfill her dreams? Maybe he wouldn't mind being the first husband in Sommerfeld to have a veterinarian for a wife.

Graham took her hand. He didn't curl his fingers around it but just placed his palm over her hand on the seat. The simple touch ignited feelings inside of Trina that took her by surprise. She stared at their hands — his much larger one, with blond hairs on the backs of his lumpy knuckles, covering hers. Only the tips of her fingers with their uneven, broken fingernails showed. Suddenly the gesture made her feel smothered, and she jerked her hand away, fearful of where the feelings might lead.

Graham's forehead creased, and for long moments, he remained with his hand lying in the middle of the seat, the fingers curling into a fist.

Trina said, "We'd better go, or Mama will worry."

He grabbed the gearshift and gave it a quick jerk, then pulled the car back into traffic. Neither spoke the rest of the way to Sommerfeld. But when he pulled up in front of her house, Trina didn't get out.

"Graham?"

Several seconds ticked by before he finally looked at her. His stern expression didn't offer much encouragement, but she knew if they were to have a relationship, she needed to be completely honest with him.

"I want to be your wife."

His expression softened.

"But just not yet. There are . . . other things . . . I want to accomplish first. Things that" — she pressed both palms to her heart — "that live in here. I have to let them come out before I can be a good wife to you."

Graham shook his head. "Trina, you are the most confusing girl. What things can a woman need besides being a good wife and

mother? That's your God-ordained purpose."

"And I'll want to be a good wife and
mother. Someday." Without conscious
thought, she leaned slightly toward him.
"But don't you think God gives us other
tasks, too? Why would He plant the interest
in animal care in my heart if I wasn't supposed to use it?"

"You do use it," Graham argued. "You
helped with Livvy's horse the other night.
You're always taking care of sick animals. I
wouldn't stop you from helping animals. Of
course, once our children start arriving,
then you wouldn't be able to run off all
night like you did with Regen, but —"

"But I want to do more!" Trina implored
him with her eyes, begging him to see how
much this dream meant to her. She needed
someone to understand, to support her, to
encourage her. She wanted desperately for
that someone to be Graham.

He ran his hand over his short-cropped
hair — the hair that reminded Trina of the
sandstone posts surrounding Uncle Al's
cornfields. Even though Graham worked
mostly inside at the lumberyard rather than
outdoors as a farmer, there was so much
about him that reminded her of the outdoors. His sandstone-colored hair, his sky-

colored eyes, his lips as full and deeply hued as a pink rosebud ready to burst. But now his eyes bore into hers with a hurt that tore at her heart, and his lips pressed into a firm, stubborn line.

"Exactly what do you want, Trina?"

It was the question she'd wanted him to ask so she could share her deepest desire, but now that the opportunity lay before her, she hesitated. She hated her hesitation. Shouldn't she feel free to share with the man who would one day be her husband?

Taking a deep breath, she whispered her dream aloud. "I want to be real."

He stared at her, confusion evident in the rapid blinking of his eyes.

She rushed on. "A real animal doctor. Someone trained in the field."

"You mean attend college?"

Trina wasn't sure whether he was astounded or agitated. "It will probably take that. Yes."

Graham threw himself against the seat, his head back, his hands on the steering wheel, and his arms straight as if bracing himself against a fast downhill ride. "I can't believe it."

"I've talked about my interest in animals, Graham."

"Interest, yes." He slumped, twisting his

head to meet her gaze. "But you're talking about having a *career,* Trina."

She had never applied that word to her dream. Suddenly the barrier between her and school seemed to double in size. Who was she fooling? They'd never let her have a career.

"But . . ." The word squeaked. She cleared her throat and tried again. "It would be worthwhile to the community. There isn't anybody in town who can doctor animals. We have to go clear to Lehigh, and Dr. Groening is getting older. He'll retire before too much longer. Surely —"

The look on Graham's face silenced her. She pushed the car door open. "Thank you for the ride, Graham. If you — if you want to get me tomorrow, make sure you check with Mama first."

His eyebrows rose, and even she realized the ridiculousness of her statement. She was planning to attend an institution of higher education, which was unquestionably against her parents' desires. Accepting a ride home from work carried significantly less importance than enrolling in college. He didn't respond, and she slammed the door. He drove off without a backward glance.

Heart aching, Trina stared at the house. She didn't want to go in. Turning, she headed for town, but she passed the café and went around to the back door of the stained-glass studio instead. Andrew's truck still stood in the alley. Relief flooded her. Of all the people she knew, Andrew should be the most sympathetic to her desire for something more.

She reached for the door handle, but the door swung open before she could connect with the silver knob. Andrew stepped onto the small concrete slab. When he spotted her, a smile lit his face, and he gave her an affectionate little pinch on the chin.

"Hey, Trina! How did your first day at Dr. Groening's go?"

To Trina's chagrin, she burst into tears.

SEVEN

Graham pulled his car into the shed behind his house and shut off the ignition, but he didn't get out. He sat behind the steering wheel, images of Trina filling his vision. Her expectant, hopeful face as she shared her desires crushed him. She didn't want him. She didn't want a home and family. She wanted . . . He couldn't bring himself to finish the thought. It was wrong what Trina wanted! He wouldn't give credence to it by letting it invade his mind.

He got out of the car and slammed the door hard — harder than necessary. It didn't help. He stomped across the grass to his own back door. Once inside the house, he stood in the little mudroom and peered through the open doorway into the kitchen. How many times had he stepped through his back door and imagined Trina in his kitchen. At his stove, stirring a pot. At his sink, her hands submerged in sudsy water.

At his table, serving a meal.

Shaking his head, he forced himself to walk through the kitchen to the living room. He sank onto the sofa and closed his eyes. The silence of the house pressed around him. The house was less than four months old. He and the men of the community had built it. The ladies — including Trina — had provided meals to keep the men going during the working hours.

The house still smelled new. New wood, new paint, new rubber from the purchased throw rugs he'd dropped here and there on the floor. Even some new furniture. What there was of furniture. Only a sofa in the living room. The bedroom he'd claimed had the familiar full-size bed, bureau, and bedside table from his old bedroom at his parents' home. He'd deliberately put off purchasing furniture, knowing his wife would want a say in what to buy.

Trina would want a say in what to buy.

Now he'd heard Trina's say, and he wasn't sure whether she'd ever choose furniture to fill his house. The house he'd meant to be theirs. He groaned, covering his face with his hands. When he'd fallen in love with Trina Muller, he'd never imagined she would hurt him like she had today.

"Dear Lord, why does she want something

else instead of me?"

Trina covered her face with her hands, clamping her lips together to silence the sobs that jerked her shoulders in uncontrolled spasms.

Warm, broad hands curled around her upper arms, drawing her forward, into the shop. Then those hands slipped to her wrists, pulling her hands away from her face. She peered into Andrew's concerned eyes.

"Trina, what's wrong? Didn't your day go well?"

"Oh, Andrew!" For a few minutes, she gave vent to the frustration that bubbled upward. As she'd learned to appreciate over the years, he didn't tell her to stop crying but just stood by and let the tears run their course. When she finally sniffed hard, bringing the raining tears to a halt, he gave her a tissue.

"Here. Clean up."

She rubbed her face clean. "I'm sorry. I didn't mean to do that."

"Don't apologize to me. Sometimes a person just needs to cry." He put his hand on her back, guiding her to the tall stools beside the worktable. She climbed onto one, and he leaned against a second one, resting his elbow on the tabletop. "You aren't one to cry over nothing. Do you want to talk about it?"

The sweet concern in his voice nearly sent her into another bout of weeping, but she took a few deep breaths and kept control. While Andrew's attentive gaze remained on her face, she poured out every event of the day, from cleaning up doggy doo and dusting shelves to the car ride home and facing Graham's disapproval.

"I want him to understand, but he doesn't. I know my parents won't, either." She twisted the soggy tissue in her hands. "Why is it wrong for me to want to go to school and learn how to take care of animals? Why would God give me this desire if I wasn't meant to pursue it? Why can't Mama and Dad and Graham let me be the person I want to be?"

To her surprise, Andrew didn't immediately validate her questions. Instead, he walked slowly around to the opposite side of the table and braced both palms against it. "Why are you asking me these questions, Trina?"

She blinked in confusion. "Who else would understand? Your father wanted you to be a farmer like the rest of your family. But you wanted something else. Surely you know how I feel!"

"But I didn't break any fellowship rules to become a stained-glass artist, Trina. What you're talking about — going to college — that's different."

Trina stared at him in amazement. The one person she felt would be completely, 100 percent on her side seemed to distance himself from her. Tears threatened again.

Andrew went on quietly, his gaze lowered. "Being a wife . . . and mother . . . is the highest calling for any woman. If you didn't have Graham wanting to marry you, I'd probably say keep learning what you can about animal care from the Internet or books and help out the way you did with Regen. But not at the expense of a family."

Trina slammed her fist against the table-top. "Oh, this is so aggravating! Why can't anyone understand?"

"And why can't you understand what you're throwing away?"

At Andrew's angry tone, Trina drew back, gawking at her cousin. "Th–throwing away?"

"Yes." He glared at her, his lips quivering. "You have a man — a good man — who wants to marry you. You could become a wife and then a mother, but you'd rather take care of sick kittens. What's wrong with you, Trina?"

Of all the people she'd feared might attack her, Andrew was at the bottom of the list. She sat in silence, too hurt to respond.

"Don't be selfish." He held himself stiffly erect, his chin high. "You have an opportunity Livvy would kill to have — the opportunity to be a mother. And if you throw it away over some ridiculous idea about —" The last words came out in a growl; then he seemed to crumble. He spun, leaning his hips against the table with his back to her.

Trina slipped from the stool and rounded the table. She touched Andrew's arm. "Andrew? Is something wrong with Livvy?"

Tears winked in her cousin's dark eyes. His chin quivered. "All the trouble she's been having with . . . female issues?"

Trina nodded. The family had been praying for Livvy's difficulties.

"She got her tests back today. The doctor says she won't be able to . . ."

Although he didn't finish the statement, Trina needed no more explanation. She tightened her fingers on his arm. "I'm sorry."

"Me, too." His voice had lost its hard edge, but it still lacked his usual warmth. He placed his hand over hers and looked directly into her eyes. "Trina, think carefully about what you want. Going to school, getting a degree — people do it every day. But not everybody has the opportunity to build a family. Don't throw something so valuable away over a childish dream."

Trina pulled her hand back, stung by his simplification of her desires. But she didn't argue. She nodded. "I'll think about it. And pray about it."

"Do that." He headed for the door, cupping her elbow and pulling her along with him. "I need to get home to Liv. I'll talk to you later, Trina."

After he drove off, Trina started for the café. But she didn't want to face her mother after the two emotionally exhausting conversations she'd just had. But where to go? Since Andrew's opinion was now colored by his personal conflict, who else might be able to offer support and sympathy?

"Beth," Trina whispered. Beth wasn't Mennonite. She would have a different viewpoint from everyone else in town. Trina would ask Beth. She set off in the direction of the little bungalow on Cottonwood Street.

The door opened to Trina's knock, and Sean McCauley stood framed in the doorway. He smiled, his mouth half hidden by his mustache. "Well, hello. It's Trina, right? Come on in."

Trina stepped over the threshold and stood on the little square of linoleum in front of the door. A television set blared from the corner, the screen showing a close-up image of a man holding a microphone and pointing to a building behind him. Sean quickly shut off the noisy box then headed toward the back of the house, still talking. "Beth and I were just getting ready to sit down to dinner. Come on back and have a bite."

Trina shrank against the door. "Oh, I'm so sorry! I didn't think about the time. I'll come back later." She grabbed the doorknob.

"Trina, wait." Beth hustled into the room and caught Trina's hand, pulling her away from the door. "Don't run off. Tell me about your first day at the vet clinic. Andrew said you were very excited to finally get to work with Dr. Groening."

"But your dinner . . ." Trina flapped her hand in the direction of the kitchen, where Sean disappeared around the corner. "It'll get cold."

"Sandwiches don't get cold." Beth grinned. "Sandwiches and canned fruit —

that's what we're having, and it'll keep. Fill me in."

Trina couldn't imagine her mother putting such a simple meal on the table for supper. Beth was so different. She twisted a ribbon tie around her finger. "Well, it was nice to finally be there, but it wasn't what I expected. I mostly just cleaned up."

Beth tipped her head. "Cleaned up?"

"Yes. Floors, cages, exam tables, kennels, shelves." Trina made a face. "I knew I wouldn't be doing surgery, but I had hoped to at least work with the animals a little bit."

"Oh, Trina, I'm sorry." Beth offered a brief hug. Trina savored the touch of sympathy she'd been seeking. Beth continued. "But surely it's just because you're new. Don't you think, after you've been there awhile and have proven yourself capable of handling the little tasks, he'll give you something more challenging to do?"

Trina considered the question. When she'd started at the café with Miss Koeppler, she'd run the dishwasher and mopped floors. Gradually, the owner had increased Trina's responsibilities until she finally became a waitress and handled the cash register. "Maybe you're right." Her heart leaped with hope. "Maybe I just need to prove myself."

"I'm sure that's it," Beth said, her smile encouraging. "Hang in there. You've wanted this for too long to give up now."

"Oh, I'm not giving up!" Trina heard the determination in her own voice. No matter what Graham or Andrew or Mama said, working with animals was in her heart. She wouldn't set it aside.

"Good for you." Beth gave Trina another hug. "Come see me again on Friday and let me know what you're doing by then, okay?"

"Thanks, Beth." Trina glimpsed Sean peeking out from the kitchen doorway. Beth might not be in a hurry to eat, but it appeared he was. She backed up to the door, her positive spirit restored. "I'll see you Friday with a great report!"

Trina's optimism waned as the week progressed with the same duties assigned each day. On Friday, Dr. Groening remained at the clinic all afternoon, and he called Trina to his messy desk in the corner of the reception area at closing time.

"I'll plan to pay you each Friday, if that works for you."

"That's fine." She was accustomed to Mama paying her once a month, which worked okay since she rarely went to the bigger towns more often than that. Tony went into McPherson frequently, though, sometimes giving rides to their Amish neighbors who didn't own vehicles. He could take her pay to the bank for her.

Dr. Groening placed a check in her hand. "You've done well, Trina. I appreciate your efforts."

Trina folded the check without looking at it and slipped it in her apron pocket. "Thank you."

The doctor crossed his arms and peered down his nose at her. "Are you satisfied with the job?"

Trina raised her shoulders in a slow shrug. She didn't want to complain, but she did want to know when she would finally be doing something besides cleaning up. "I appreciate being able to work here, but I wonder when I might actually get to work *with* the animals."

Dr. Groening's gray eyebrows twitched. "With the animals?"

"Yes. Like I did out at Andrew's with Regen."

The man stared at her in silence for several seconds, and then he drew back, shaking his head. "Oh, Trina, we have a misunderstanding."

Trina waited, her heart pounding.

"Without any kind of veterinary training,

licensure, or certification, you can't work with the animals. It's against the law. I'm sorry if I wasn't clear on that."

Trina's heart sank. "You mean, until I get something from a school that says I have training, I'll never get to help with the animals?"

"You'll be able to bathe them and feed and water any boarders I might keep, but doctoring? No, I'm afraid not." His face and voice reflected sympathy. "If you want to quit, I'll understand."

"I'm not quitting." Trina set her chin in a determined angle. "I want to stay, because I can watch you and learn from you even if I'm just cleaning up after you."

The doctor smiled, his eyes warm.

"But I won't always be cleaning up," she said. "I'm going to get the schooling I need."

Dr. Groening's brows rose. "Your parents are letting you —"

"I'm taking classes online." The moment the words were out, Trina knew she would follow through. Beth had said a person could do nearly everything online these days. Beth had taken a class, and she had offered Trina the use of her computer. If Beth could do it, Trina could do it.

"That's very admirable," Dr. Groening said. "I knew you had an interest in animal care, but I had no idea you were working toward a certificate."

"Well, I am." Trina felt a small prick of conscience. She hadn't actually started the work yet, but she knew she would. Her words would prove true. A *beep-beep* from a vehicle horn outside the clinic interrupted. "That must be Tony. I've got to go. I'll see you Monday morning."

"Good-bye, Trina. And let me know if I can help you with your studies."

"Thank you, Dr. Groening. I will." She ran outside, climbed into Tony's pickup, and slumped into the seat.

"Rough day?" her brother asked with a smirk. "What was it this time?"

Each evening she'd shared one of her messy cleanup tasks with him. It kept her mind off the hurtful remembrance that Graham hadn't asked Mama if he could pick her up from work. Instead of answering Tony's question, she removed the check from her pocket and held it up. "Dr. Groening said he'd pay me every Friday, so could you take this with you when you go to McPherson tomorrow?"

"Sure. Don't you want to go with me?"

Although normally Trina would jump at the chance to go into the big discount store in McPherson, she shook her head. "No, I have something to do in Sommerfeld."

"What's that?"

Trina couldn't tell Tony about her plan to take college classes online. He'd tell their parents, and she needed to wait until the right time to share it with them. She said, "Nothing you need to worry about. Will you take my check to the bank or not?"

He shrugged. "Sure." He glanced at her. "How much did he pay you?"

Trina unfolded the check and released a little gasp. It was nearly double what she would have made in a week at the café working for Mama. She held it out to Tony, and he whistled appreciatively.

"That'll add up quick." He winked. "I can help you spend it."

"Oh no," Trina shot back, giving him a playful punch on the arm. "I can spend it all by myself." She slipped the check back into her pocket then kept her hand pressed over it. Hadn't she just been worrying about how she would pay for college? And now God was providing. She knew exactly how she would spend this money.

EIGHT

"So the first thing we have to do," Beth said, her fingers tapping rapidly on the keys of the computer keyboard, "is help you get your GED." Behind her, the dining-room table held the dirty plates and nearly empty pans from supper. Trina had offered to help clean up, but Beth had laughingly said Trina had done enough cleaning up this week.

Trina propped the heels of her hands on the edge of the huge computer desk that took up an entire wall in Beth's dining room. She was cautious not to bump any of the machines that stood in a neat line along the desktop. "What is that exactly — a GED?"

Beth rocked back and forth in her leather chair. "It's short for General Education Development. You didn't attend high school, so you don't have a diploma, which is required in order to enter college. The GED is just like having a high school diploma without going to school."

"How do I get it?"

"You have to take a test to show your knowledge of the general education subjects."

Trina sucked in a worried breath. Would that include physics? "Can I take the test on the computer?" She peered over Beth's shoulder at the Web site sponsored by the Kansas Board of Regents.

"No, I'm afraid not." Beth pointed to the screen. "You have to go to one of the testing sites. It looks like the closest one for you would be Hutchinson."

Trina cringed. "Hutchinson? But we hardly ever go there."

Beth continued tapping buttons, leaning close to the screen. "Looks like you'll need to plan a trip. And you'll need some sort of identification." She scowled at Trina briefly. "Do you have a Kansas ID card or a driver's license?"

Trina drew back. "No. I've just worked here in town, so I've never needed an ID. And I haven't learned to drive yet, so I don't have a license."

Beth shook her head, her long, blond ponytail swishing back and forth over her shoulders. "Well, you'll need an accepted form of identification to prove you live in

Kansas, so you'd better plan to get one or the other." She clicked a few more keys, adding, "In addition to the GED, you'll also need to take the ACT — nearly every college requires the scores from that test, as well."

"Another test?" Trina yanked a chair from the dining table and flopped into it. "There are so many steps! This is going to take forever!"

Beth swiveled again to look at Trina. Her serious expression held Trina's attention. "Is it worth it?"

Trina gulped.

"Is it what you're supposed to do?"

Trina hung her head.

"If so, then don't see the steps as roadblocks but as stepping-stones to your goal." Beth touched Trina's arm. "Anything worth having is worth working for."

Tears pricked Trina's eyes. Head still down, she said, "Do you know you're the only person who is encouraging me instead of telling me I'm doing the wrong thing?"

"Even Andrew?"

Trina sighed. In the past, she and Andrew had been each other's cheerleaders. She'd always encouraged him to pursue his dream of art despite his family's misgivings. It hurt that he didn't reciprocate now. "Livvy's problems have changed his focus. He thinks I'm foolish to put aside marrying Graham and having children just to . . ." She cringed, remembering the sting of his words. "To take care of sick kittens."

"Aw, Trina . . ." Beth leaned back and nibbled her lower lip. "Well, it is kind of odd, isn't it, for someone from your religious group to want to go to college?"

Trina shrugged. "I'm sure I'm not the only one who's thought about it, but as far as I know, I'm the only one from Sommerfeld who's ever tried to follow through." Wrinkling her nose, she admitted, "They'll probably kick me out."

"Out of what?"

Trina released a dramatic sigh. "Out of my family, out of the fellowship, out of *town.*"

Beth started to laugh, and despite herself, Trina joined in. The laughter relieved some of her tension. Little wonder the Bible said laughter was good for the soul.

Beth tipped her head, her expression thoughtful. "Trina, why is your sect so opposed to higher education? What does college hurt?"

Trina shrugged. "Mostly there's a fear of young people losing their sense of self and their faith if they get caught up in the world out there." She swung her hand in the direction of the window. "The more things you're exposed to, the less satisfied you become with simplicity, so by limiting our experiences, we remain content where we are."

Beth nodded slowly. "I suppose that makes sense. It's the main reason Sean and I attend the church in Carston rather than joining the fellowship here. We're Christians, but we've lived our lives with stuff." She gave the computer monitor a pat. "And having sampled all of that, it's hard to let it go. Besides" — she shrugged — "I believe I can follow God without wearing a certain kind of clothes or doing without the world's conveniences."

Trina slid her fingers down the length of her cap's ribbons. "I understand. And truly, I don't want to leave the fellowship. I love my faith and how we express it. When I put on my dress and cap, it reminds me where I belong, and there's a security I wouldn't trade. I just want to be allowed to follow my heart." Releasing the ribbons, she wove her fingers together and pressed her hands to her apron. "Do you know in Pennsylvania, some Old Order Mennonite youth have been allowed to attend college? Their bishop approved it because it was training that would benefit the community as a whole."

"Having a real veterinarian in the community would be good for Sommerfeld," Beth observed in a thoughtful tone.

"I think so, too."

"So maybe your bishop will approve it."

Trina grimaced. "The bishop might, eventually, but my dad? When Dad read about those youth going to college, he was very upset. He said it would lead to trouble." She shuddered. "He'll be very upset with me when he finds out what I'm doing."

Beth sat quietly, looking hard into Trina's face. "Should you tell your parents what you're planning before you get too far into it?"

Trina's chest constricted. "I want it to be a . . . surprise."

Beth crunched her forehead. "Well, sometimes surprises aren't all that pleasant. I kept secret where I was and what I was doing when I was learning the art of stained glass in order to surprise my mom, and it turned out to be pretty hurtful before the truth came out. Remember everybody in town thought I was stealing from them because I wouldn't tell anybody where I really was? Maybe it would be better to tell your mom and dad up front and —"

"No." The word came out more forcefully than Trina intended. She took a breath to calm her racing heart and spoke in an even tone. "I'll tell them after I've gotten enrolled in a college. If they see how much it means to me, it should make it easier for them to accept."

"I suppose you know best." Beth sounded uncertain.

Trina gave an emphatic nod. "Yes, I do."

"All right, then." Beth swung around to face the computer, pointing to the screen. "This says there's a fee to take the test. You can retake it if you don't pass, but you have to pay again each time. There's also a practice test." Beth sent Trina a speculative look. "I think that sounds like a good idea. For your peace of mind, if nothing else."

Trina squinted at the screen's small print. "How much does the practice test cost?"

"Twenty-five dollars."

Trina sat back, thinking about her bank account. "A small price to pay for peace of mind."

"So . . ." Beth tapped her lips with her finger. "Before you can sign up to take the practice test, you've got to be able to identify yourself. Should we download the test booklet for a Kansas driver's license so you can start studying?"

Trina thought about Graham's offer to teach her to drive. Would he still be willing?

He hadn't come by to see her since Monday. Maybe asking him would give them some time together to mend their torn relationship. "Yes." She bobbed her head in one quick nod. "Please do."

"Tuh–ree–na!" Graham held to the dashboard of the car as it bucked like an untamed colt. "Let out on the clutch!"

Trina's knee left the seat, and the car died. A whirl of dust from the county road drifted through the open window, and she coughed.

"But not that fast." Graham wiped his forehead with an already-soggy bandanna. When Trina had called yesterday evening and asked so sweetly if he would teach her to drive, he'd had no idea what he was getting himself into. He hadn't been opposed to spending time with her — he'd missed her tremendously over the week — but she was aging him fast with her mistakes. He just hoped she wasn't damaging the car's gears.

She peeked at him with a contrite expression. "I'm sorry. I'm not doing it on purpose. I just can't seem to get my feet to work together."

Looking into her brown eyes, Graham melted. "You'll get it. It just takes some practice to get the out-and-down right.

Remember, out on the clutch, down on the gas. The secret is to let up at the same rate you push down. Try it again."

Trina thrust her jaw into an adorable stubborn set, pushed down on the clutch, turned the ignition key, and tapped the gas pedal until the engine caught. "Okay, here we go." And go they did! The car lurched forward.

Trina screeched, "Whoa!" And the car died.

Graham laughed uncontrollably, holding his belly. After several moments, Trina bumped him on the shoulder with the heel of her hand.

"Stop laughing at me!"

He coughed to bring himself under control, but when he looked into her stern face, he erupted again. Her scowl deepened. He held up both hands in surrender. "Okay, I'm sorry. No more. But you said 'Whoa,' and the car stopped. Don't you think that's funny?"

"No." Then she giggled, hunching her shoulders. "Well, didn't you tell me there was horsepower in the engine? It probably recognizes 'Whoa.' "

They laughed together. When the mirth died away, they sat looking across the seat at each other. Graham felt a pressure build in his chest. He would have no difficulty looking into her face for the rest of his life. How he hated the disagreement that had kept them apart this past week.

"Trina, I want — ," he said.

"I'll never — ," she said at the same time.

He waved his hand. "Go ahead."

She sighed. "I'll never learn to drive at this rate."

Graham grinned, giving the ribbon on her cap a gentle tug. "But the longer it takes, the longer we get to be out here together. That's a good thing, right?"

Her shy smile made him want to lean across the seat and kiss her lips. But if someone saw them, the consequences would be severe. He threw his car door open and stepped out of the vehicle. They were parked in the middle of the road, but he didn't expect traffic. He'd deliberately chosen a seldom-used dirt road for her practice. "Come out here."

With a puzzled look, Trina obeyed, following him to the front of the car.

"Sit on the hood." he directed. As soon as she was settled, he knelt in front of her and held up the palms of his hands. "Okay, now let's pretend my hands are the clutch and the gas pedal."

Trina giggled, crossing her ankles and

pressing her heels to the painted black bumper.

He clapped his hands twice then angled his palms outward again. "C'mon. Feet right here."

She stared at him, her eyes wide. "You're kidding!"

"No, I'm not. You said you were having trouble getting your feet to work together, so we'll just practice. Put your feet against my hands." With another self-conscious giggle, she lifted her feet and placed them gingerly against his palms. He curled his fingers around the soles of her tennis shoes. "Okay, up on the clutch" — he tilted her left foot back — "and down on the gas." At the same time, he pulled her right toes forward. "See how it feels?" He repeated the motions several times.

Trina scowled with concentration, one fist in the air as if holding onto a steering wheel, the other gripping an imaginary gearshift. Graham swallowed his chuckle. If she only knew how cute she looked. He let her practice until the discomfort of the hard ground biting into his knees made him grimace.

"I gotta get up." He pushed to his feet, brushed off his trousers, then rubbed his knees, bent forward like an old man.

Her fingers grazed his shoulder. "I'm sorry."

He tipped his chin to give her a smile. "It's okay. You're worth it."

Pink flooded her cheeks, and she hopped from the hood. She twisted her apron around her hands. "Do you trust me to try it now with the car?"

"That's why we're out here." But suddenly teaching her to drive was secondary. Just *being* with her out on the open landscape with the wind whispering through the cornfields and the Kansas sun warming their heads was a pleasure beyond compare. He stifled a groan. Would he be able to make Trina his in every sense of the word?

She bustled around the hood and climbed back into the driver's seat. Graham followed more slowly, and when she reached for the ignition, he caught her hand. She sent him a look that was half puzzled, half scared.

"Trina, this week was the longest of my life. Know why?"

The breeze through the open window caught her ribbons, making them twirl beneath her chin. She licked her lips, shaking her head slightly.

"Because I didn't see you."

"You could have if you'd taken me to the singing like we'd planned."

He cringed at the slight accusation in her tone. He regretted not going after her, yet the hurt had still been too deep. Meeting her gaze, he hoped his eyes reflected an apology. "I don't want to go another week like that." He hesitated then braved a question: "Do you?"

A smile trembled on her lips. "I missed you, too, Graham." She swallowed. "I really don't want to displease you."

Her innocent expression, the sweet words, gave Graham the courage to slip his fingers between hers, linking their hands. "I know you don't."

She removed her hand from his grasp, curling it over the gearshift. "And I appreciate your teaching me to drive, even though we had a falling-out."

"It's easy to forgive you, Trina."

She shot him a quick look, her brows low, but she didn't say anything.

Graham went on. "And I'm willing to wait while you get your animal-care whim worked out of your system." He released a chuckle and said teasingly, "Tony told me you're doing a lot of scrubbing. I figure it won't take you too long to get tired of that."

The answering smile he expected didn't come. A weight pressed on his chest. "What's wrong?"

"Graham, I've tried to tell you. This isn't a whim." She closed her eyes for a moment, drawing in a slow breath. When she faced him again, the seriousness in her expression made him hold his breath. "Do you really love me?"

He leaned toward her. "You know I do."

"Then can I trust you to keep a secret?"

Graham glanced out the window, scanning the empty landscape. He lifted his shoulders in a shrug and met her gaze. "Yes."

She looked hard into his face, seemingly deciding whether or not she truly could trust him. He resisted fidgeting, frustration building. Finally, she gave a little nod, as if giving herself a private message, and then she spoke. "Learning to drive is just the first step in becoming a real animal doctor. I've been using Beth McCauley's computer, and I figured out how I can get the equivalent of a high school diploma. After that, I plan to enroll in online classes. It will probably take me several years, and I might even have to leave Sommerfeld for a little while, but eventually I'll be a real veterinarian."

"College." Graham tried to hold his temper, but he knew the word barked out. "You're really going to do it." He had hoped the long week of distance between them had awakened her to what really mattered — namely, becoming a wife. *His* wife.

She nodded. "That's what I'm working toward. Maybe it won't happen, but I have to try. This . . . this tug on my heart is too strong to ignore. I *have* to try."

Her pleading expression tore at him. He faced forward, away from the silent entreaty for understanding. "College, Trina, is against the fellowship." He didn't say it was against what he wanted. She already knew that.

She ducked her head. "I know. And it's hard to think of going against the rules of the fellowship, but —" Her head came up, her hand grasping his arm. "Why would God give me these desires if I wasn't meant to follow through with them? That would be cruel! Don't you see?"

Graham carefully removed her hand from his arm. "All I see is you are foolishly chasing a dream that will lead to nothing but heartache for —" He started to say "me." Realizing how selfish it would sound, he amended, "Your parents. Have they approved this?"

Her quivering chin gave the answer. Suddenly, he wondered about something else. "Do they know I'm teaching you to drive?"

She pulled in her lower lip and slowly

shook her head.

"Then you're sneaking around behind their backs. That's a sin, Trina!"

"I don't want to sneak, but if I tell them now, they'll say no. They need time to think about it. Once they see how much it means to me, they'll come around."

Graham considered her statement. Did she think he, too, would come around? He'd just told her he was willing to wait for her, but now, looking down the road to years of college classes and her using the earned degree, he feared he may have told a lie.

Slamming out of the car, he stomped around the hood and yanked open the driver's door. "Scoot over."

She blinked at him, her mouth open in surprise.

"I'm driving you back to town," he said, his voice grim. "I won't help you deceive your parents."

Tears trembled on Trina's lashes, but she worked her way over the gearshift to the opposite side of the seat. Graham sat behind the steering wheel and gave the ignition a vicious twist that brought the engine to life. He jammed the car into first gear, revving the engine. Not until he had shifted into third and they were traveling at fifty-five miles per hour with a cloud of dust whirling behind them did Trina speak.

"Graham?"

He grunted, his eyes aimed ahead.

"Even if you won't teach me to drive, you—you'll keep my secret, won't you?"

His jaw clenched, the back teeth clamping down so hard it hurt. But he gave a brusque nod.

He heard her sigh. "Thank you, Graham."

He wouldn't need to tell. There were no secrets in Sommerfeld. It wouldn't be long. Her folks would get wind of her plans, and they'd bring an end to this nonsense. Then maybe she'd listen to reason and accept his marriage proposal.

NINE

"Hi, sweetheart." Beth set the paper bag she was carrying onto the kitchen table and opened her arms for Sean's hug. "I didn't expect to see you until late this evening." He had left before dawn that morning for Kansas City to meet his father and representatives from a church in Olathe.

"The meeting ended early."

"Did they like your plans?" Beth knew Sean had worried over the drawings of the church addition, mixed messages from various committee members making it difficult to pinpoint their exact needs.

He sighed, his breath stirring her hair. "Back to the drawing board."

"Oh, hon, I'm sorry." She burrowed closer. "And then you come home to no wife and no dinner started."

"That's okay." Sean nuzzled her ear, his hands roaming up and down her spine. "If nothing else, we'll walk to the café and grab something there."

"It's Wednesday — they close at three, remember?" With a gentle push against his chest, she freed herself, reaching up to tousle his thick red-blond hair. "But I can throw together some grilled cheese sandwiches and open a bagged salad." She didn't pretend to be a good homemaker, and so far Sean hadn't complained. Of course, they were still in their honeymoon period. Sometimes she wondered how he could bear to leave her as often as he did with his business travels, and other times she savored the privacy.

Sean crossed his arms and yawned. "So where've you been? I called the studio to let you know I was on my way. Andrew said you'd left early, but you didn't answer the cell."

Beth crinkled her nose. "I left it at home — sorry." She moved to the sack and reached inside. "I went to an auction in Carston this afternoon. They'd advertised a Depression-era bedroom suite. I thought if I could get it reasonably, I'd fill up the second bedroom."

Sean came up behind her and curled his hands over her shoulders. "I take it you didn't get it?"

"Nope. Went higher than I wanted to

spend. But" — she lifted a stack of books from the sack — "I got all of these for a dollar." She laid the books across the table, brushing the covers with her fingertips. "Look — high school textbooks. They're outdated, but they're better than nothing." Trina would be delighted with her find.

Sean reached to pick one up, a frown on his face. "Algebra." He looked at the others on the table. "American history, geometry, and earth science? What are you going to do with these?"

Beth laughed, rising on tiptoe to deliver a quick smack on his lips. "They're for Trina so she can prepare for her GED."

Sean's frown deepened. "So you're helping her, huh?"

She shot him a sharp look. "Is there some reason I shouldn't?"

He sighed, plopping the book back onto the table. "You know how the Old Order Mennonite feel about higher education. Letting Trina explore on the Internet is one thing, but buying her books so she can prepare for a GED? That's overstepping some pretty big boundaries, Beth."

Beth took a step back and gawked at her husband. "So I should leave her floundering alone? The poor kid is getting trampled from every direction — her parents, her boyfriend, even Andrew, who should know better than to stomp on somebody's dream. *Someone* needs to offer a helping hand."

"Now don't get all defensive on me." Sean reached out and tucked a stray strand of hair behind her ear. She jerked her head away from his touch. He clamped his jaw for a moment then dropped his hand. "Stop and think about it, Beth. We already have trouble fitting in around here since we aren't Mennonite or Amish. Do you want to give the community another reason to distrust us?"

"I'm not going to let their attitudes dictate what I do," Beth protested. "Trina's a smart girl with a lot of ambition. It isn't fair that she can't pursue veterinary school if she wants to."

"It might not be fair," Sean countered, "but we don't write the rules. And I'm afraid you're going to open a can of worms if you get involved."

Beth opened her mouth to argue, but Sean placed his fingers over her lips.

"No, let's don't fight about this." He slipped his arms around her again, drawing her close. She allowed his embrace but held her body stiff, still disgruntled with him. He murmured into her ear. "I'm tired and hungry. Let's drive into McPherson or

Newton and get some supper, relax, and talk about nothing, okay?"

Sean's hands roved gently over her back, reminding her how much she had missed him during his absence. Beth relented, relaxing into Sean's embrace. "All right. That sounds good. Let me change my shirt, though — I got really sweaty out in the sun." She lifted her face for his kiss then headed to their bedroom to change.

"I'll put these books back in the bag," Sean called after her, "and put them on the utility porch."

She sighed. "Fine." *Out of sight, out of mind,* she supposed. She didn't want to fight with her husband, but Trina was the first person in Sommerfeld to befriend her. She owed the girl something. If that something turned out to be assistance in seeing her dreams become reality, then Sean would just have to accept it.

Trina slammed the book shut and released a strangled groan. From the computer, Beth looked over her shoulder.

"What's the problem?"

"Algebra. Rational expressions, factoring, complex numbers. All I had in school was add, subtract, divide, and multiply. None of this stuff makes sense to me!" She put her forehead on the books. The musty smell of the old textbook filled her nostrils, reminding her of the generations-long rules of the Old Order community. Who did she think she was, trying to change the traditions? "Maybe I should just forget it."

A hand grabbed her shoulder and pulled her upright. She looked up into Beth's stern face.

"Trina Muller, I never took you for a quitter."

"But, Beth," Trina said, "it's pointless! Even if Mama and Dad do say it's okay, I'll never pass the test." Flopping the book open, she pointed to a problem. "Look at this! If $x - y = 1$, and $2x - y = 5$, then what are x and y?" She clenched her fists. "I don't know!"

Beth sat down next to Trina and looked at the problems in the book. She sighed, sending Trina an apologetic look. "I took algebra in high school, but it was a long time ago. I'm afraid I don't remember a lot about the formal steps involved in resolving algebraic equations, but I know with this we can do a little simple problem-solving and find the answer."

"How?" The feeling of hopelessness made Trina want to cry. For the past week, she'd spent her late evenings holed up in her room reading the history and science books Beth had purchased. Those subjects were interesting, almost like reading stories or taking a walk through nature, and she'd enjoyed them. But neither algebra nor geometry was enjoyable. Certainly both mathematics areas would be on the GED test, and Trina would have to master them in order to pass. She blinked back tears. "Can you show me?"

Beth picked up Trina's pencil. "Look. You know in each of the equations, x and y have to be the same number. So let's just explore. Start with 2 − 1, which equals 1. Put the 2 for x and the 1 for y in the second equation. Does it work?"

Trina frowned at the problem. "No."

"Okay, then go to the next two sets of numbers that will equal one — 3 − 2."

Trina worked her way through Beth's system. When she tried 4 for x and 3 for y, both problems worked. She clapped her hands and crowed, "Success!" Her euphoria lasted only moments, however; an entire page of problems — more complex than the one she'd just solved — waited. She wilted again. Looking at Beth, she implored, "Tell me again I can do this."

Beth caught one of Trina's string ties and tickled her nose with it. "You can do this! I believe in you!"

Tears of gratitude flooded Trina's eyes. "Thank you, Beth. It means so much to have you encouraging me. I just wish I had a private teacher — what is that called?"

"A tutor."

"Yes, a tutor. But I don't know anyone in town who's had this kind of math."

Beth flicked a glance into the front room, where her husband sat watching television. Trina's heart skipped a beat. Sean McCauley drew blueprints for elaborate buildings. Surely he was familiar with these different types of mathematics. She waited for Beth to ask him to help, but instead she turned back to Trina.

"Well, it isn't as if you have to know the whole book to pass the test," Beth said. "There will be basic math and a spattering of the higher-level mathematics. If you do well on the other parts, then a so-so score on the math part should still let you pass."

"Do you really think so?" Trina pressed both palms to her stomach. "When I think about taking that test, I start to feel queasy."

"And how do you feel when you consider not taking the test and giving up?"

Trina's lips trembled into a weak smile. "Queasy."

Beth laughed. "So you might as well feel queasy and forge forward, huh?" She tapped the book. "Study. Do at least five of these." She got up and returned to the computer.

With a sigh, Trina got back to work. It took nearly half an hour to work five problems, and she was almost relieved when the telephone rang and Beth held it out to her.

"It's your brother."

Trina took the phone. "Hello?"

"Mom said to call and have you come home." His voice dropped to a whisper. "I think she's upset about all the time you've been spending over at the McCauleys' lately. Might want to step careful when you get here."

Trina stifled a sigh. Never demonstrative, Mama had been downright cold to her ever since she started working with Dr. Groening. Between Mama's chilly treatment and Graham's avoidance, Trina carried a constant heartache. She said, "Maybe I'll swing by the park and pick her a few daisies. That usually cheers her up."

"Okay." Tony brought his voice back to full volume. "See you in a few minutes."

Trina handed the telephone back to Beth. "I have to go — Mama's missing me."

Beth smiled. "Well, you have been spending a lot of time here. She's used to seeing you all day, every day. I imagine she does miss you."

Trina forced a light chuckle as she gathered up her papers and pencils. "Probably mostly she just wonders what I'm up to over here."

Sean pushed off from the sofa and walked to the wide doorway between the front room and dining room. "You haven't told your parents yet?"

Trina glanced up and caught Beth and Sean exchanging a quick, tense look. She shook her head slowly. "No. I'm going to wait until I've passed the GED and have been accepted into a college program."

Sean leaned against the doorjamb and folded his arms across his chest. "Was that Beth's advice?"

Beth shot Sean a look that made Trina gulp.

"Um, no. Actually, Beth advised the opposite — to just come right out and tell them what I'm doing. But I want to wait." She observed Sean's expression change to approving, and Beth's mouth unpursed. Uncomfortable with the silent messages being sent back and forth between the pair, Trina snatched up her things and bustled toward the door. "Thanks again for the help, Beth. I'll see you tomorrow . . . maybe." She closed the door behind her and stepped into the humid air of midevening.

Instead of going directly home, Trina headed for the area dubbed "the park" by Sommerfeld's young people. Just an empty lot where a livery barn had burned down almost twenty years ago, the area now sported halfhearted grass, a spattering of wildflowers, and a crude picnic table and benches constructed out of scrap lumber by a couple of boys learning to use their fathers' tools.

The farmers' market sellers used the area, as did young people on pleasant evenings for a place to gather and talk. Trina hoped a handful of daisies, her mother's favorite flower, might stave off an unpleasant series of questions concerning her frequent evenings spent with Beth McCauley. Mama had warmed considerably toward Beth since Uncle Henry, Mama's younger brother, had married Beth's mother, but she still didn't approve of Beth's non-Mennonite lifestyle. Anyone who wasn't Mennonite was suspect, as far as Mama was concerned.

Trina rounded the corner toward the park and heard laughter. She slowed her steps, turning her ear toward the various voices drifting across the warm summer breeze. The high-pitched giggle belonged to Darcy Kauffman. Wherever one found Darcy, Michelle Lapp was nearby. Michelle had acted sweet on Graham's best friend, Walt Martin, for quite some time, and Walt had recently begun responding, so that masculine rumble no doubt came from Walt's throat.

Previously the café had kept Trina too busy in the evenings to spend much time with friends. Now, studying for her GED had curtailed her social time. The thought of catching a few minutes of chatting with Michelle, Darcy, and Walt sped her feet, and she headed around the side of the general merchandise store with a smile on her face.

"Hello!" she called, and the group at the picnic table turned. Her smile faltered when she realized Graham was with the others.

He leaped up from the table, where he'd been sitting next to Darcy. "Trina . . ." The word sputtered on his tongue. Then, seeming to pull himself together, he gestured toward the table. "Come join us. Michelle was telling us about her cousin's trip to the Kansas City zoo and the antics of the chimpanzees."

Trina stopped several feet away from the table. She hugged the book and stack of crumpled papers tight to her pounding heart. "No, I — I can't. Mama's expecting me. I just wanted to pick a few daisies."

"I'll help you." Graham strode toward her,

his hands outstretched. "Let me take those so you can pick flowers."

She shook her head, backing away from him. "No. That's okay."

Darcy turned around on the bench, peering at the items in Trina's arms. "What have you got there? A new book?"

Reading was a favorite pastime of the Old Order young people, and they often shared new purchases with one another. But Trina knew she wouldn't share this one. She shouldn't have come this way. "Yes, but it's not — not anything you'd enjoy." She hoped Darcy would take her word for it and not ask to see the math textbook.

Graham looked down at her, his expression unreadable. Trina begged him with her eyes to keep silent. He offered a barely discernible nod. Turning back to the group at the table, he said, "Daisies are thickest over against the Feed and Seed's west wall. Hope your mother enjoys the bouquet."

Trina swallowed, called a good-bye, and hurried off. As she picked a handful of the cheerful flowers, she listened to the laughing conversation at the table. Beth's question replayed in her mind: *Is it worth it?* Her heart heavy, she discovered the answer didn't come as easily as she would have preferred.

TEN

Out of the corner of his eye, Graham watched Trina head down the sidewalk toward her house. Just seeing her created a lonely ache in his chest. Darcy and Michelle jabbered away, unaware how little he cared about their endless prattle. The only voice he wanted to hear was Trina's, but she'd just told him his assistance wasn't needed.

In other words, *Go away.*

He never would have thought anything would come between him and Trina, but something had. *Lord, why'd I have to fall in love with her? It's not supposed to be this hard.* He sighed.

Walt clapped him on the shoulder. "Hey, didn't you hear her?"

Graham jerked his gaze to Walt. "What?"

Walt laughed. "Michelle just said her mom's got a key lime pie in the refrigerator. We're heading over there to have a piece. You coming?"

Graham's favorite, and Mrs. Lapp took no shortcuts when it came to cooking. At fellowship gatherings, good-natured arguments broke out between people vying for the last slice of her pie or a second piece of her cornmeal-coated fried chicken. Graham waited for his mouth to water, but instead he felt as though cotton filled his throat. He shook his head. "That sounds good, but I need to get home."

Darcy caught his arm. "Are you sure?"

Graham looked into Darcy's hopeful face. She was a pretty girl with large blue eyes, thick lashes, and sunshiny hair. And she was interested in him — she let him know without being forward. He half wished some sort of feeling would rise up — even a hint of a desire to spend more time with her. But nothing happened. Pulling his lips into a rueful smile, he said, "I'm sure. Thanks anyway."

Darcy's hand slipped away. She ducked her head, the white ribbons of her cap bunching against her shoulders. "If you hurry, you could still catch her."

Graham wasn't sure he heard correctly. He leaned forward slightly. "What?"

Head still downcast, she shifted her eyes to peer at him through her lashes. "I said, you could still catch her."

Graham jolted to his feet. Heat filled his face. "I — I —"

Across the table, Michelle tipped her head. "Yes. What happened between you and Trina? I thought for sure you two would be getting published soon, but lately you're never together."

Graham grimaced. Darcy at least tried to be tactful. Michelle had always been one to boldly state her opinions — there were times when he thought she belonged more with Trina's mother than Trina did. Michelle and Darcy waited, their gazes fixed on Graham's face. He formed an answer. "She's just . . . busy." Even to his ears, the excuse was lame, but it was the only thing he could think of.

Darcy and Michelle exchanged looks. Michelle asked, "With what? I understood it when she worked at the café — her mother hardly gave her a moment's rest. But now? She works in Lehigh and has every evening off. And we still don't see her. How is she staying so busy?"

Graham couldn't answer that question truthfully without betraying a confidence. As much as he resented Trina's choice to pursue a career in veterinary care, he couldn't bring himself to divulge her secret. He shrugged, forcing a light laugh. "You know Trina . . . always up to something." He realized his statement pertained more to the old Trina. The girl he fell in love with had been bubbly, full of life. This new one was slowly losing the sparkle. Sadness struck with the thought.

He stepped away from the table, lifting his hand in a wave. "You all enjoy your pie. I'll see you Sunday in service."

Before they could say anything else, he hurried down the sidewalk, his heels thudding against the red bricks. Darcy's comment about catching Trina if he hurried ran through his mind, and of their own volition, his feet sped up. Did he want to catch Trina?

He knew he did. Despite her crazy ideas of going to college and becoming some sort of animal doctor, he still wanted her. Still loved her. He wished he could set the feelings aside, but how did a person turn off love? The whole community still talked about how Henry Braun had remained a bachelor for over twenty years when the girl he loved married someone else. Henry didn't marry until that girl, widowed, returned to Sommerfeld. Now they were happily married and the proud parents of twins.

Henry Braun had waited two decades to marry the girl of his heart. Wouldn't Henry say his wife, Marie, had been worth the wait? But Graham was ready to be married now. Waiting for Trina to go to college, get a degree, and spend some time working as a veterinarian seemed interminable. He sucked in a breath of hot air then blew it out with a snort. Henry Braun was a much more patient man than Graham professed to be.

Somehow he needed to get Trina's focus turned around. Now that she wasn't working at the café, there shouldn't be any barriers to spending evenings with her. Maybe he should do what Darcy said — catch up to her, walk her the rest of the way home, go on into the house, and ask permission to take her to the barn party planned at the Kreider farm on Saturday night.

His heart pounded with the thought of having an evening with Trina. Surrounded by their friends, being seen as a couple — the time was just what Trina needed to remember there were other things in life besides taking care of animals. The decision made, he broke into a jog. He caught Trina just as she was walking up her sidewalk.

"Trina!"

She paused at the bottom of the porch steps and turned. Her face didn't light with pleasure when she saw him, giving him momentary pause, but he refused to let her lack of warmth deter him.

"I didn't get a chance to tell you about the party tomorrow night at Kreiders'."

She tipped her head, bringing her cheek near the bedraggled cluster of daisies in her fist. "What kind of party?"

"Shucking." Graham laughed at her grimace. "But the girls will probably do more watching than working."

"Yes, you boys will want to show off."

The hint of teasing in her tone encouraged him. "So do you want to go and watch me show off?"

She released a brief giggle then turned her head toward the house. "I'll need to ask permission."

"Here." He took the book and papers from her arms. "Take those flowers in to your mom, ask, and then come let me know the answer." By taking her belongings, he solved two issues — first, her parents wouldn't see them; and second, she would have to come back out to get them.

"All right." She skipped up the steps and entered the house. He heard the mutter of voices through the screened door. The voices drifted away to the back of the house, and still he waited. Finally, Trina returned, her mother on her heels.

Mrs. Muller remained in the doorway. "Graham, what time will the party be over?"

"Early, ma'am. I'd have Trina home by ten o'clock for sure." With service in the morning, Saturday evening activities never went late.

"Who else is riding with you?"

Graham recognized the woman's underlying concern — would he and Trina be alone at any time? "I plan to ride out with Walt Martin and Michelle Lapp."

Trina stood on the edge of the porch, her gaze on her mother. It appeared she held her breath, but Graham wasn't sure if she was hoping for a positive or a negative response.

Finally, Mrs. Muller gave a brusque nod. "All right. She can go since she'll be home early and you'll be in a group. Does she need to bring anything?"

"A snack, if she wants to."

"She wants to."

For a moment, sympathy swelled for Trina. Small wonder she kept secrets from her parents. Deborah Muller tended to think for her children, controlling every part of their lives. Another brief thought struck — wasn't he, too, trying to control Trina? He pushed the thought away and looked at Trina.

"Trina, shall I pick you up at six o'clock?"

Still looking at her mother, Trina replied, "Yes. Six would be fine." Trina moved back one step from the door. "Mama, I'm going to sit out here with Graham for a little bit."

Graham's gaze jerked from Trina to Mrs. Muller. He'd never heard Trina state her intentions before — she always asked. From the look on Deborah Muller's face, she was as surprised as Graham. For a moment, he feared the woman would yank Trina into the house. But to his surprise, she bobbed her head in one quick nod, her black ribbons jerking with the stiff movement.

"Very well. But you've been gone all day. Make it a short visit." She closed the door before Trina could respond.

Trina sat on the top step of the porch stairs. With a triumphant grin, she patted the spot beside her. "We won't have much time. Better sit."

A few uninterrupted minutes with Trina had always been a gift. But for some reason, Graham hesitated. Her sudden change in demeanor made him think of the young woman who ran the stained-glass studio on the edge of town — Beth McCauley. Beth told people what to do rather than asking.

"Or do you need to hurry off?"

The quaver in her voice pulled him forward two feet, but he couldn't make himself sit. Instead, he held out the math book and stack of lined papers. "I'd like to, but it's been a long day. And I have to work tomorrow, so I'd better head home." He put the items into her arms. "I'll pick you up a little before six tomorrow, okay?"

Her brown eyes looked sad, yet he felt the need to step back and process the subtle change he'd just witnessed. He couldn't do that sitting beside her — he needed some distance. He almost snorted. For the past two weeks, he'd had nearly constant distance from Trina and had begrudged the time apart. Now he was choosing to separate himself? It didn't make much sense, yet he still moved backward down the sidewalk.

Still perched on the porch floor with her feet on the bottom riser, she offered a meek nod. "I'll see you tomorrow, Graham. Have a good day at work."

He glanced back before turning the corner toward his own house. She was still sitting there, staring into the gloaming.

"So tell me about your new job, Trina."

Darcy Kauffman pulled Trina into the corner of the barn, away from the raucous young men who tried to outdo one another in the number of ears shucked per minute.

145

The cheers from the girls added to the din.

Trina normally enjoyed watching Graham — although he worked inside at the lumber-yard, he could hold his own against the farmers' sons, and her heart had always thrilled to his success. Tonight, however, she sensed his displeasure, although no one else would have recognized it, and she welcomed a few moments away from the crowd.

"I like Dr. Groening a lot," Trina said, leaning against the barn wall and running her fingers along the attached modesty cape of her dress. "He's very patient, and he lets me watch all of the examinations."

"Your mother told my mother you're basically Dr. Groening's cleaning service."

Darcy's words were uttered without a hint of malice, but Trina still cringed. "I suppose that's true. But I still like it."

Darcy smiled, leaning closer. "I also heard Graham is teaching you to drive."

Trina's jaw dropped. They'd only had one lesson. One unsuccessful lesson ending with a disagreement that had yet to be resolved. "Who told you that?"

Darcy giggled, hunching her shoulders. "Is it true?"

Trina shrugged. "He tried. It didn't work out very well."

"Oh." Darcy sighed, her lips twisting into

a pout. "I'm sorry."

A mighty cheer rose from the group in the center of the barn. Both girls looked toward the gathered group. Walt stood up and waved a red ear over his head. Darcy and Trina shared a snicker — Michelle would be given a kiss before the night was over.

Darcy caught Trina's hand. "Don't you wish Graham had found the red ear? Then you and he . . ." Her voice trailed off, her cheeks glowing bright red.

Trina felt heat fill her face, and she was certain she blushed crimson. Many times she'd fantasized about Graham kissing her. But she knew she didn't want their first kiss to be the result of a chance find in a corn-shucking contest. "No!" She hissed the single word.

Darcy's eyes widened. "You don't want him to kiss you?"

Oh, Trina wanted Graham's kiss. Sometimes she wanted it so badly it frightened her. She closed her eyes and imagined it — a sweet, tender joining of lips. But in her dreams, it always took place on the day they became officially published. Her eyes popped open, her heart skipping a beat. Would they become published if she continued to pursue a degree in veterinary science?

She planned to take the GED test at the end of August. If she passed, she would immediately begin trying to enroll in the community college in El Dorado. A two-year college didn't require ACT scores, so she could get several classes out of the way before transferring to a bigger college. She and Beth had worked everything out. But now a fear struck. Graham might decide to pursue some other girl — maybe even Darcy — if she persisted in her pursuit of education. A stinging behind her nose let her know tears threatened. She quickly turned her back on Darcy.

"Trina?" Darcy's worried voice came from directly behind Trina's ear. "Is something wrong?"

Yes, many things were wrong. But Trina didn't have the slightest idea how to fix them. *Lord, I'm so confused. I believe I'm meant to care for animals. But I love Graham, too. How can we make this all work?*

She sniffed hard and turned to face her friend. "It looks like the girls have started bundling the shucks for fodder. Should we help?"

Darcy's brows pulled down briefly, but then she offered a smile and nod. "Sure."

They moved toward the group just as another whoop rose. Walt pounded Graham on the back, and the other young men laughed and hollered. Trina's feet came to a stumbling halt as people began turning, aiming their laughing gazes in her direction. Behind her, Darcy grabbed her shoulders and murmured, "Uh-oh." Trina knew without even looking.

Graham, too, had found a red ear of corn.

ELEVEN

Graham held his prize with a mixture of elation and regret. A month ago he would have presented Trina with the red ear then given her a possessive kiss that would make clear to everyone his intentions regarding her. But now? He held the ear against his thigh while whistles and cheers sounded, and Trina stood twelve feet away on the straw-covered barn floor, her brown eyes wide in her pale face.

She didn't know what to do, either.

A feeling akin to anger welled up inside of Graham. This ridiculous notion of hers had changed everything. He couldn't put his stamp of possession on a woman who might not be his someday. But how could he save face with his friends? He had to kiss her. Yet, looking into her apprehensive face, he hesitated. His mind raced through the options, and he decided there was only one thing he could do.

With deliberately slow steps for the benefit of their audience, he advanced on Trina. Her cheeks flamed brighter with every inch that closed between them. He stopped less than a foot and a half in front of her. Between his buddies' encouragement and the girls' giggles, he hoped she'd be able to hear him. Leaning forward, he let his lips brush her temple, which would satisfy the gawkers, as he whispered, "Don't worry — I won't kiss you in front of everyone."

The look of relief she gave him sent another rush of mixed emotions through his chest, but he squeezed her arm, straightened, and called over his shoulder, "Okay, I won that round. Who's going to top me this time?"

By nine thirty, the corncrib overflowed with stripped ears, and the bundled shucked leaves lay in neat rows in the loft to dry. Everyone began climbing into their vehicles to return to their homes.

Graham couldn't help but notice Trina's reticence during the good-bye process. In the past, she would have bounced from car to car, offering private farewells to each person in attendance. Tonight, however, she stayed close to Walt's vehicle, waving and smiling, but clearly eager to be done with the formalities and on their way.

He and Walt got into the front seat, and Michelle and Trina shared the back. Michelle chattered away, leaning forward occasionally to tap Walt's shoulder and whisper comments that made him laugh. Trina responded to questions but did very little talking. That, too, was different.

Graham faced forward, his chest tight, as he compared the Trina he had begun courting six months ago to the one sitting in the backseat of Walt's car. He missed the old Trina. Ever since she got the idea of pursuing a career, she hadn't been the same. Why couldn't she see it? Surely if she set the notion aside, her old bubbly self would return.

Wouldn't it?

Walt pulled up in front of Trina's house. "Here you go. See you at service tomorrow."

"Thank you for the ride, Walt. Bye, Michelle." Her gaze flitted to Graham, her eyes questioning. "Bye, Graham."

She expected him to just ride off with Walt and not have a private good-bye? He popped his door open. "Thanks for the ride, but I'll walk from here." He knew Michelle and Walt would want a few minutes alone, too. Based on the silent messages flowing between the two of them following their kiss tonight, it wouldn't be long before they were published. He envied his friend.

Walt nodded. "See you, buddy."

Graham slammed the door and remained on the road until Walt drove off. Trina stood on the sidewalk, her gaze on him. The same reserve he'd seen during the leave-taking at the party was still very much in existence. How he wished she'd warm up a little. Was it only a month and a half ago she'd nearly danced into his arms when he visited her in Andrew's barn?

He walked toward her, watching her suck in her lower lip. She tipped her head back to look into his face when he stepped onto the sidewalk. Her brown eyes appeared darker in hue with the evening around them.

"You could have let Walt take you home," she said. "It's late — Mama will expect me to come in right away."

He shrugged. "Walt will want some time alone with Michelle." He should have said he wanted some time alone with Trina.

"I suppose." She turned toward the porch and took tiny steps along the walkway. He wished she'd say she wanted some time alone with him.

Although she didn't offer an invitation for conversation, he fell in step with her. The porch light cast a golden path for them to follow, and he touched her back lightly as they neared the steps. She scurried forward, away from his fingers, and stepped onto the first riser. But then she turned to face him.

The eight-inch riser put her at an equal height with him. How simple it would be to lean forward and place a kiss on her lips. But if he did it now, she'd think it was because of the red ear. Besides, her mother was probably watching.

He slid his hands into his trouser pockets. "Did you enjoy this evening at all, Trina?" He heard the resignation in his tone and did nothing to mask it.

Her eyes widened. "W–why, of course I did. The shucking parties are always fun." She licked her lips. "And it's been ages since I had an evening with everyone."

He wanted to ask, *And whose fault is that?* But he didn't want a fight. He wanted things to go back to the way they were before that night Andrew called her out to work on Regen's leg. So he said, "I'm glad you came. I wish we had more evenings together."

"I know." But she didn't say, "Me, too," or "We will," or anything else that would have been encouraging.

Graham blew out a noisy breath. "Well, you'd better go in."

Her eyes seemed sad as she nodded. But she remained on the step, her hands clasped girlishly behind her back, her white ribbons trailing down her cheeks. "I don't want to go in with you mad at me."

Graham took a stumbling step backward. "I'm not mad at you."

"Yes, you are." She looked at him, unsmiling. "You invited me to go to the party, but I can tell you're mad. You've been mad at me for a long time."

He knew exactly how long, too. "Trina, I'm not mad, I'm —" But what could he say? If he was honest, he was mad. Mad at her for heading in a direction she shouldn't. Mad at her for being stubborn. Mad at her for disrupting his life. With a rueful snort, he admitted, "Okay, I'm mad."

"Tell me why."

In her expression, he saw a hint of the old Trina — the spunky, I can-handle-whatever-comes-my-way Trina who had captured his heart. Yet the firmly held posture, the tension in her brow spoke of the new Trina — the one he didn't want to know.

"Because you've changed. All your plans to go to school, to become some kind of animal doctor — it's taken something away from you. I miss that something."

For long moments, Trina stared into his eyes without moving, without changing expression, without speaking. When he felt as though she'd turned to stone, she finally raised her shoulders in a tiny shrug and turned her face slightly to the side. She sighed. Without looking at him, she said, "It isn't the planning for school that's taken something away from me."

Without offering further explanation, she climbed the remaining two risers and entered her house. Despite the sultry evening air, Graham experienced a chill. He got the distinct impression he'd just been told good-bye.

Trina followed her mother from the cloakroom. On the benches across the worship room, Graham sat beside the other unmarried men in the last row in the men's section. Her heart ached when she saw him. Not that long ago, he would have met her gaze and sneaked a wink or sent her a secretive smile. But today he didn't even glance in her direction.

He was still mad.

She slid onto the bench next to Mama and blinked rapidly to control the sting of tears. She missed Graham. She missed his laughter, his teasing, the way he could make her tummy tremble with a simple look. How it hurt that he now held himself aloof. She had hoped better of him.

Her gaze drifted to Andrew, sitting stoic and serious two benches ahead of Graham. She had expected more from her favorite cousin, too. Fulfilling her heart's desire meant so much to her, but everywhere she turned she met resistance. Why had so many people let her down lately?

Trina had no time to process that question. The deacons and minister marched in, and the congregation knelt for the opening prayer. Head bowed and eyes closed, Trina added her own prayer to that of the minister — *Please, Lord, bring our hearts together so I can walk where You lead.*

After the service, as people mingled in front of the simple clapboard building before going to homes for meals, Trina moved to the center of the grassy yard and waited. Graham came out the front doors with Walt. The two slapped their black hats on their heads in unison then paused at the foot of the steps to chat. She watched, waiting, hoping, her hands clasped at the waist of her purple dress and her breath coming in short spurts of anticipation.

Look at me, Graham. Look at me. If he would only look — just once — then she could send him a silent message. *I still care. I still love you. Please, we can work this out.*

Someone touched her arm, and she

jumped. She turned to find Michelle Lapp. "He won't be coming over here anytime soon."

Trina frowned. Was she that transparent? Denying she was waiting for Graham would be pointless as well as untruthful. "Why not?"

"Walt is talking to him about . . ." Michelle glanced around, her lips pursed tightly. Then she leaned forward and whispered, "Our plans to be published. He talked to my folks last night after the shucking." Michelle's eyes danced with excitement.

Trina squeezed her friend's hands. "Oh, Michelle, how wonderful for you." She tried to truly mean it, but she recognized a wave of jealousy underscoring her words.

"Yes." Michelle smoothed her hair beneath her pristine cap then ran her fingers along the white ribbons. "All along I thought you and Graham would beat us to it, but we'll be first, after all."

Trina's brows pulled down. Did Michelle see marriage as a competition to be won?

Apparently reading Trina's mind, Michelle laughed and threw her arm across Trina's shoulders. "Oh, don't be silly. I know we aren't in a footrace. I'm just surprised, that's all. Graham's had eyes for no one but you for over a year now, and we all finally saw you looking back with the same interest. Graham's a year older than Walt, so we just figured . . ."

Trina didn't care for the use of the word *we,* implying others had been talking about her behind her back. She also wondered what else had been discussed. As Andrew had often joked, there were no secrets in Sommerfeld. Did they know the deepest secret in her heart, too? While she sought a way to ask without giving herself away, her mother's voice carried across the yard.

"Trina! It's time to go — come along."

With a sigh, Trina sent one more look toward the men's doors. To her surprise, Graham was no longer there. She spun around, seeking his car. It was gone. Her heart fell. He'd left without saying a word to her.

"Trina!"

Michelle gave her arm a little nudge. "I think your mother is getting impatient. I'll see you later, Trina. Don't tell anybody about me getting published yet, okay?"

Trina looked directly into Michelle's eyes. "I don't tell secrets."

Michelle's blush let Trina know she understood the hidden meaning. Of all their friends, Michelle had the biggest tendency to talk too much. "Bye." She scurried away.

"Trina, are you coming?"

The irritated note in Mama's voice set Trina's feet in motion. "Yes, Mama, I'm coming."

TWELVE

Tuesday after work, Tony dropped Trina off at the stained-glass art studio. Before she closed the door of the truck, he said, "Be sure to be at the café by six thirty to eat supper."

Trina caught the warning note. Mama's disgruntlement at the amount of time Trina had spent with Beth McCauley — and the number of times she'd missed the supper hour since she'd started working with Dr. Groening — made everyone walk on eggshells. Trina felt bad that Tony sometimes got caught in the crossfire of Mama's ill temper when he'd done nothing to deserve it. The family's caution around Mama reminded Trina of a comical plaque she'd seen in a discount store that read IF MAMA AIN'T HAPPY, AIN'T NOBODY HAPPY. At the time, she'd laughed. It wasn't funny, however, when it proved true.

"I'll be there. Maybe I'll stick around and

help with cleanup, too."

Tony nodded in approval. "Good idea." He glanced at the clock in the truck's dash. "It's almost five thirty already — you'd better hurry."

Trina gave the door a slam and scurried up the short sidewalk to the front door of the studio. Stepping inside, she called, "I came to use the Internet, if that's okay." Too late she noticed Beth seated at the computer. She moved past the workstations to the desk and looked at the screen. The complex design, half colored, let Trina know Beth was in the middle of planning a new stained-glass art window.

Beth offered a sympathetic smile. "I'm sorry, Trina. I know I told you the computer was available to you anytime, but I've got to have this preliminary window ready for Sean to show to a committee tomorrow. I really need to work."

Trina backed up, aware of Andrew at the worktable behind her. "That's okay."

"You wanted to go back to that math site, didn't you?"

Beth had located a tutorial site with basic math plus algebra, geometry, and trigonometry. Trina had spent at least an hour each evening on it for the past week. She nodded. "Yes. But I can wait — it'll keep."

However, she knew what she needed to do wouldn't keep for long. In just two weeks, Beth would drive her to McPherson to get her Kansas ID, then to Hutchinson to take the GED test.

Beth dug in her pocket and withdrew a key ring. She held it out to Trina. "Here. I'll work on this at home this evening, which will free up the studio's computer. You can let yourself in the back door after supper and go online."

Trina pressed her hands to her dirty apron. "Are you sure? I don't want to infringe."

"It's fine." Beth pressed the key into Trina's hands. "No one will be here to distract you. Just leave the key on the desk and remember to lock up when you're done."

"Thank you, Beth." Trina's heart swelled with gratitude. Aware of Andrew's silence behind her, she appreciated more fully the support she had from one person in town. "I guess I'll go over to the café and give Mama a hand with the supper rush."

"Good idea," Andrew said. Trina turned to face him as he continued in a mild tone that still sounded accusatory to Trina. "I'm sure your mother will appreciate your company. She told my folks Sunday she feels like you're a stranger."

Trina felt sometimes like a stranger to herself, so far removed from the girl she'd been before the desire to become a veterinarian took control of her thoughts. In the past, she would have shared these odd feelings with her favorite cousin, but given the distant way he'd treated her of late, she shrugged and said, "Some unplanned time with her should cure that. I'll see you later. Thank you again, Beth."

Back in the sunshine of the sidewalk, she felt a chill. Once again the question Beth had asked her — *"Is it worth it?"* — winged through her mind. She nearly stomped her foot. Yes, it was worth it! Being a veterinarian was her dream, and dreams were worth sacrifice!

But the sacrifice of family and friends? Is it truly worth that? With a grunt of frustration, Trina pushed the question aside. Of course she wasn't sacrificing her family and friends. Not permanently, anyway. They would come around eventually. Andrew's family came to accept his desire to work as an artist. Aunt Marie, the prodigal daughter, had been accepted into the community after a twenty-year absence. It just took time, and Trina had time.

Turning toward the café, she forced the troublesome thoughts out of her head. It all depended on whether or not she passed the GED in two weeks. If she didn't have a high school diploma, she couldn't enroll in the community college. So why worry about losing her family and Graham until she knew for sure what would happen? The decision made to put worry on hold, Trina marched through the busy dining room to the kitchen and gave her mother a huge smile.

"Hi, Mama. I'm here to help."

Graham hung his canvas work apron on a nail, plopped his cap on his head, and waved good-bye to his boss. Stepping from the lumberyard's dim storage barn onto the sunny sidewalk, he squinted and tugged the hat brim a little lower.

He heaved a tired sigh and turned toward home, but a smell wafting from down the block brought him to a halt. Cabbage, onions, and bread. If his nose was correct — and he had no reason to doubt it — Deborah Muller had prepared *bierocks* at the café today. His mouth watered as he considered biting into one of the beef-and-vegetable-filled bread pockets. She probably had pie, too. If he was lucky, lemon with meringue inches high. Nothing in his cupboards at home would compete with home-baked bierocks and lemon meringue pie.

He changed direction and entered the café. The overhead fans whirled, providing a stir of air that felt good after he'd been in the heat all day. A quick glance at plates in front of other diners confirmed he had gotten a whiff of bierocks. He licked his lips in anticipation, slid into an open booth, and inhaled deeply, enjoying the mingle of mouth-watering aromas. Two bierocks, he decided, a wedge of pie, and a tall glass of milk.

Tapping his fingers on the tabletop, his gaze on the doorway that led to the kitchen, he waited eagerly for someone to come take his order. Someone zipped through the opening, hands filled with plates of bierocks and thick french fries, and he blinked twice, rearing back in surprise. Trina! His heart leaped with hope — she was working at the café again! She must have quit her job with Dr. Groening.

She buzzed by his booth, glancing sideways as she went. "I'll be with you in —" Her steps slowed, her eyes widening as recognition dawned. She gulped. "In a minute," she finished in a hoarse whisper then hurried off with the plates.

Graham resisted craning his neck around to watch for her return. Before she made it

166

back, Kelly Dick trotted to his booth. She offered a big smile. "Hi, Graham. Mrs. Muller made bierocks, so that's the special. Want some?"

"That's what I came in for. I could smell them clear down the block," he said, resisting the urge to send her away so Trina would take his order. "I'd like two, with fries. And is there any lemon meringue pie?"

Kelly pulled her lips to the side. "Um . . . there was a little bit ago. Let me go check." She zinged off toward the kitchen.

As soon as Kelly left, Trina stopped beside the table. "Did Kelly get your order?"

"Yes."

"Okay."

Graham caught her arm before she could escape. "Wait a minute."

Trina shot him an impatient look. "Graham, I can't stop to chat right now. We're bringing in the highway traffic from the softball tournament in McPherson — we probably won't even get our own supper break. Mama needs me to get a load of dishes run so we'll have silverware for the next customers. I'm sorry. I don't have a minute."

He released her arm. "Okay. But when you're done, can we talk?"

For a moment he held his breath, certain

she'd refuse. But she gave a quick nod. "Later." She hurried off as Kelly returned, carrying a plate heaped with two bierocks bigger than his fist and a pile of french fries.

Kelly placed the plate in front of Graham. "There was one piece of lemon meringue pie left, so I set it aside for you."

Graham sighed, smiling. "You're a sweetie."

Kelly blushed crimson and fled. Graham ate slowly, savoring every bite. While he ate, he watched other diners come and go; watched Trina, Kelly, and another teenage girl, Janina Ensz, scurry around meeting needs; and watched the hands on his wristwatch. Eight o'clock — closing time for the café — couldn't come quickly enough to suit him.

He knew from past experience that Trina would be busy an hour past closing, and he hoped Mrs. Muller wouldn't mind his sticking around and waiting until she was free to go. Or maybe she'd let Trina leave early since both Kelly and Janina were working, too. Curiosity burned in his full belly. Had his final comment to her the night of shucking awakened her to her need to let go of the foolish notion about going to college? Was she back in the café? Was she back to normal?

At a little after eight, the last diners left and Mrs. Muller turned over the sign from OPEN to CLOSED. Then she turned and put her hands on her hips, glaring at Graham. "I suppose you're waiting for Trina."

Graham remained in the booth and offered a grin. "Is that all right?"

The older woman sighed. She ran the back of her hand over her forehead, removing a sheen of perspiration. "I suppose, as long as you leave her alone while she cleans up."

"Or I can help."

Mrs. Muller's scowl deepened at Graham's hesitant suggestion. "Just stay out of the way." She charged back into the kitchen and began issuing orders.

Graham remained in the booth and watched the workers restore neatness to the café. Time crept slowly, and he wished he had something to read besides the menu. Twice he almost nodded off, but he straightened in the seat and forced himself to stay awake. His heart pounded in anticipation of asking Trina the question that filled him with hope: Had she returned to the café for good?

Trina put the mop in the closet, wiped her forehead with her apron, and turned in a slow circle. Dishes on the shelves, tomorrow's breakfast items stacked and waiting on the back of the stove, floor clean and shiny, condiment bottles refilled, and dispensers plump with brown paper napkins. Everything was done.

With a sigh, she removed her apron and dropped it in the wash basket beside the back door. As she did so, she glanced through the doorway to the dining room where Graham sat in a booth, his gaze straight ahead, his hands clasped on the clean tabletop. Another sigh escaped. She hated the dread that filled her when considering talking to Graham. How she longed for the days when uncontrolled eagerness carried her to his side at every opportunity for a moment of time with him.

Kelly and Janina tossed their soiled aprons into the basket. The two teenagers looked first at Trina then at Graham, and giggles erupted. Without a word, they each sent smirking grins in Trina's direction before slipping out the back door, their high-pitched laughter following them as they left the café.

Trina shook her head. Although only three years older than the other two girls, she felt decades older. When was the last time she had giggled with such carefree abandon?

She blew out a breath, squared her shoulders, and crossed the floor to Mama, who sat at the desk in the corner, counting the evening's receipts.

"Mama? Do you mind if Graham and I take a walk?"

Mama's gaze jerked upward, her brows low. "A walk? Where to?"

Trina shrugged. "I don't know — just around town. Maybe the park."

Mama glanced at the wall clock. "Be home by ten." She turned her attention back to the tabs on the desk.

Trina turned and headed for the dining room. She jumped when she discovered Graham standing right inside the door that led to the kitchen. Hands clasped against her ribs, she said, "I have to be home by ten."

Graham nodded, his blue eyes solemn yet holding a hopeful spark Trina didn't understand. "I heard. Let's hurry, then, huh?" Cupping her elbow, he guided her to the front door, pushed it open, and ushered her through.

Once on the sidewalk, his fingers slipped away. Despite the balmy evening, a shiver shook Trina's frame. The release of her arm seemed indicative of all the pulling away people had been doing for the past several weeks. She hung her head, staring at the brick sidewalk beneath her feet.

"Trina?"

She looked up, meeting Graham's gaze. That same odd emotion in his eyes set her heart to pattering. "Yes?"

"We don't have much time. Let's walk. And talk. Okay?"

His hand returned to her elbow, and another slight shiver struck. "Okay."

Still loosely holding her arm, he set his feet in motion, and she followed suit. Yet he didn't speak until they reached the corner on the opposite end of the block from the café. Then his fingers tightened, he drew her to a halt, and he angled his body to face her. His warm hand framed her cheek, and he leaned forward slightly. She feared he might kiss her, and her gaze darted back and forth in search of prying eyes, but instead he whispered, his breath touching her forehead.

"You were in the café tonight, working. Does that mean you're back?"

She read the multitude of meanings in the simple question. And the answer to every meaning was no. Taking a step away from his fingers, she shook her head. "I was just helping out. Mama was very busy tonight."

Graham seemed to deflate before her eyes.

"Oh." The single word was uttered in a low, flat tone that spoke volumes.

Although she had distanced herself from him only seconds ago, she now found the need to connect with him. Her hand shot out to grasp his wrist. "Graham, please. Can't you try to understand how important this is to me?"

Graham twisted his wrist free and clamped his hands over her shoulders. His fingers didn't bite into her skin, but she sensed the anger coursing from his fingertips. "And can't you understand how wrong you are being?"

Trina blinked rapidly. "Why is it wrong to want something more than what other women in the community have? It takes nothing from you, Graham, for me to become a veterinarian. I can still be a wife. I can still be a mother someday. It will be a challenge, yes, but why is it wrong?"

Graham raised his chin, blew a noisy breath heavenward, and then looked directly into her eyes. His stern, unyielding, critical gaze made her heart skip a beat. "It's wrong because you're breaking the ninth commandment."

Trina released a squawk of protest. "I haven't been lying! I've been very open with you!"

"And with your parents?" His harsh tone bruised her conscience. "You've been honest with them?"

"Well . . ." She licked her lips, her chin quivering. "I will be. Soon."

"That's not good enough, Trina." Graham withdrew his hands and shoved them into his trouser pockets. "All this sneaking around behind their backs makes me feel as though I can't trust you, either. How can we have any kind of relationship if you knowingly go against the teachings of the fellowship and are dishonest with your own family?"

Trina sniffed, the truth of his words piercing her more deeply than she cared to admit. Since she'd started pursuing the idea of becoming a veterinarian, she knew she'd put aside several lifelong practices, and being open and honest was only a part of it. With all of her studying, she hadn't read her Bible in weeks. During prayer at worship, instead of praying for others, she'd prayed for herself — for her dream to become reality.

Her heart constricted painfully as she recognized how these changes must be grieving her heavenly Father. She hung her head, shame striking hard. But how could she be honest with her parents and still proceed? "I — I don't know what to say. . . ."

Graham's sigh carried to her ears. "I don't, either." The sad resignation in his tone sent another shaft of hurt through Trina's chest.

Lifting her gaze, she said softly, "I am sorry, Graham, that so much has changed. I wish — I wish I knew how to fix it so everyone could be happy."

He twisted his lips into the semblance of a grin. It fell short of any warmth or amusement. "Yeah. Me, too. But it isn't going to happen, is it?"

Trina had no answer to that question. To say yes would mean giving up her dreams; to say no would mean letting go of Graham. She wasn't ready to do either.

After several long seconds, with only the strident chorus of locusts breaking the silence between them, Graham gave a jerk of his head. "Come on. I'll take you home before you're late. Might as well honor your mother's wish in that regard, at least."

THIRTEEN

Trina stared at the gray ceiling of her bedroom. The rustle of her curtains, lifted by the night breeze, and the ticking of her bedside clock seemed loud in the otherwise quiet room. Now and then the squeak of a mattress on the other side of the wall told her Tony tossed and turned, but she lay perfectly still, eyes wide open, mind racing.

How she hated to concede that Graham's words had hit their mark. But her conscience ached with the knowledge of her sins. She must tell Mama and Dad what she'd been doing when she visited Beth McCauley. Sweat broke out over her body as she considered their reaction. Dad would be disappointed, Mama so angry. They might even make her talk to the minister. Not for forgiveness — only God could forgive — but because her actions went against the fellowship's teachings.

A fierce gust sent her curtains sailing into

the air and twisted them into a knot. Then, as the breeze lessened, they settled back into the gentle, nonthreatening swish. Trina watched them, feeling as though her heart were twisted into a tight knot. She wished her conscience could be as easily settled.

She squeezed her eyes closed, willing sleep to come, but after counting off a series of steady clicks — the passing of minutes — she knew she wouldn't be able to sleep until she'd cleared her conscience.

Throwing back the light sheet, she snatched up her robe, which lay across the foot of her bed, and slipped her arms into it. The sash firmly tied, she tiptoed down the hallway to avoid disturbing Tony and stopped outside her parents' closed door.

Trina could count on one hand the number of times she had entered her parents' bedroom. The room was off-limits, and it felt strange now to tap lightly on the solid wood door. At her first tap, she heard a snuffle, but no one replied. So she tapped again, a little harder, cringing as she glanced over her shoulder in hopes the noise wouldn't bother her brother.

This time, she heard her father's cough, followed by, "Who's out there?"

Without touching the doorknob, Trina whispered, "It's me, Dad. May — may I come in?"

"Trina?" Dad's voice sounded croaky.

"Yes."

"Just a minute." A scrabbling could be heard, underscored by her parents' muttered voices, and then the door opened. Dad blinked at her in confusion. "What are you doing up in the middle of the night?"

"I couldn't sleep." Trina linked her fingers together beneath her chin. "I need to talk to you and Mama."

Mama snapped on the bedside lamp. Her hair, usually slicked back in a smooth roll, lay tumbled across her shoulders in shimmering waves. With a start, Trina thought, *Mama's pretty.* How strange to see her formal mother in such an informal setting — propped up on bed pillows, a cotton nightgown buttoned to her throat, hair loose and flowing. She appeared approachable and . . . kind.

Mama lifted her hand, gesturing. "Come in, Trina."

On bare feet, Trina crossed the threshold and stood at the foot of the bed. The polished wood floor felt cool and satiny against her feet, and she twitched her toes, waiting until Dad sat back on the bed next to Mama.

"I'm sorry to wake you up, but there's

something I need to tell you, and I couldn't wait any longer."

Mama and Dad looked at her expectantly, their expressions curious but open.

Trina took a deep breath. "All these evenings I've been in my room or over at Beth's, I've been —" Her mouth went dry, and she swallowed. "I've been studying."

Neither expression changed.

Trina's heart pounded so hard she was surprised her parents didn't hear it. She took a deep breath and finished. "I've been preparing to take a test that would give me a high school diploma."

Mama gasped, and Dad's brows came together. "Why?" Dad growled the query.

"If I have a diploma, I can get into college." Trina held her breath, waiting for the explosion. She didn't wait long.

"College!" Dad leaped from the bed and stood glowering. "Where did you get the idea you could go to college?"

Mama folded her arms across her chest. "I know where. From Marie's daughter, that's where. I knew letting Trina spend time with Beth would serve no good purpose."

"But, Mama, it wasn't Beth's idea!" Trina held out her hands in entreaty. "It was all my idea. She just helped me because no one else would."

"Of course no one else would!" Dad paced between the bed and dresser, his hands clenched into fists. "My child . . . college!" He spun around, fixing his squinted gaze on Trina. "And what did you plan to do with a college degree?"

Although Trina quivered from head to toe, she wouldn't withhold any information. "Become a veterinarian like Dr. Groening."

Mama dropped back against the pillows, shaking her head. Dad brought his fist down on the dresser top with a resounding *thud.* "So that's why you wanted to work for him — so you could take his place. Not because you like animals, the way you led me to believe."

"It *is* because I like animals!" Trina scurried around the edge of the bed to stand in front of her father. Fury emanated from him, and she trembled in her nightclothes, but she stood tall and refused to cower before him. "I like them so much I want to be able to do all I can to help them. If I'm an animal doctor, then I can —"

"You deceived us, Trina." Mama's strangled voice captured Trina's attention. The hurt in her mother's eyes brought a sting of tears. The anger Trina had expected was nowhere in sight — only pain of betrayal showed in her mother's pinched face. "You know our feelings about higher education, yet you went behind our backs and pursued the notion." Mama thrust out her jaw, stopping the quiver in her chin.

"Dad? What's going on?" Tony stood in the bedroom doorway, rubbing his eyes.

"Get back to bed!" Dad roared. "This doesn't concern you!"

Tony's eyes flew wide, and he scuttled off without another word.

Dad wheeled on Trina. "Go back to your room, young lady. Your mother and I will deal with you in the morning. But you will not be going to Dr. Groening's again. You're done."

Trina's jaw fell open. "But — but, Dad! He depends on me!"

"That isn't my problem." Dad's hard tone sent a chill down Trina's spine. "You should have thought about that before you lied to me."

Trina stood on wooden legs, unable to believe her father would be so cold.

"Go to your room!"

At his thundering command, Trina fled. She threw herself across the bed, hiding her face in the rumpled sheets. Had she really thought telling her parents the truth would make her feel better? When she was little, confessing her infrequent crimes had led to swift punishment followed by forgiveness — a cleansing absolution. But this confession had only led to hurt, anger, and despair. Where was the release?

Her misery welled up, bringing a rush of tears. "Oh Lord, I don't know what to do. . . ."

Trina moved through the remainder of the week as if walking in her sleep. Dad and Mama made it clear she was in disgrace. They forbade her to go to the stained-glass art studio or to Beth's home. Her mother walked her to the café each morning, and they walked home together each evening. She spent her afternoon break in a corner of the café's kitchen under her mother's watchful eye.

Her request to attend a Wednesday night singing was met with a stern, silent stare that communicated denial. The only place she found freedom from a chaperone was the bathroom or her bedroom. Her schoolbooks mysteriously disappeared, so she sat alone in the evenings, staring out the window or at her ceiling, mourning the opportunity that had been lost and wondering if things would be different had she been up front with her parents from the beginning.

She doubted it, yet she wondered.

Adding to her humiliation and heartache, Dad insisted she be the one to tell Janina Ensz and Audra Koeppler their part-time services were no longer needed since Trina would be working at the café full-time again. Seeing the disappointment in the teens' faces increased Trina's pain. Now they were left hunting for jobs. She hadn't meant for these innocent girls to be hurt by her decisions.

Graham came into the café each day for lunch, and Trina waited on him, but she didn't give him any more attention than the other diners. He seemed hurt by her aloof behavior, but she couldn't garner enough desire to change it. Her lips felt incapable of smiling, her tongue unable to form conversation, her soul dead. She had nothing to give, and she made no effort to pretend otherwise.

The emptiness inside frightened her, but she had no idea how to regain a sense of purpose. So she moved through the day as her parents expected, waiting tables, cleaning up, being obedient, saying "Yes, ma'am," and "Yes, sir" without complaint or argument. And a constant, pervasive sadness blanketed her world.

Midmorning on Saturday, Beth McCauley entered the café and slid into a booth. The breakfast rush was over, and the lunch rush hadn't begun, so the dining room was empty except for Beth. Trina clinked ice in a glass, filled it with water, and brought it over with a menu.

But Beth pushed both items aside and pointed to the seat across from her. "Join me."

Trina glanced around.

Beth glanced around, too, her eyebrows high. "Nobody's here who needs you. Have a seat."

Trina looked toward the kitchen. Although she couldn't see Mama, she knew she was there. Mama would frown plenty if she saw Trina sitting with Beth. With a sigh, she shook her head. "I can't. I'm not on break."

Beth sighed, too, tipping her head to the side. Her shiny ponytail fell across her shoulder, reminding Trina of her mother's hair falling over her shoulders the night she chose to be truthful. Trina jerked her gaze away.

A soft *swish* indicated Beth had slid the menu across the table. Trina peeked. Beth sat with the open menu propped up on the table like a shield, but she looked over the top of it to Trina. "So . . . haven't seen you in quite a while. Are the rumors true —

have your parents shut you down?"

Trina sent a worried glance toward the kitchen, holding her breath. But Mama didn't appear in the doorway, so she braved a quick reply. "Yes."

"So I won't be driving you to Hutchinson to take the GED test?"

Trina clenched her jaw for a moment. "No."

Beth's lips puckered in sympathy. "I hate to hear that, Katrinka. I wish it were different."

Trina wished it were different, too, but she should have known better than to try. Why had she thought God would call an Old Order Mennonite girl to be something more than wife and mother? All she'd managed to do with all of her dreaming and scheming was make a fool of herself and let everybody down.

She said the words aloud in an attempt to convince herself of that truth. "It was a dumb idea. Graham is right — the highest calling for a woman is being a wife and mother. That's all I need to be."

Beth smacked the menu closed. She leaned forward, her eyes flashing. "Listen to yourself! If it's such a high calling, where's the passion? Where's the excitement? You might as well be discussing how many cups of flour go into the recipe for buttermilk pancakes — that's how *blah* you sound. Trina, there's no life left in you!"

Trina backed away from the table. Her hands trembled as she fumbled with the little order pad in her apron pocket. "You — you decide what you want to eat. I'll be back." She turned with a squeak of her tennis shoe on the tile floor and hurried into the kitchen, her heart in her throat. What if Mama had heard Beth? To her relief, her mother was in the storeroom measuring navy beans into a large colander and seemed oblivious to the brief conversation.

Trina cleared her throat. "Beth McCauley is in the dining room. I thought you might want to take her order." It occurred to Trina she could put a bite in her tone and deliver a secondary message to her mother, but years of practicing respectful behavior removed the temptation.

Mama turned to face Trina. "Yes, I suppose I should." She looked at Trina for long moments, her gaze narrow and her lips unsmiling. Yet she didn't appear as much disapproving as sad. She put the colander in Trina's hands. "Rinse these well and sort out the stones, will you? I'm going to make ham and beans for tomorrow's lunch." She moved past Trina and headed into the dining room.

Trina walked to the stainless steel sink and began the task of sorting beans. The mumble of Beth's and Mama's voices drifted through the open doorway, but she didn't try to hear the words. The comment Beth had made kept replaying through her head — *"There's no life left in you!"* Trina knew her friend was right.

Closing her eyes, Trina hung her head. *Father in heaven, help me. Help me want to be the person Mama and Dad and Graham want me to be. Change me. Please change me. Because I don't want to live like I'm already dead.*

Fourteen

"Amen."

At the minister's rumbling closure to silent prayers, Graham rose from his knees and slid back onto the bench. During the prayer time, he'd found himself unable to pray. He couldn't remember a time since he'd been baptized that his thoughts had remained empty during silent prayer. What was happening to him?

A deacon stepped behind the wooden podium, opened his Bible, and began to read. " 'Who can find a virtuous woman? For her price is far above rubies. . . .' "

Graham's heart thudded in double time as the deacon read from chapter 31 of Proverbs. The words pelted him like grit from a windstorm — " 'The heart of her husband doth safely trust in her. . . . She will do him good and not evil. . . .' " Despite his efforts to keep his gaze aimed forward, his head jerked toward Trina. He'd told her he couldn't trust her. She'd hurt him immeasurably with her plans to attend college.

The deacon read on, describing all the duties the virtuous wife performed. Graham had heard these verses preached before — he knew the list was long. But for some reason, this morning certain pieces seemed to stand out from the others.

" 'She perceiveth that her merchandise is good. . . . She reacheth forth her hands to the needy. . . . She maketh fine linen, and selleth it. . . . A woman that feareth the Lord, she shall be praised. Give her of the fruit of her hands; and let her own works praise her in the gates.' "

The deacon sat down and the minister rose to begin the main sermon, but Graham's focus turned inward. Why had he never noticed references to selling before? Selling indicated a business. That meant a woman would be involved in a business other than managing a household. And reaching forth her hands to the needy — could that include animals in need of care?

He shook his head hard, trying to clear the thoughts. What was he thinking? That Trina *should* go to school? *Should* become a veterinarian? It was ridiculous! Trina's own words returned to replay in his mind — how God had given her the desire to treat animals with a doctor's care. If this idea had truly come from God, should Graham consider it ridiculous?

His stomach churned as he realized where his thoughts were taking him. Outside of the dictates of the fellowship. Outside of the borders established for his community. Outside of his own personal ideals and beliefs.

Once more, his gaze drifted to Trina. She sat, spine straight, hair neatly tucked beneath her cap, her attention unwavering. His heart turned over in his chest. She was everything he wanted in a wife — lovely, gentle, hardworking, God-fearing.

Virtuous? He considered the word carefully. Could he still consider her virtuous despite the changes he'd seen in her over the past several weeks? And then another thought came — *To whom should Trina ultimately answer: to God or to man?*

The sermon continued, the minister's droning voice addressing the congregation, and Graham finally found words to pray. *Father God, help me understand Your will for Trina and me. I believe we're to be married, yet she believes she is meant to be more than a wife and mother. Reveal Your will to us, and give us the courage to follow it, whatever it may be.*

As he closed the silent thought, an image of Trina the night of the shucking flashed through his mind. She'd stood on the edge of the porch riser, her face sad, as she'd told him it wasn't the pursuit of education that had changed her. Now he pondered the statement. If it wasn't studying that had changed her, then what?

Before he could find the answer, the minister instructed the worshippers to kneel for prayer. Graham knelt, rested his linked hands on the hard bench, and lowered his head. As the minister prayed aloud, Graham formed his own prayer: *Help me help Trina find her way back to the way she used to be. Help me help her find her happiness again.*

Beth stood beside the car and waited for Sean to open her door. Before sliding into the seat, she rose up on tiptoe and gave him a kiss on the jaw to say thank you for the courtesy. Fastening her seat belt, she smiled, enjoying the way Sean made her feel like a lady with his gentlemanly gestures. She'd married a jewel.

Sean plopped in behind the wheel and started the engine. He glanced at her and grinned. "What're you smiling about over there?"

"Oh, just thinking about how lucky I am to have you for a husband." She reached across the console to take his hand. "I love you, Sean." Having been raised by a single mother, Beth hadn't witnessed the give-and-take relationship between a husband and wife during her growing-up years. Yet she sensed what she and Sean had was better than many. Maybe better than most, despite the frequent separations due to his job obligations. She gave his hand a squeeze.

He lifted her hand to kiss her knuckles and angled the car onto the highway. "I love you, too, darlin'. But what brought that on?"

Beth shrugged, squinting against the high sun. "Nothing special, I suppose. It's just been awhile since I said it, so I figured it was time."

His low-toned chuckle made her smile. "Well, I never get tired of hearing it."

With a grin, she singsonged, "I love you, I love you, I love you, I —"

His laughter covered the words. "You're a nut." But he said it affectionately. "So what are we doing for lunch today? Want to drive to McPherson?"

"No. Remember? Mom invited us over." Beth frowned. "I think she also invited Troy and Deborah and their kids. So things could get a little tense."

Sean shot her a sympathetic look. "They still mad about Trina using our computer?"

Beth nodded grimly.

"Well," Sean said in an I-told-you-so voice, "it shouldn't surprise you. It isn't as if you don't know the rules of the sect."

Pursing her lips, Beth refused to respond. Yes, she knew the rules. She also thought they were silly. Her mother had explained the reasoning behind the restrictions of the Old Order Mennonite group, but Beth still couldn't see the harm in wearing up-to-date clothes, driving a sporty vehicle, or getting a college education.

Sean's fingers tightened on her hand. "They'll get over it eventually. Don't let it bother you."

Beth sighed, shifting in the seat to face her husband. "I really don't care that they're mad at me. We don't have any kind of relationship anyway, so I'm not losing anything with their anger. I am concerned about how it will affect Mom, and I'm mostly concerned about Trina. She's just so . . . so sad all the time."

Sean nodded. "But don't you think she'll get over it, too, in time? I mean, you wanted to open a big boutique and it didn't work out. You're still happy, aren't you?"

"Well, of course I am. But I'm doing what

God designed me to do — I believe the art studio is His will for me." Beth released a huff of aggravation. "Trina isn't being given a choice to find God's will. She's just being forced to do her parents' will. That isn't right."

"Well . . ." Sean nibbled the lower edge of his mustache as he turned the vehicle onto Highway 56.

Beth yanked her hand from his and folded her arms across her chest. "What do you mean, 'Well . . .'?"

"Honey, don't get testy. Don't you think we've argued enough over Trina?"

At his reasonable tone, Beth melted a bit. "I don't want to argue. But she's my friend. I care about her. I want to see the bubbly, cheerful, full-of-life Trina return. And as long as people are trying to force her into a role she isn't meant to fill, we might never see that side of her again."

Sean shook his head. "I don't know, Beth. I understand what you're saying, but you have to remember these people have a lot of rules to live by, and those rules are important to them. I don't see how Trina would have been completely happy going through with her plans if it meant censure from the community and her family."

Beth sat in silence, digesting Sean's statement. All the years her mother had spent away from Sommerfeld were years of censure. She knew there were times her mother had been sad, even though she had tried to hide it. Now that she was back in Sommerfeld, living as an accepted member of the fellowship, her contentment was evident. Maybe Sean was right, and it was best that Trina didn't pursue veterinary training without her family's approval.

Sean patted her hand. "Beth, I admire your concern for Trina. But what you're suggesting means breaking a generations-long rule. I don't see that happening."

"I don't, either," Beth said, sorrow rising with the recognition. "But it just seems to me that people should be more important than rules."

Sean brought the car to a stop in front of Henry and Marie Braun's bungalow. Beth looked out the window and released a sigh. Troy Muller's car was parked along the curb.

"We don't have to go in, you know," Sean said.

Beth grimaced. "Yes, we do. Mom's expecting us. And I want to see Theo and Dori. I don't get enough time with them." Just thinking about spending time with her twin siblings gave her heart a lift.

"Then let's go."

Beth met Sean by the hood of the car, and they linked hands as they walked up to the porch. Without bothering to knock, Beth pushed the screen door open and called, "Hey, where are the munchkins?"

The patter of feet on hardwood floors told of the twins' approach, and Beth laughed as she crouched down to catch the giggling toddlers.

"Whiz–beff! Whiz–beff!" the dark-haired pair chorused, clinging to Beth's neck and trying to climb onto her knees. Their childish attempts to pronounce her given name of Lisbeth made Beth laugh.

"What about me?" Sean asked, and the two immediately abandoned Beth to reach chubby hands to Sean.

Beth straightened as her mother approached, arms outstretched. "Hi, Mom." Beth returned Mom's hug then smiled at Henry, who entered the room. "Hi, Dad." She released her mother to accept her stepfather's hug, relishing the freedom of stepping into his embrace without embarrassment. "Are we late?"

Henry captured Theo, and Mom scooped up a wriggling Dori. On the way to the kitchen, Henry spoke over his shoulder. "We were ready to strap the twins into their highchairs when they heard you, so you're just in time."

Mom added, "Troy and Deborah are already here with Tony and Trina."

Beth shot Sean a quick look, and he slung his arm across her shoulders. They entered the kitchen, and Beth pasted on a smile as she let her gaze drift over each member of the Muller family. None of them smiled back. Not even Trina. Beth's stomach clenched.

Henry had put an extra leaf in the table to accommodate the guests. Beth and Sean sat next to Trina on one side of the table, with Troy, Deborah, and Tony on the opposite side. Mom and Henry each swung a twin into a waiting highchair; then they sat down, and everyone joined hands for Henry's prayer. Beth noticed Trina's hand felt moist, and it trembled. Her heart lurched in sympathy. Why couldn't her family see the harm they were inflicting?

Henry ended the prayer with "Amen," and Theo immediately began pounding on his highchair tray. Henry caught the little boy's hands. "Patience, son." Theo obediently clasped his hands and waited.

Serving bowls circled the table, and spoons clacked food onto plates. The smell of roast beef, carrots, and potatoes was tantalizing, but Beth had a hard time swallowing, aware of the steely glares coming from Troy and Deborah.

Trina, on her left, pushed the food around her plate rather than eating, her head downcast, her voice silent as conversation took place between the older adults. Sean contributed occasionally, but the cotton in Beth's mouth kept her silent, as well.

"So, Beth," Henry said as he buttered a crusty roll, "when do you plan to add the showroom to the studio?"

Beth put down her fork. "We had hoped to get the construction started next spring, but we may put it off a bit longer. I need to have two more employees in place to help with the windows before I can even think about additional projects for the showroom."

"But the Internet sales are going well on the suncatchers, aren't they?" Henry took a bite, his attentive gaze on Beth's face.

"They're going great," Sean answered for Beth, giving her hand a squeeze. The pride in his voice made Beth smile. "Not to mention the consigned pieces she ships all over the United States."

"Sounds to me like you're overly busy." Troy's stern voice carried over the twins' cheerful jabber. "What with making fancy church windows, too."

Beth forced herself to meet the man's gaze. She didn't really care if she offended Troy, but she wanted to avoid conflict for her mother's sake, so she tempered her voice when she replied. "I am busy, but if I want to have a successful business, it means meeting demands. I don't begrudge the time it takes."

Sean inserted, "She's incredibly talented, and people are recognizing it more and more. It's been a joy to see how God is using her abilities."

Troy harrumphed.

"I think she also serves a purpose in the community," Sean continued.

Beth stared at him. Not one to seek confrontation, Sean almost seemed to be goading Troy.

"How so?" Troy barked the question.

Sean shrugged. "She employs four people from Sommerfeld now. As the studio grows, she'll be able to offer employment to more young people. I would think that would be preferable to having them drive out of town to find work."

Troy lifted his water glass and took a sip. He thumped the glass onto the table. "Maybe, but how long can she keep it going?"

Sean opened his mouth to reply, but Beth put her hand on his knee under the table. "The studio is my life's calling. I have no plans to close it or do anything else. Unless, of course, God opens a different door to me."

"Like motherhood?"

Beth heard Trina's sharp intake of breath at her father's brusque question. Suddenly Beth felt as though she was being used as a bad example to Trina, and heat filled her face. "I don't see how one affects the other."

Mom stood, lifting the almost-empty roast platter, and cleared her throat. "I'll get these serving bowls out of the way, and we can have dessert. I made cherry pie. Who would like ice cream with it?"

Troy acted as though Mom hadn't spoken. "If you have a child, you'll still work every day at the studio, just as you've been doing?"

"Of course I will." Beth raised her shoulders in a shrug. "My mother worked all during my growing-up years. I learned to be independent and responsible as a result. That's not to say every mother should take a job outside of the home, but I don't see anything wrong with it." She gestured toward Deborah. "Even Mrs. Muller has the café, and she has children. It's worked out all right for you, hasn't it?"

Deborah flapped her jaw, surprising Beth with her lack of response. When had she ever seen Deborah Muller speechless?

"But my wife stayed at home with her children until they were grown," Troy argued. "She now has the café so our Trina would have a safe place to work, and she also hires other Sommerfeld young people. Her café serves a purpose in the community."

"As does my studio," Beth said. "And as would . . ." Her gaze drifted sideways briefly to Trina, who sat staring at Beth with wide, disbelieving eyes. She faced Troy Muller again. "As would having a certified veterinarian right here in town."

FIFTEEN

Trina gasped at Beth's boldness. Dad's face blazed red. Mama looked as though she'd swallowed something bitter. Tony stared at his empty plate, his lips twitching. Uncle Henry and Aunt Marie gawked at each other across the table as if uncertain what to do. Only the twins seemed oblivious to the tension in the room, pushing against their highchair trays and complaining to be released. Uncle Henry lifted them in turn from their chairs, and they scampered around the corner, giggling. An apprehensive silence fell in their wake.

Oh, Beth, please don't say anything else, Trina's thoughts begged, but a glance at her friend confirmed her worst fears — Beth had only gotten started.

Aunt Marie also must have suspected Beth had more to say, because she leaned forward and spoke loudly. "So are we ready for that pie now?"

Everyone around the table jumped and stared at Aunt Marie. Beth stood up, and all heads swiveled to look at her. Had the moment been less stressful, Trina might have laughed — everyone moved as if their heads were attached to a single string, being pulled here and then there in unison.

"Thank you, Mom, but I think I'll pass on the dessert. Sean and I will go. But before I do, I have to say something to Mr. and Mrs. Muller."

Trina held her breath, her fists balled so tightly her fingernails dug into the tender flesh of her palms. Beth's hand clamped over her shoulder, and Trina looked up. Tears glittered in her friend's eyes.

"Trina is special. I've known that from the first time I met her. She had a joy that was contagious — she lit a room. I know you all saw it, too." She met Trina's gaze for a moment, her lips turned down sadly. "And I know you also see that now . . . the joy is gone." Beth's sigh brought a sting of tears to Trina's eyes. "I miss it. I miss the real Trina — the bouncy, cheerful girl she used to be."

Trina dared a quick glance across the table. Dad's jaw muscles twitched, and Mama's chin quivered. Were those tears in Mama's eyes?

"You've taken it out of her with your inability to see beyond your narrow views. We were talking earlier about service to the community. A veterinarian in Sommerfeld would be a tremendous service. Half of your residents depend on livestock for their livelihoods. Think what good it would do them to have someone close at hand to take care of their animals as needed."

Beth's voice, although low in tone, trembled with fervor. "That in itself should be reason enough to give Trina a chance to become a veterinarian. But there's a deeper reason. She believes God has placed that calling on her heart. Who are we to say He didn't?"

"A woman's calling is to be a wife and a mother." Dad spoke in a firm, flat tone.

"And," Beth said, "sometimes something else, too. Like an artist. Or a terrific cook, like Mrs. Muller. Or . . ." Once more she looked tenderly into Trina's face. "A caregiver for God's lowly creatures." Turning to face Dad, Beth said, "Being a wife and mother is a very important calling, Mr. Muller, but it doesn't have to be a woman's *only* calling."

Beth took hold of Trina's chin and aimed her face toward Dad. "Look at your daughter. It breaks my heart to see her in so much pain, and she's just my friend. She's your child. How can you look at her and not respond to her heartache?"

Trina pulled loose and ducked her head. She didn't want to look at Dad right now, to see anger instead of compassion, condemnation instead of understanding. Beth's fingers on her shoulder tightened for a moment and then slipped away, leaving Trina feeling cold and alone.

"Mr. Muller, I know you think I'm impudent." Beth released a light, humorless chuckle. "Maybe I am. But what I've said has been out of love for Trina."

Dad came out of his seat, pointing a finger at Beth. "Trina was just fine before you came along and opened your studio and put crazy ideas in her head. Well, she won't be spending time with you anymore, so your influence will fade away. *Then* our Trina will come back. She will honor her father and mother just as the Bible commands her to, and she will be happy in the decision."

Dad grabbed Mama's arm and pulled her up. He shot a look from Uncle Henry to Aunt Marie. "I thank you for the good dinner, but we need to go home. Come on, Tony, Trina. Let's go."

"Thanks for dinner, Mom. Everything was

good." Graham pushed away from the table.

His brother, Chuck, shoved his last bite of cake into his mouth and spoke around it. "Want to play some checkers?"

Normally Graham would jump at the chance to trample Chuck in a checker match, but today his heart wasn't in games. He felt burdened from the thoughts that had attacked during worship service, and he needed time to be alone and process all of the emotions warring for release.

"Sorry, Chuck. I'm going to head on home."

Mom looked up, disappointment on her face. "You aren't staying to visit?"

Graham fiddled with the buttons on his shirt. "Not today."

"And you're going to *your* house?"

Mom's sharp tone caught Graham's full attention. "Yes. Why?"

Mom sighed, her shoulders slumping. "I hoped you might be going to visit Trina. She's looked so forlorn the last couple of weeks. Makes me feel sad for her." Mom tipped her head, one black ribbon slipping along her cheek. "You're still courting, aren't you?"

Graham clutched the back of his chair, his head low. He knew how much his family liked Trina — Mom especially — and he didn't want to upset her by saying he was no longer courting Trina. Yet saying yes might give her false hope that things were okay between them. He wasn't sure what would happen as far as Trina was concerned, despite how his heart still ached with loving her.

"Graham?"

He lifted his head and met his mother's concerned gaze. He forced a smile. "Don't worry, Mom. Things'll work out for the best."

An ambiguous answer, but it seemed to satisfy his mother. She nodded and began clearing dishes. "Well, you run on, then, and get some rest." A scowl marred her brow. "You look haggard, son."

Graham waved good-bye and headed outside. Shoving his hands into his pockets, he made his way slowly toward his own little house. His empty little house. His mother's parting comment followed him. He looked haggard? Well, he supposed it was possible. Worry and sadness could do that to a person.

He let the screen door slam behind him; then he crossed to the sofa and threw himself onto the center cushion. Head back, eyes closed, his mind drifted over the morning's sermon and all the strange feelings that had coursed through him when the Bible passage was read.

Something pressed at the fringes of his mind, trying to clarify itself. He squeezed his eyes tight, pinching his lips. *What is it, Lord?* Unable to grasp the elusive message, he got up and retrieved his Bible. Flopping it open to Proverbs, he located the text and read it himself. Slowly. Finger underlining each word. Face pursed in fierce concentration. Heart begging for understanding.

When he reached the final verse, a jolt as powerful as a lightning bolt straightened him in the seat. He lurched backward and then forward as he bent over the Bible and read the verse again.

" 'Give her of the fruit of her hands; and let her own works praise her in the gates.' " He closed the Bible and aimed his gaze unseeingly across the room. His mind raced to comprehend his strange reaction to the words. Like layers being peeled away to reveal a hidden treasure, understanding dawned bit by bit until a clear picture emerged.

Graham leaped from the sofa and charged to the door. He hoped Trina was home. He needed to talk to her.

A light tap roused Trina from an uneasy

sleep. She rolled over on the bed, her cap coming loose. Still reclining on the mattress, she said, "Yes?"

The door squeaked open a few inches. Mama peered in. "Trina, Graham is here and would like to see you." A frown creased her face. "But before you come out, straighten your hair and cap."

Graham. Trina sighed. She wasn't up to Graham's disapproval after the awful lunch scene at Uncle Henry's. Beth meant well, but she'd gotten Dad so upset he wouldn't even speak on the way home. Trina couldn't face another angry man.

Her heart heavy, she shook her head. "I'd rather not visit today, Mama. Would you tell him, please?"

Mama's lips pursed so tightly they nearly disappeared. But then her face relaxed, her expression showing sympathy. "All right, daughter. I'll tell him."

Trina lay, her heart booming as she held her breath, and listened to the mumble of voices. Graham's raised slightly, the words indiscernible but the tone insistent. Mama's firm reply came, then a brief rebuttal from Graham, Mama's voice again, and finally Graham's resigned farewell. The click of the screen door signaled his departure.

Her breath whooshed out in relief. She

rolled to her side, closing her eyes once more, but another tap at the door intruded. Without moving, she called, "What is it?"

"Trina?"

Tony's whisper. Trina peeked over her shoulder. "What?"

"Can I come in?"

Trina released a loud huff. "All right." Her tone wasn't welcoming, but Tony tiptoed in anyway. When he sat on the edge of the bed, she snapped, "What do you want?"

"I think you should've talked to Graham." Tony's youthful face puckered in concern. "He looked really disappointed when Mom sent him away."

Trina tried to conjure sympathy, but none would come. Graham had been sending her away, figuratively, for weeks. Why should she care about his disappointment? It certainly couldn't equal hers. She shrugged.

Tony shook his head, staring at her in confusion. "You and Graham've been seeing each other for a long time. I thought you liked each other. I thought when you really like somebody you try to work things out."

"Tony, how is this your business?" Trina's words came out in a harsh hiss.

Tony's face blotched red. He picked at a hangnail, his eyes downcast. "Dunno.

Just . . . makes me feel bad, having everybody upset with everybody else."

Trina shifted her gaze to the ceiling. "Everybody's not upset with *everybody*. Everybody's just upset with *me*. So don't let it bother you."

"But it does bother me!" Tony nudged Trina on the leg, capturing her attention. "I–I've been thinking . . . about what Beth said at lunch today."

Trina groaned. "Tony, let's not talk about lunch, please?" An image of her father's furious face flashed through her memory. She threw her arm across her eyes to block the sight, but it replayed behind her closed lids.

Tony yanked her arm down. "I have to. She's right. And — and I know I bug you a lot, but I miss my happy sister."

Trina opened her eyes and looked at Tony. Tears pricked her eyes at the sorrow reflected in his dark eyes. She swallowed hard.

"Are you going to be unhappy forever if you don't get to be a veterinarian?"

The whispered question hung in the air for several long seconds. Tony waited, silent, his unblinking gaze pinned to her face. Finally, Trina heaved a sigh. Running her fingers up and down the length of her dress's modesty cape, she shook her head.

"I wish I knew. It sure feels like it right now. But I hope not."

Tony hung his head. "Me, too."

Trina touched his shoulder. "I'm sorry you're feeling bad, Tony. I don't mean to make everyone feel bad. I just —" But what could she say? Tony wouldn't understand the hollow ache that left her feeling dull and empty. How could he understand when she couldn't understand it herself? Why, she wondered again, had God given her a desire He knew she couldn't fulfill?

Giving her brother's shoulder a pat, she swung her legs over the edge of the bed. "I'll be okay, Tony. Don't worry."

He sent her a dubious look.

She forced her lips into a smile, although she was certain it lacked its former spark. "You know how girls are. Moody."

He snorted. "Yeah." He interjected disdain into the word while grinning.

She punched him on the arm, as she knew he expected, then pushed to her feet. "I think I'll go ask Mama and Dad if I can take a walk."

"Want me to go with you?"

Trina crinkled her nose. "If I say no, will you be offended?"

Tony rose, shrugging. "Who wants to walk with a moody girl anyway?"

A light chuckle found its way from Trina's throat. A rush of love swept over her, and she impulsively threw her arms around her brother. "Thanks, Tony."

He gave her back a few awkward pats and pulled away. "Yeah. Okay." His cheeks blazed red. He backed up toward the door. "I hope the walk helps."

"I'm sure it will." But when he stepped out of the room, Trina felt her shoulders collapse. A walk wouldn't cure anything even if she walked all the way to Alaska and back. She feared she would carry the weight of unfulfilled dreams forever.

SIXTEEN

"Where are you going?" Dad nearly growled the question.

Trina shrugged. "Just around town. Maybe to the cemetery and back."

"Not to McCauleys'?"

It took effort not to sigh. "No, Dad."

Mama, seated on the opposite side of the sofa, stretched her hand out to touch Dad's knee. "Let her go. Sometimes a girl just needs to . . . get off alone."

Trina nearly jolted in surprise. Never had Mama been so understanding. She looked at Dad — would he heed Mama's words?

Dad smacked his newspaper against his knee a couple of times, peering at Trina with narrowed eyes. Finally he let out a huff. "All right. But be back before supper so you can help your mother."

Trina nodded and headed for the door. She stepped onto the porch, breathing in the heavy, hot air of midafternoon. Knowing her parents were probably watching through the big front-room window, she moved down the sidewalk toward the cemetery. It had been a snap decision to name the community resting place as her destination, but now that she thought about it, it seemed a likely choice. One buried the dead in a cemetery. She needed to bury her dream.

Sweat broke out across her brow and trickled between her shoulder blades despite the thick shade offered by the towering elms and maples lining the street. In another week it would be August — and probably even hotter. Then September, when college classes traditionally began. She kicked a pebble, a feeble attempt to dislodge the thought.

Determinedly, she turned her attention outward. As she passed neat houses, she named off the families. And their pets. Funny how she might forget the name of a child residing under the roof, but she knew the names of every cat, dog, rabbit, and parakeet. Didn't that mean something?

Puffing out her cheeks, she blew out a frustrated breath. Then she clenched her fists and picked up speed. Her feet smacked the brick walkway. Her arms pumped, stirring the air. Her nose stung with the desire to cry. By the time she reached the cemetery, her back was covered in sweat, and fine strands of hair, loosened from the roll on the back of her head, clung to her sticky neck. She scanned the grounds, seeking the tallest stone to crouch behind and give vent to the tears that longed for release.

Most of the headstones were uniform in size and shape, but the Braun family stone loomed higher and wider. The sun glinted off the back of the massive sandstone marker. Surely a large slice of shade waited on the other side. Trina moved briskly across the short grass to the stone, prepared to crumple behind it. But when she rounded the chiseled edge, she came to a surprised halt. Someone was already leaning against the stone, picking apart a blade of grass.

"Graham?" She blinked twice, shielding her eyes with her hand.

He leaped to his feet, snatching off his ball cap at the same time. "Trina."

"What are you doing here?" they asked at the same time.

Trina clamped her jaw shut, taking a hesitant step backward. Two longings filled her — to run away as quickly as she could and to throw herself into his arms. But she did neither. She simply stood with clasped hands at her waist, staring into his unsmiling face.

"I come here a lot." Graham held his cap against his thigh, his fingers convulsing on the brim. "It's a good place to think . . . and pray."

Trina nodded. Hadn't she come here to think? But praying . . . she hadn't considered that. Guilt struck. She took another slow step backward. "Well, I'll leave you alone, then."

"No!" His hand shot out, not quite touching her.

She jumped, and he lowered his hand.

"I mean, please don't leave. I — I came by your house to see you, but your mother said you were asleep."

Mama fibbed? Trina could scarcely believe it. She stood stupidly, trying to make sense of her mother's strange behavior.

"But I'm glad you're here. I have something I want to tell you."

Trina brought her focus back to Graham. Her heart began to pound. If anyone saw her out here with Graham and told her dad, he'd be madder yet. She shook her head. "Please. I don't think —"

"Just for a few minutes."

"But if my folks find out I met you here . . ." She licked her lips.

Graham looked around, seeming to scan

every inch of their surroundings. "There's no one nearby, Trina. And we aren't doing anything wrong." He caught her elbow and pulled her into the shade of the headstone. "Just let me say this, okay?"

Holding her arm stiffly while he grasped her elbow, she debated jerking free and dashing away. But she was tired. With a sigh, she offered a meek nod.

He sat, tugging her down next to him. Trina tucked her legs to the side, smoothing her skirt over her knees. Graham shifted over slightly, putting a few inches of space between them. The sandstone felt rough but cool against her back, and she leaned a little more heavily against it, her head angled sharply to meet Graham's gaze.

"Trina, this morning's sermon . . . I can't get the Bible reading out of my head."

Trina nodded miserably. The "virtuous woman" had been preached before, always as a means of encouraging women to be godly, industrious wives and mothers. The reading of those verses this morning had been like rubbing salt in an open wound.

"Especially the last verse — the one about giving her the fruit of her hands and letting her works praise her."

Trina's brow furrowed as Graham's face contorted with emotion.

"Trina, I fear I've been wrong."

She tipped her head, her heart skipping a beat. Had she heard him correctly?

"I fear . . . we've all been wrong."

Trina swallowed. "W–what do you mean?"

Graham shifted slightly, resting one shoulder against the gravestone, his face turned toward her. "Tell me again why you want to become a veterinarian."

She had no difficulty finding the answer to his question. "Because for as along as I can remember, I've always loved caring for animals."

"And you think — no, you *believe* — God put that desire in your heart?"

"Yes, I do."

"Trina, you said it wasn't the desire to become a veterinarian that changed you." Graham's hand moved forward, his fingertips brushing against hers. "I didn't understand at the time, but I think I do now. The reason you've changed — the reason you never smile anymore — is because . . . because we're holding you back."

She sucked in a sharp breath.

"We're keeping you from answering God's call, and it's crushing you inside."

Trina nearly wilted. Finally, someone understood! So great was her relief, tears spurted into her eyes.

Graham leaned forward slightly, bringing his face closer. "Am I right?"

With a choked sob, Trina nodded. "Yes. And — and it's hurt *so much,* Graham."

He cupped her cheek with his broad hand. "I'm sorry."

She searched his face, seeing sincerity in his eyes. The comfort of his simple touch lessened the pain in her chest. She nodded, accepting his apology.

With a sigh, he dropped his hand. "I can't change what's past, Trina, and I'm not sure that things will change for you in the future. Your parents may never grant permission; the fellowship may say it can't be done. So you might not be able to follow through on what you want, but I want you to know I understand. And I won't stand in your way if you want to try."

Trina stared, her mouth open. "Do you really mean that?"

His solemn nod offered a response.

"But what about — what about getting published?" She hardly dared to breathe, waiting for his answer.

"I love you, Trina."

The beautiful words swept Trina from despair to delight. She had asked God to bring their hearts together so she could walk where He led, and God had answered.

Despite her neglect of Him in the past days, He'd still heard and answered. A genuine smile broke across her face, bringing with it the rush of happy tears. She clasped Graham's hand between both of hers. "Oh, Graham, I love you, too."

Graham rose, helping her up at the same time. "Then let's go talk to your parents. Let's tell them we want to be published. And let's tell them we want to talk to the bishop about the possibility of you going to college."

Trina's knees buckled, and had it not been for Graham's strong hands holding tight, she might have collapsed onto the grass. "Are — are you sure?"

"I'm sure." Graham slid his finger along Trina's cheek. "I know I love you. And if you believe God is calling you to this service, then I must give you the fruit of your hands."

"Oh, Graham . . ." Tears distorted her vision.

He gave her hand a squeeze. "They might say no, Trina."

She blinked rapidly, peering into his serious face.

"But we'll try."

Trina took in a deep breath and released it slowly. "We'll try."

"And if it doesn't work?"

Now it seemed Graham held his breath.

Trina shifted her hand to link her fingers with his. "Then I'll be grateful that I at least had your support. And I'll try to accept it."

"Okay." Graham put his hand on her back, aiming her toward the cemetery gate. "Then let's go try."

Graham perched in a straight-backed chair transplanted from the dining room to the living room and faced Trina's father. The man sat in his overstuffed chair like a king on a throne, his presence stern yet attentive. Graham hoped he maintained a calm appearance. Underneath, he felt as though he might quiver to pieces. Yet a potential father-in-law should see only conviction and courage when being asked for his daughter's hand in marriage. So Graham squared his shoulders, clamped his hands over his knees, and met Troy Muller's stern gaze without squirming.

"I have a good job at the lumberyard — as you know, the business will be mine someday. My dad has promised that. My house is already built, so I have a home waiting."

Mr. Muller waved his hand. "All superficial." He leaned forward, resting his elbows on his knees. "You know what's important to me."

Graham flicked a quick glance at Trina. She sat beside her mother on the end of the sofa. The soft expression in her eyes gave him the courage to continue.

"I love your daughter, sir, and I commit to being a godly husband to her. If God sees fit to bless us with children, they'll be raised in the fellowship. Trina will not be left wanting physically, emotionally, or spiritually."

Mr. Muller gave a brusque nod and leaned back. "That's what I was waiting to hear." He shifted to pin a serious look on Trina. "Trina, Graham is asking permission for you to be published. Do you have any opposition to his request?"

A smile quavered on Trina's lips. She shook her head. "No, sir."

The man slapped his knees. "Very well. I'll speak to the bishop, and when he gives his approval, your intentions will be published." He started to rise.

Graham held out his hand. "There's something else we need to discuss."

Mr. Muller sank back into his chair.

Graham rose and took two steps to stand at the end of the sofa. He put his hand on Trina's shoulder. Although he didn't look at her, he sensed her turning her face upward.

223

Her muscles felt tight beneath his hand, and he gave a gentle squeeze of assurance before speaking.

"As you know, Trina has spent time studying —"

"Behind our backs," Mr. Muller inserted, his brows coming down into a sharp *V.*

Graham nodded. "Behind your backs. But I was aware of her actions. She shared them with me."

Mr. and Mrs. Muller exchanged a quick glance.

"You're aware she had plans to take a test to get a high school diploma and then attend college."

Mr. Muller's cheeks became streaked with banners of temper. "And you're aware we've forbidden her from further pursuit."

Graham nodded. "Yes, I know. But I'd like to humbly ask you to reconsider."

Mr. Muller gaped at Graham as if he'd suddenly broken out in purple polka dots.

Trina's mother leaned forward to peer into Graham's face. "Why would you ask such a thing?"

Graham offered a quick, silent prayer for guidance before replying. "Trina believes God has called her to this task. And the Bible verses read in service only this morning say that a woman should be allowed the fruit of her hand. I believe God is telling me this is His will for Trina."

Trina's father came out of his chair. "You speak nonsense! We have always followed the belief that a woman's place is in the home." He whirled on Trina. "Not in a barn!"

Trina recoiled, her shoulder connecting with Graham's side. He curled both hands over her shoulders. She trembled beneath his touch, stirring his ire. He opened his mouth to respectfully request the older man to calm himself, but Mrs. Muller bolted to her feet and stepped in front of her husband.

"Troy, please do not raise your voice. The neighbors needn't be aware of our business." She spoke reasonably, as a wife should, yet an undercurrent of tension carried through.

Mr. Muller's lower jaw jutted forward. "If my voice is raised, it's because of great frustration. They've both lost their senses!"

Trina's mother lowered her head for a moment, her shoulders lifting and falling as if she took mighty breaths. Finally, she returned to the sofa and sat next to Trina. Her face was white, but her eyes flashed with a fire Graham had often seen in Trina's eyes.

Taking Trina's hand, she spoke directly to

her daughter. "Trina, you know I've always been strict with you." She paused, and Trina offered a small nod that seemed to encourage her mother to continue. "We've never told you this, but . . . before you were born, your father and I lost three babies. I couldn't carry them to term."

Graham took a step back. The subject matter was personal — something reserved for families. "Maybe I should leave. . . ."

But she held her hand to him. "No, Graham. If you're to marry Trina, you need to know this, too."

Mr. Muller moved to his wife and sat beside her, putting his hand on her knee. His expression softened. Graham returned to his spot at Trina's back and once more placed his hands over her shoulders.

Mrs. Muller continued. "When I found out I was expecting you, I told God if He let me have this baby, I would raise it right. The child would learn early to respect and follow His teachings. I would make no mistakes, and He wouldn't regret allowing me the privilege of motherhood." Tears spilled from the woman's eyes. "I've taken that promise seriously, Trina, but I fear in my attempts to teach you respect, I didn't give you freedom to grow into your own person."

"Oh, Mama . . ." Trina raised her arms to embrace her mother. "You've been a good mother to me. You did raise me right. I'm sorry I've disappointed you."

Pulling free, Mrs. Muller shook her head fiercely. "You haven't disappointed me. You've always been obedient, always meeting your father's and my expectations, never giving us a reason to distrust you. Until . . ."

Graham finished the sentence in his mind. *Until now.* Silence fell — a heavy, uncomfortable silence. Trina hung her head, and her mother sniffled while her father sat stern and stoic. Graham stared over their heads, wondering if he should speak in Trina's defense. What she'd done — sneaking behind her parents' back — was wrong, yet her reasons were good. How to reconcile the wrong with the right? Before he found an answer, Mrs. Muller turned to face her husband.

"Troy, has Trina ever defied us before . . . before this time?"

Mr. Muller shook his head.

"No, never. Not until now." Spinning, she faced Trina again. "Trina, I don't agree that you should have misled us. That was wrong. But . . . I think . . . maybe . . . you should go ahead and take that test."

SEVENTEEN

Trina held her breath, anticipating her father's explosion. Graham's warm hands on her shoulders gave her strength to face the tirade, but she still wished it could be avoided.

But instead of jumping up and spouting in frustration, Dad shook his head, narrowed his gaze, and stared at Mama. "Has everyone in this house gone crazy?"

He nearly whispered the words, and Trina resisted the urge to giggle. He must be remembering Mama's admonition about the neighbors hearing. It was the only logical explanation. But all other logic seemed to have fled the room. Was it logical that Graham would ask her parents to allow her to go to college? Was it logical that Mama would agree? Was it logical that Dad, after exhibiting his temper, would respond calmly? Trina felt as though she were caught in a dream, where nothing made sense.

"Please listen to me, Troy." Rarely had her outspoken Mama seemed so hesitant. Trina listened, spellbound. "The very fact that our daughter has always abided by our wishes tells me she wouldn't do this thing without having solid reasons — without having solid beliefs that it is right. She isn't rebellious. She isn't thoughtless. Yes, she made a mistake in going ahead without our permission. She's young, and the young can be impetuous. Even us, once . . ."

For a moment, Mama and Dad locked gazes, and Trina suspected they were both reliving some youthful activity known to no one but them. She tried to imagine her parents young and foolishly impetuous, but the picture wouldn't gel. Dad broke away to stare at his clenched fists in his lap.

"Of course, Trina's wish to attend a college could be denied by the bishop." Mama went on softly, thoughtfully. "Our sect, unlike some others, has never allowed our young people to go beyond grade nine. But I think, given the usefulness of the profession, and her strong conviction that it's God's will, we should let her ask." In an uncharacteristic display of affection, Mama placed her hand over Dad's fists. "Please, Troy?"

Graham slipped to one knee beside Trina.

"Mr. Muller, as Trina's intended husband, I should have the greatest reasons to object. Trina knows how much I have objected when she's spoken to me of her desire. I fought her, telling her she needed to be a wife and mother only. I was afraid I would lose her to this dream."

Trina looked at Graham's chiseled profile, her heart expanding with love for him. To hear him openly support her ideas gave her more joy than she could have imagined.

He continued in a steady, courteous voice. "But God has softened my heart. I would like to pray with you and your wife for God's will to be done. If Trina is meant to become a veterinarian, then surely the leaders will grant permission."

"And if they say no?"

Trina chose to answer her father's question. "If they say no, I will accept it as God's will."

Dad looked at her for a long time, his thick brows pulled down, his lips pressed tightly together. No one spoke, waiting for him to make a decision. Trina's heart pounded with hope. Although she inwardly begged for a positive response, she knew a part of her had been restored with Graham's and Mama's understanding and acceptance of her longing. Even if Dad said no — even if the leaders said no — there would always be the knowledge that someone believed in her.

Finally, Dad shook his head and pushed to his feet. "I still don't understand, Trina. I'm still very disappointed in your deceptions. But I am willing to allow you to speak to the minister and deacons for permission to ask the bishop. Whatever they deem acceptable, I will also accept."

Trina leaped from the sofa and threw her arms around her father's neck. He stood with his arms at his side, allowing her embrace, but he didn't hug her back. Trina understood that, too — she had hurt and displeased him. It would take time to regain his trust and affection. Arms still tight around his neck, she whispered, "Thank you."

He caught her shoulders, set her aside, and left the room without another word.

Trina hung her head. Tears stung behind her nose at her father's abrupt dismissal. Arms embraced her — Mama, offering a rare hug. Trina rested her head on Mama's shoulder, savoring the comfort provided. In time, Mama pulled away and cupped Trina's cheeks.

"You and Graham go sit on the porch, talk about your plans. You have much to consider if you're to be married. I'll . . . I'll go speak with your father."

Trina grasped Mama's wrists. "He'll be okay, won't he?"

Mama sighed. "His father was a deacon, Trina. He feels very accountable to the fellowship and its teachings. But he'll be okay. You go on now." Her gaze lifted to include Graham, who stood behind Trina. "I want you to know I approve of your relationship. I haven't openly welcomed you — just as you feared Trina's dream would rob you of her presence in your life, I've feared you would take her from us. But children grow up and make their own lives — that's the way it should be. You're a fine young man, and I trust you to take good care of my daughter."

"Thank you, ma'am."

With tears distorting her vision, Trina watched Mama leave the room. She had received more warmth from her mother in the past few minutes than she could remember in all of her growing-up years. She marveled at the change.

Graham took her hand. "Come, let's go sit as your mother said." They went to the porch and sat side by side on the top riser, their legs in the sun. Graham asked Trina about the GED test and what would happen next. She shared all she had learned from the Internet searches.

"Before I can train as a veterinarian, I have to take two years of basic courses. Beth says a community college will be less expensive, and Barton County Community College in El Dorado allows online classes," Trina said. "So I will take as many classes from Beth's computer as I can. But eventually, I'll need to go to a college campus and finish."

Graham nodded solemnly. "That means moving away from Sommerfeld." He chewed his lower lip, his brows pulled down, but the expression was thoughtful rather than stern. "Do you want to wait to be married until after you've finished your schooling?"

Trina tipped her head and toyed with one white ribbon. "If I become a licensed veterinarian, it will take at least five years, Graham. That's a long time for us to wait."

He drew in a deep breath, his blue eyes narrowing. "A very long time . . ."

"No one knows that you've asked Mama and Dad for us to be published. If . . ." Trina swallowed. "If you want to court someone else, I'll —"

"I don't want to court anyone else." His firm tone convinced her of his sincerity. "I love you. I want to marry you."

Trina sagged with relief. "I want to marry you, too."

"Do you want to wait five years?"

"I want to marry you tomorrow," Trina said. The warmth of his smile nearly melted her. "But I'll do what you want. I know your dad relies on your help at the lumberyard. Being away from Sommerfeld would create a hardship for him."

"There are others who could work there if I needed to be away for a while." Graham looked outward, his hands on his knees. "And I could find a job in a city, I'm sure." He chuckled, shaking his head. "I just can't imagine living anywhere else."

Trina sighed. "Me neither. I truly love Sommerfeld."

Graham looked at her. "So you're sure, if you go away to college, you'll want to come back here?"

She blinked at him in surprise. "I've never wanted to leave Sommerfeld. Or the fellowship."

"But being away might give you other ideas."

Trina thought about her friendship with Beth McCauley, and how Mama and Dad had worried Beth might pull her away from the fellowship. Now it seemed Graham was worried time away from Sommerfeld might keep her away. But in her heart, she knew where she belonged — here, with her family and friends and fellowship. God might be opening a door to learning, but she was certain it was a door that wouldn't close behind her as she went through.

"I'll be back." She said it with conviction, and Graham's shoulders seemed to wilt. She placed her hand over his. "I know where I belong. I want to use the skills I learn to help the people in my own community. I know it's right."

"Well, then," Graham said, turning his hand over to link his fingers with hers, "we need to make arrangements to speak with the deacons and minister. But for now . . ." Rising, he pulled her to her feet and aimed her toward the house. "Go find your schoolbooks and study. You have a test to pass."

"So how do you think you did?"

Beth adjusted the dial on the car's air-conditioning system, and a blast of cool air twirled the ribbons on Trina's cap. Trina caught the dancing tails of the ribbons between her fingers and toyed with the ends. "I'm really not sure. It was hard! But I know I did my best."

"That's all a person can do." Beth's warm

tone offered Trina some reassurance. "And remember, if you don't pass the first time, you can always retake it."

Trina sighed. "I know. But the next date is three weeks away, and the longer it takes to get my GED in hand, the longer I prolong enrolling in a college. Waiting for the fellowship's approval took up almost two weeks. We're already near the end of August! I don't have much time to spare."

Beth glanced in her rearview mirror before switching lanes. "Well, no sense in worrying over it. Just proceed as if you already have the certificate in hand. Then, when you do have it, you'll be ready."

Trina looked out the window at the passing landscape, eager to return to town and tell Graham how things had gone. Although Graham had wanted to take her to Hutchinson for the test, his father had insisted he stay in Sommerfeld and work. Trina suspected Mr. Ortmann, like many others in Sommerfeld, wasn't in favor of Trina's plans to be a college graduate. But the deacons, minister, and bishop, after long discussion, had granted permission. The others in the community would eventually have to accept the decision.

"Do you realize" — Beth's voice cut into Trina's thoughts — "you are being a trendsetter?"

Trina faced Beth and released a light, puzzled laugh. "What?"

Beth grinned, her eyes sparkling. "A trendsetter. You're paving the way for change. Just like the Mennonites before you who wanted to use electricity or wanted to drive a car." With an impish smirk, she smacked the car's horn. "Now, because of you, other young people from Sommerfeld will be able to get an education if they want to."

Trina stared at Beth. "But I didn't want to change rules. I just wanted to be a vet."

Beth laughed. "I know that, silly. But don't you see? Now that you've been given permission, they'll have to give permission to others, too. You've opened the door of opportunity to every person in Sommerfeld! I'm really proud of you, Katrinka."

Trina shook her head wildly, her ribbons slapping against her shoulders. "Don't give me too much credit. The deacons made it clear this is experimental and conditional. *If* I can attend college without jeopardizing my personal faith or becoming a stumbling block to others, *then* I'll be allowed to continue. But they're watching, believe me."

Beth snorted. "Oh, I believe you." Then she flashed Trina a smile. "But if there's anyone who could do it — who could attend college without losing one inch of her belief system — I think it would be you."

Trina's heart thumped in appreciation of Beth's support, but curiosity drove her to ask a hesitant question. "Why me?" She hoped Beth wouldn't assume she was fishing for compliments. Mama would certainly frown at that activity!

"Because of what you told me when we first started exploring on the Internet." Beth tucked a strand of hair behind her ear. "Do you remember? You said you loved living in Sommerfeld and loved your fellowship. You didn't want to leave it; you just wanted to help the residents by being able to treat animals. So I believe, even if you have to live somewhere else for a while, you'll come back to Sommerfeld, still wearing your cap and modest dress, still firmly entrenched in your faith."

Tears pricked Trina's eyes. "Thank you for believing in me, Beth."

Beth shrugged. "Believing in *you* was easy. Believing *they* would actually let you do it — that's another thing entirely."

Trina understood Beth's doubts. Although Beth and Sean lived in Sommerfeld and socialized occasionally with Beth's cousins, she knew the worldly couple still felt like outsiders. Beth, although rarely openly disdainful, didn't pretend to support the community's restraints, which created conflict in relationships with residents. Trina wished everyone would recognize the good Beth's business did for the community — not only providing jobs for a handful of people, but also bringing business to town. Shoppers who visited her stained-glass art studio also visited other Sommerfeld businesses.

In Trina's opinion, Beth's presence was a positive thing for the community, but others still looked at her blue jeans and T-shirts and kept their distance. Why, Trina wondered, was it so hard for people to look on the heart instead of the exterior? But then, she mused, worldly people had a difficult time looking past her simple attire and seeing the person underneath the cap, so Mennonites weren't the only ones who struggled with looking on the heart.

Beth curled her hands around the steering wheel and straightened her arms, pushing herself into the seat and releasing a yawn. "But I'm sure glad the leaders surprised me with their decision to let you try college. God answered our prayers, and you're able to forge ahead into your dream."

"Oh, He sure did." Trina propped her chin

in her hand and peered out the window. Having Beth's wholehearted support from the beginning had given her courage to pursue her dream. Now she had support from Graham and her mother, too. If only Dad would be more encouraging. Even though Dad had said he'd go along with whatever the leaders decided, he still held himself aloof from Trina, almost as if punishing her for stepping outside the generational boundary limiting education.

"But there's still a lot to pray about." Trina shifted to face Beth. "Graham and I aren't sure whether we should get married before or after I finish college."

Beth sucked in her lower lip, her gaze ahead on the road. "That's not a question I can answer, Trina. Once you're married, you'll probably start a family, and that would sure make it harder to go to school."

"Or to be a veterinarian," Trina concurred. She felt a small prick of conscience. Was it fair to set Graham and their future family aside for the sake of a college degree? She felt the strong tug on her heart to care for animals, but she also felt a tug toward Graham. Which tug should be honored first?

"What does Graham want?"

Trina sighed. "Graham says he's willing to wait if that's what I think is best, but I know he's eager to be married. He has a house built and waiting. He's older than me, you know, and he's ready for a family."

"I see." Beth ran her fingernails over the curve of the plastic steering wheel, her brow furrowed in thought.

Even though Beth wasn't Mennonite, Trina respected her opinions. Beth was older, and because she'd been raised in the secular world, she often had insights beyond the limited scope of Trina's experience. Now that Beth was a Christian, Trina trusted her not to lead her astray. "How do you and Sean make decisions?"

"We argue."

Trina raised her eyebrows.

Beth nodded, smirking. "Oh yes, we argue. All my fault. I'm pretty stubborn, and I always want my way."

"Beth!" Trina couldn't believe her friend would openly admit to arguing and demanding her way with her husband. Dad had always had the final word in their household. Even though Mama was strong willed, she bowed to Dad's leadership in the home. Albeit reluctantly at times, Trina suspected.

Beth's laughter rang. "Sean's headstrong, too, so he doesn't cave in to me when he believes he's in the right. And eventually we find a compromise that works for both of us." Suddenly she frowned. "At least, most of the time."

Trina thought she understood. "Except on his being gone so much?"

Beth shrugged and flipped a strand of hair over her shoulder. "Except that. But I do okay on my own. That's where my independent spirit comes in handy. I don't *need* Sean to be around. I just *want* him. There's a huge difference."

Trina nodded thoughtfully. As a single person living at home, she followed her parents' lead. As a married woman, she'd follow her husband's. She sent up a silent prayer of gratitude for Graham's change of heart concerning her desire to become a vet. Having come to a compromise on that huge issue, Trina had every confidence they could find a solution to any problem — including whether to get married before or after her graduation from college.

EIGHTEEN

"Graham! Graham!"

Graham dropped the length of lumber with a clatter and spun around, his heart in his throat. Trina raced toward him, tears staining her cheeks, the ribbons of her cap streaming over her shoulders. He held out his arms, and she plowed into him, setting him back two stumbling steps. Catching her shoulders, he regained his balance and held her to his chest.

"What is it? What's wrong?" Her panicked voice and the tears sent a shaft of fear through his belly.

"My test . . . I got the letter. . . ." Trina blubbered against his shirtfront, and suddenly he understood.

"Aw, Trina." He rubbed her shoulders, resting his cheek on the top of her head. The cap felt abrasive against his skin, but he didn't move, hoping his embrace would soothe her bruised heart. The weeklong wait for the test results had been excruciating for both of them, and it hurt him to have it end this way. "I'm sorry."

"No!" She pulled away, shoving a folded piece of paper beneath his chin. Only then did he notice the smile behind the tears. "I passed! Just barely — my score isn't all that good, but I passed. I really passed!"

"You passed? Let me see." He opened the letter and scanned the contents. Sure enough — there it was, in black and white, that all-important word: *Passed.* "Trina, you're a high school graduate. Congratulations."

She beamed up at him. "Thank you." Taking the letter back, she stared at it with awe lighting her eyes. "I can't believe it. I really didn't think I would pass. It was a hard test, Graham."

"Well, you studied hard. You deserved to pass." When the leaders had given their approval for Trina to take her GED with the intention of applying to a college, Graham had offered his support. Yet as much as he hated to admit it, a sense of foreboding now pricked as he realized it wasn't just a dream. Trina's attending college would be a reality.

"Now I've got to let Barton County Community College know I have the GED. If they approve my application, I'll be a college student!"

Her unbridled glee chased away the hint of melancholy. Graham gave a genuine smile and squeezed her upper arm. "I'm proud of you."

"Oh, thank you! I can't wait to tell Beth and Mama and Dad and . . ." Suddenly her face clouded. "But probably only Beth will really be happy with me. Mama wants to be, I know, but with Dad so upset, she can't be."

Graham slipped his thumb up and down on her arm. "No one said it would be easy to do what God calls us to do. But you know you won't be happy unless you keep trying." He reminded himself of the truth of his words, battling the urge to worry.

She nodded, blinking rapidly. A smile trembled on her lips. "I'm so glad you're happy. Having you celebrate with me means so much."

He brushed her cheek with his knuckles then pushed his hand into the pocket of his work apron. "You're impossible to resist. You know that."

Trina giggled, hunching her shoulders. The gesture reminded him of the old Trina — the one who'd been too long absent. His heart thumped in double beats. *Thank You, Lord, that Trina is back.* He jerked his chin toward the lumberyard doors. "Now scoot on over to the café and show your mom. I'll come by after work, and we'll talk more, okay?"

She nodded, her face wreathed with a smile. "Okay. See you later!" She skipped away, carefree as a young girl, cradling the letter against her chest.

Graham watched her, chuckling. She really was impossible to resist. A groan replaced the chuckle. Could he wait five years to make her his wife? They had a serious discussion coming. *Give us guidance, Father.* With that prayer hovering in his heart, he returned to work.

Graham considered having supper at the café. Thinking about the Thursday night special of German sausage, kraut, and fried potatoes made his mouth water. But in the end, he decided he'd rather go home, clean up, and have some quiet time alone before speaking with Trina about when they should be married.

The short walk seemed longer in the stifling heat of late August. As a boy, he'd once commented that summer did its best to get as much heat as possible in before it closed, making August unbearable. His father had berated him for complaining and told him to appreciate his indoor job — he didn't have to be outside under the sun, like the farmers. Graham kept his thoughts to himself after that, but he still believed August to be the most uncomfortable month of the year.

After scrubbing himself clean in a bath and eating two bologna and cheese sandwiches, he felt ready to face Trina. But a glance at the clock told him he'd better wait awhile. Trina's responsibilities at the café wouldn't end until after eight. Now that she'd passed her test, she would probably return to her job at Dr. Groening's, if he hadn't filled it with someone else. He'd have to ask her about providing transport to work — that would give them time alone each day. The thought appealed to him.

He glanced at the clock again. Only two minutes had passed. Blowing out a noisy breath, he looked around the neat living room for something to do to fill time. His gaze fell on his Bible, which sat on the end of the sofa, still open from his morning's reading. He sank down beside it and flicked a few pages, until he reached Proverbs. Bending forward over the book, he reread chapter 31, seeking further illumination as to how to proceed in his relationship with Trina. Finding no real answers, he idly turned pages, scanned brief passages, and allowed his mind to wander.

When he came upon Proverbs 10:22, he read the words out loud. " 'The blessing of the Lord, it maketh rich. . . .' " He counted Trina as one of his blessings. Her spark for life, her openness to everyone around her raised his spirits and made him want to be more openly cheerful himself. She added a richness to his life that had nothing to do with monetary gain — he couldn't put a value on what she meant to him. A smile tugged at his cheeks as he thought about her sweet laugh, her dancing eyes, her joyous spirit.

But his smile faded when he focused on the final words. " 'And he addeth no sorrow with it.' " There had been a great deal of sorrow lately in his relationship with Trina. Even if he and the fellowship leaders endorsed her desire to attend college, others murmured in opposition to the decision, just as there were those who still murmured about the use of electricity or the driving of automobiles. Those unpleasant, demeaning voices would surely bring a touch of sorrow to the situation.

Then, of course, her own father and some other family members who stated their objections openly or made known their disapproval with firmly pressed lips created sorrow, too.

"How can we keep the sorrow away, Lord?" He asked the question to the empty room, his face tipped upward, seeking a reply. "Even I struggle with all of the changes it will mean for me. As much as I want Trina to follow Your will, there are things I may have to give up, and the thought of them makes me sorrowful, too."

For some reason, saying the words out loud offered a release Graham didn't realize he needed. So he said them again. "I support Trina. I'm happy for her, but I feel sad for me at the same time." With that admission, something struck him. The verse said *He* added no sorrow to it. That meant the Lord wouldn't add sorrow to His blessing. But *man* certainly could — and probably would.

With a sigh, Graham closed his eyes. "Lord, help me not to add sorrow to Trina's blessing. Let me support her sincerely and without reserve. Let my support ease the sting of sorrow inflicted by others in the community. Open my heart to the blessing You have in store for us as a couple dedicated to Your service. Amen."

Revived by the prayer, he looked at the clock, eager to meet with Trina and discuss plans. Not quite seven o'clock. With a shrug, he rose and headed for the door. He'd have some dessert and wait for her at the café. His steps felt light despite the sluggish weight of humidity in the air. *"The blessing of the Lord, it maketh rich." It won't be easy to do what's right, but I'll do it because I trust in Your promise, Lord.*

Trina caught Graham's eye as she closed the door behind the final patrons. Something in his expression — a tenderness, a warmth, a secret promise of good to come — made her chest feel like a bell holding a raucously clanging clapper. She pressed her hands to her apron bodice, the thud of her heart pounding against her trembling palms.

A grin crept up his cheek. "You're staring at me like you've seen a ghost."

She stepped to the edge of the table and shook her head. "No, not a ghost. A glimpse of . . . the future."

He tipped his head, his forehead crinkling even while the smile still curved his lips.

She laughed at his puzzlement. "Don't ask me to explain, because I can't. But if you'll give me a half hour to help Mama with cleanup, maybe we'll be able to make sense of it together."

"I can wait."

The words took on a much broader meaning, and an impatience filled Trina. He'd said he could wait for her to finish her schooling, too, but did she want to wait? Peering into his handsome, open, adoring face, she wanted everything right now — Graham, her degree, her own home. Taking a step backward, she waved her hand in the direction of the kitchen. "Let me get that cleanup going. I'll go fast."

He nodded, and she scurried away. She banged things together getting the mop and mop bucket out. Just as she set the bucket in the sink to fill it, Mama came over and put her hand on Trina's arm.

"Go ahead and leave. Tony is coming in to help, so between Kelly, him, and me, we'll get it covered."

Trina raised her eyebrows. "Are you sure? Graham said he'd wait."

A smile softened Mama's normally stern expression. "Graham's been waiting long enough. Go ahead."

"Thank you, Mama!" Trina shut off the stream of water and reached to remove her apron.

Mama grabbed her arm again. "And, Trina? This is your last day. I called Janina and Audra, and both of them are willing to come back here. I know you want to work

251

for Dr. Groening, but even if he's filled the position, you won't be needed here. You'll want to use your time to study."

Tears filled Trina's eyes, making Mama's image swim. Even though Mama hadn't offered congratulations for passing the GED, her words now spoke of her pride in Trina's accomplishment. "Thank you, Mama." Trina gave her mother a quick hug. "I'll see you later tonight. Ten o'clock?"

"That'll be fine." Mama turned her attention to the mop bucket.

Trina scampered out to the dining room and captured Graham's hand. "Mama says I don't need to stay."

Outside the café, Graham lifted his shoulders in a shrug and smiled down at her. "Where should we go?"

Someplace private was preferable, yet Trina knew the community would frown on it. "How about the cemetery?" The open location, in sight of anyone who happened by, would be considered acceptable and still be without an audience.

"That's fine." Graham held Trina's hand as they walked the distance to the cemetery. In the treetops, cicadas sang their buzzing chorus, but neither Trina nor Graham spoke. For Trina, just walking with Graham, her hand held loosely within the confines of his firm calloused fingers, was pleasure enough. Conversation would come when they reached their destination.

Instead of crouching behind a tombstone, they chose a bench beneath a towering elm at the corner of the cemetery. The concrete bench felt cool despite the warmth of the night air, and Trina released a satisfied sigh.

"It's nice to be alone with you this way."

Graham nodded, keeping his face attentively turned to her.

"And right now I can't imagine waiting five years to get married."

Graham ducked his head for a moment, his eyes closed. When he raised his gaze to meet hers again, she glimpsed a maturity and strength beyond what she'd seen before. She swallowed, waiting quietly for him to share his thoughts.

"Trina, my desire would be to marry you this winter. My home is ready; my heart is ready to make you my wife. But I don't want to be selfish."

"Selfish?"

He nodded. "Think how much time you took studying to pass the GED. Don't you think college will be even harder than that? I want you to have the time you need to do your best. If you're working for Dr. Groening *and* running a household, you aren't going to have time to focus on studies. Maybe . . ." Suddenly the conviction in his tone faltered. He cleared his throat and started again. "Maybe it would be best for us to wait so you can give this dream the time and attention it deserves to be fully born."

Trina stared at him in amazement. "You really want to wait?"

He chuckled softly, placing his hand over hers in the center of the bench. "No, my precious Trina, I don't *want* to wait. But I wonder if it's best to wait." He drew in a deep breath and released it, his gaze heavenward where a few stars glittered softly against the fading evening sky. "I read a verse in Proverbs about the Lord giving us rich without adding any sorrow to it. It seems to me that stressing over finding time to study and not being able to apply yourself fully to this task is going to lead to sorrow for you. That isn't right."

"Oh, Graham . . ." Trina knew what it cost him to make this concession. His readiness for a home and family hadn't been kept secret, yet he was willing to set aside his desires for the sake of hers. If she'd harbored any question about whether he truly loved her, the unease now whisked away like a cottonwood seed on a stiff Kansas breeze.

"We could still be published but just put off the wedding until you have college finished. I would like to take you to Lehigh to work each day so we'd have some time together. I'm not saying it will be easy." His voice dropped to a low growl. "But I do think it will be for the best."

Trina nodded slowly, absorbing the wisdom of his words. Looking back on the number of hours she had spent in preparation for the GED, she knew taking college classes would tax her time and energy. But five years . . .

She groaned. "How did Uncle Henry live for twenty years without Aunt Marie?"

Graham laughed — a low, throaty sound. "I've wondered that myself. I guess when I get to feeling impatient, I can always go talk to him. He should be able to give good advice."

Suddenly something occurred to Trina. "If we wait until I'm finished, then . . . when it comes time for me to take classes on a campus instead of over the Internet, I'll be moving away from Sommerfeld all alone." Uncertainty washed over her. Could she manage by herself in a strange town, hours away from her family and Graham?

His warm fingers tightened on her hand. "That isn't something you need to worry about yet. It's at least two years away, since you'll be taking your first classes online. By the time you need to go away, God will give you the strength you need." Another chuckle sounded, this one rueful in tone. "And He'll give me the strength to let you go."

"Or maybe . . ." Trina licked her lips, peering at him hopefully. "I won't have to go alone?"

He smiled, shaking his head. "As I said, we'll worry about it when the time comes. But until then, you need to learn what you can from Dr. Groening, you need to study hard, and you need to prove to everyone in Sommerfeld that becoming a veterinarian will not be damaging to your faith."

Trina threw her hands outward, releasing a snort of laughter. "Oh, that's nothing! Anyone could do it!" Then she sobered, taking Graham's hand again. Amazing how the feel of his strong fingers gave her courage. "I'm sorry I'm making you wait, but thank you for being willing to wait for me."

"Oh, my Trina . . ." Graham sighed, raising his free hand to cup her cheek. "I've told you before: You are worth the wait. God will get us through this time of waiting, and when we are finally together as husband and wife, I'll feel like the richest man in the world."

NINETEEN

Trina closed her Bible and slipped to her knees beside her bed. She'd made a commitment to God not to give studying more importance than fellowship with Him, so her early mornings were committed to Bible reading and prayer.

While her books waited on the table she'd set up in the corner of her bedroom, she spent long minutes talking to God, offering praises for His work in her life, acknowledging her weaknesses, and petitioning Him for assistance and strength. She was careful to ask for His help for others before ending with her daily request: "And help me do well in my classes so I can honor You."

Rising, she crossed to the table and smoothed her hand across the cover of the top book. Despite the fact that she'd been following a study routine for two weeks now, there were still moments when it all seemed like a dream. She really didn't own college textbooks; she really wasn't a college student. But the stack of books beneath her hand was solid; the pages contained words and pictures and graphs. Not a dream but a certainty.

Suddenly, as had happened frequently in the two weeks she'd studied on her own and submitted assignments through Beth's computer, a feeling of impatience struck. Her first two years of study would be basic subjects — nothing directly related to animal care — and she longed to dive into the classes that would benefit her the most. Yet the college adviser had said every student was required to pass the basic subjects first.

Closing her eyes, she whispered, "Make these first two years go quickly, please." The addendum to her formal prayer time brought a smile to her face. During her weeks of preparing for the GED, she'd nearly put aside conversation with her heavenly Father. But now it came naturally again, making her even more certain she was doing exactly what He'd called her to do.

She slid onto the wooden chair Dad had grudgingly hauled in from the car's shed and opened the English composition book. Since she would be returning to work at Dr.

Groening's clinic on Monday, this would be her last full day of study — she intended to make the most of it. But despite her best efforts to keep her attention on past and present verb tenses, her mind kept drifting a few miles east to Lehigh and the clinic.

With a sigh, she allowed herself to replay the telephone conversation with the aging doctor.

"Trina! Of course, I'd be delighted to hire you again. My receptionist has been filling in for you since I haven't been able to find anyone else. She'll be very willing to let you have those duties again."

Trina had smiled then stated adamantly, "But I won't be doing only cleanup forever, you know. I'm now enrolled in college. I will be a veterinarian one day."

"The fellowship approved it?"

The shock in the man's tone hadn't surprised Trina. It gave her great pleasure to repeat his words as a statement. "The fellowship approved it."

"Well, congratulations, Trina."

"And, Dr. Groening, I'd appreciate it if you would consider selling me your practice when the time comes."

At that point there had been a lengthy pause, during which Trina feared the connection might have been terminated. But finally his voice had returned, hesitant in its delivery. "You know, Trina, I'm already past the age of retirement. I've continued because I'm the only veterinarian nearby for many of the area farmers. But another five years of practice? I'm not sure I want to continue that long."

Trina's heart pounded with trepidation. She couldn't possibly complete the necessary coursework and practicum in fewer than five years. Given the expenses involved, she feared the time might be extended while she worked to save up enough money to finish. "Will you at least consider it?" she had managed to squeak.

Finally Dr. Groening's tired voice had said, "I'll consider it. We can talk more when you come into work, all right?"

That promised conversation was just around the corner, and Trina was both eager and reluctant to finalize her plans with the doctor. Sighing, she rested her chin in her hand and stared out the open window. Although September had arrived, bringing a change in color to the trees, the daytime weather still held the feel of summer. Evenings were somewhat less stuffy, however, and she and Graham spent at least an hour together on the porch before sundown each day.

Closing her eyes, she deliberately conjured Graham's face — his handsome, honed, adoring face. He had a way of looking at her that made her feel treasured and special. Just thinking of him now increased her pulse while a flutter of something pleasant coiled in her chest. A smile played on the corners of her lips. Her intended husband . . .

How fortunate she was to have a man willing to listen to God's voice rather than remaining trapped in the traditions of man. Based on the reaction of many of the community members, she felt certain no other young man in Sommerfeld would have supported her desire to further her education. God had certainly chosen the perfect mate for her. Each evening, as he bestowed a chaste kiss on her forehead, Graham whispered, "Do a little reading before you turn in. Keep your grades up."

With the remembered gentle admonition, Trina gave a start. How long had she been sitting here daydreaming? She had work to do! Determinedly, she turned her attention back to the English book. When she met Graham for lunch at the café, she wanted to give him a good report on her morning's progress.

"So I got three English assignments done

— one that isn't even due for another week — and a science paper written. I'll need to type it, and then I can send it. Beth taught me how to e-mail attachments. It sure makes things simple." Trina pushed her empty plate aside and rested her elbows on the table edge. Despite the busyness of the café's noon traffic, she and Graham were secluded in a corner booth, giving them a small amount of privacy.

Graham took a bite of grape pie, his gaze never leaving Trina's face. How he loved to watch her dark eyes sparkle and her animated face beam with pride in her accomplishments. "That's good to get ahead. So the typing is going better?"

At the mention of typing, her cheery expression turned sour. "Oh, I hate it! My fingers are so clumsy. It takes forever." She sighed then straightened her shoulders and tipped up her chin. "But I'll get better the more I do it. Beth got me a tutorial that shows me the right way to put my hands on the keys so I'm not pecking around like this." With a laugh, she demonstrated by jabbing her pointer fingers against the tabletop in a wild dance. She laced her fingers together and shrugged. "She says I'll enjoy typing more when I'm not having to stare at the keys and poke them."

Graham winked. "I'm sure you can do whatever you set your mind to. But doesn't the tutorial eat up your study time?"

Once more, Trina crinkled her face into a scowl. "Yes. It hasn't put me behind because I've had the whole day to commit to studies since classes started, but when Monday comes and I go back to work . . ." She sent him a mournful look. "How will I fit everything in, Graham?"

"Well . . ." He scratched his chin. "Don't work full-time."

"I have to!" She leaned forward, her palms flat on the table. "I thought I had a lot in savings, but college is very expensive. I didn't get any scholarships, partly because I enrolled so late but mostly because all I had was the GED, and my score wasn't very good. I don't know how I'll pay to finish if I don't work full-time."

Graham put down his fork and slid the dessert plate to the edge of the table. He placed his hands over hers. "Do you think you might be able to get a scholarship next year?"

Trina shrugged, turning her hands to twine her fingers with his. He sensed she wasn't even aware of the action, but it had a serious affect on his heart rate. "Maybe . . . if I get really good grades in all my classes.

But according to what I read online, most scholarships are for activities like music or sports." She released a regretful chuckle, shaking her head. "I'll never get any of those."

"God will pave the way." Graham gave her hands a quick squeeze. "If you have to work full-time, then it means you'll just have to budget your study time wisely."

She bit down on her lower lip, sending him a repentant look. "But what if it means no evening time with you?" Her face puckered into a pout. "I've gotten spoiled the last couple of weeks, seeing you every day. I don't want to give it up, but —"

"Are you going to the skating tonight?" At the intruding voice, both Trina and Graham jumped, their hands jolting apart. Graham met Kelly Dick's smiling face. The girl's gaze bounced back and forth between them. "I get to go — Mom and Dad said I could. Are you going?"

"I don't know." Graham looked at Trina. "I had forgotten they scheduled the rink for tonight."

Trina tipped her face up to Kelly. "Is this your first time to go skating?"

Graham already knew the answer, but Trina's mother had kept her home so often, he wasn't surprised Trina didn't know who regularly attended the skating parties.

Kelly's eager nod exhibited her enthusiasm. "Yes. They made Kyra wait until she was seventeen, but Mom said I could go if Dad said it was all right, and Dad said it was okay if Mom approved it." She laughed. "So I'm going a full year earlier than Kyra!"

Graham couldn't imagine the significance of Kelly's statement, but by Trina's laughing eyes, he sensed she understood.

"Well, don't tell Tony," Trina said, "because I'm sure Mama and Dad will make him wait until he's seventeen, just like they did me."

Kelly teasingly ran her fingers over her closed lips then snatched up their plates and scampered away.

As soon as she left, Graham said, "Well? Do you want to go to the skating party? Especially if our time together is going to be limited when you go back to work, maybe we should have a fun evening together with our friends."

Trina licked her lips, her eyebrows rising in speculation. "Would you rather do something . . . quiet? Just the two of us?"

Could she possibly know how tempting he found her question? He loved their together time, yet he realized the more time they spent one-on-one, the harder it was to put off their wedding. At times it was tortuous not being able to exhibit the affection his heart longed to release. Although he told himself it was best to wait, he knew it wasn't going to be easy.

Leaning forward, he grasped her hands again. "Trina, I would love nothing more than to have an entire, uninterrupted evening with you. But you've spent all of your free time just with me lately. Wouldn't you like to have time with your other friends? You must miss them. I know they miss you."

Her smile turned impish, and she bobbed her head in a firm nod. "It's hard for me to have time alone with you without wanting more, too."

He burst out laughing then coughed to cover the sound. "How did you know that's what I was thinking?"

She shrugged, still grinning. "I just know."

"Well, you're right. Being alone with you makes it a lot harder to leave you afterward. I'm starting to think that's how your uncle Henry managed to wait so long for Marie — he didn't *see* her every day, which would have let him know exactly what he was missing. So being in a crowd is probably best — for both of us." He gave her hand a slight tug. "Do you want to go? If so, go check with your mom and make sure it's okay."

Without another word, Trina slipped from the booth and disappeared into the kitchen. Moments later she returned, a smile on her face. "Mama says to go. She says I've been holed up in my room too much lately and getting out will do me good." Shaking her head, she stared at him in wide-eyed wonder. "I can't believe how much Mama has changed."

Graham agreed Mrs. Muller seemed like a different person than the one who used to watch him with a scowl on her face. Although she still didn't greet him with huge smiles or cheerful banter, she did acknowledge him with a nod of hello and conversed with him. Most noticeable, however, was her willingness to allow him time with Trina. He wasn't sure what had precipitated the change, but he was thankful for it.

"Dad's changed, too." Trina's melancholy tone captured Graham's attention.

"I know." Graham had witnessed the man's drawing away from Trina since she started the college classes. He prayed daily for Mr. Muller's acceptance of Trina's choice. Although in the past her father had been strict, he'd also been warm. Graham knew how much Trina missed the dad she used to know. "Give him time. He'll come around."

Trina nodded, her gaze to the side, seemingly lost in thought.

Squeezing her hands, he said, "I'll pick you up at six o'clock." He waited until she looked at him. "We can eat at McDonald's before we go to the rink."

Trina finally rewarded him with a slight smile. "That sounds good."

He affected a stern look and pointed at her. "But now you go home and use the afternoon to study. Or go to Beth's and type that science paper. But get some work done, okay? Earn your evening out."

Trina giggled, not at all put off by his mock dictatorial attitude. "Yes, sir!" Bounding from the seat, she said, "Thank you for lunch. I'll see you this evening."

He watched her leave the café, her steps light and head held high. How he wished he had the money to give her for school so she wouldn't have to work. But it wouldn't be seemly, considering they weren't married. And he didn't have it anyway. He'd used his savings to build his — their — house. Then an idea struck with such force he sat upright, banging his head on the high back of the booth.

Withdrawing his wallet, he dropped enough bills on the table to cover the lunch tab plus a tip for Kelly. Then he hurried out of the café, eager to locate his father. He had something important to discuss.

TWENTY

Watching Michelle and Walt huddle in a corner of the rink sent a shaft of jealousy through Trina's middle. Since they were officially published, expressing affection was acceptable. How she'd love to rest her head on Graham's shoulder, to have his arm slip around her waist, to feel his breath on her cheek as he whispered in her ear.

But she couldn't.

She turned her attention away from the benches and watched the skaters. She'd removed her borrowed skates early, offering the excuse of a blister on her toe. In truth, she simply needed to separate herself from the giggling and teasing and roughhousing going on. Why, she wondered, did the childish displays — displays that only a few months ago she would have cheerfully joined — now set her teeth on edge?

Propping her elbows on the wooden ledge of the rink's surrounding wall, she observed

Kelly laughing into the face of Paul Lantz as she held on to his arm. Paul appeared quite content to move slowly around the rink with Kelly attached to his elbow. Smiling, Trina remembered her first attempts and the repeated falls before Graham had offered his elbow to keep her upright. Would romance bloom for Kelly and Paul as it had for her and Graham?

Automatically her head raised, her gaze seeking, until she spotted Graham's familiar sandy head of hair. He skated like an expert, his body angled forward, arms swinging in rhythm with the smooth movement of his feet. Her heart caromed at his display of athletic prowess. As she watched, he whizzed between two slower skaters and came alongside Darcy Kauffman. With a huge grin, he tapped her opposite shoulder, then zoomed on while Darcy glanced back with a puzzled look. His laughter brought Darcy's gaze forward, and she shook her fist at him, skating faster to catch up. But of course she couldn't catch him.

Trina scowled. Graham was still laughing when he careened to a halt on the other side of the wall, but his expression changed quickly when he met her gaze.

"What's wrong?"

With effort, Trina pushed aside the rush

of envy that made her want to snap at him for tapping Darcy's shoulder. He and Darcy were friends — he should be able to tease a friend. But she couldn't quite manufacture a smile.

"Nothing."

He placed his hands over hers and leaned closer. She had to strain to hear his voice over the noise of the skaters. "Do you want to leave now?"

She thought about the fun he'd been having only moments before. It would be selfish to pull him away just because she didn't want to skate. With an adamant shake of her head, she said, "No."

"Are you sure? Can't be much fun just standing there watching."

He was right — it wasn't as much fun as being a participant. But tonight she had no desire to participate. "I'm okay, really. Go ahead and skate. See if you can make it around faster than Lester."

Graham snorted, his grin returning. "Lester, huh? Oh, that's easy." He whizzed back to the floor and in moments caught up to Lester Hess. After a whispered consultation in the corner of the rink, the two lined up for a race. An excited wave of laughter carried the other skaters to the edges to watch the contest. Several heads blocked Trina's view, and she rose up on tiptoe to peek out just in time to see Graham zing by a few seconds ahead of Lester.

A cheer rose, and someone grabbed Trina's hand.

"Did you see him? He's the fastest skater ever, I think." Darcy's blue eyes shone with admiration. "I wish I could skate that fast, but never in a dress." She giggled, and Trina couldn't help but join in, imagining Darcy trying to keep up with Graham's long-legged stride.

The crowd headed back to the floor, except for Darcy, who remained next to Trina and waited for Graham's smiling approach.

"Well, I guess I showed him, huh?"

Before Trina could answer, Darcy said, "You sure did! That was exciting!" She crinkled her nose. "Lester is always bragging, so it's good to see him bested now and then."

"I guess so." Graham wiped the sweat from his brow. "But that wore me out. I'm ready to go now, Trina, if you want to leave."

Darcy grabbed Graham's sleeve. "Oh no! Don't go yet! A bunch of us are going for ice cream afterward. You'll want to come." She turned to include Trina. "Won't you?"

Seeing Darcy and Graham side by side on

the other side of the wall left Trina feeling strangely distanced from her friends. She swallowed. "I'm not really hungry." She looked at Graham. "But if you want ice cream, I don't mind staying."

To her relief Graham shook his head. "It sounds fun, Darcy, but I worked today, and I'm worn out. I think Trina and I will go on home." He skated around Darcy and left the rink.

Darcy's lips slipped into a brief pout, but then she shrugged and shot Trina a grin. "Well, I'll see you at service tomorrow." Her smile turned impish. "Maybe I'll go console Lester on his loss in that race." With a laugh, she skated off.

Graham approached, skates dangling from his hand. He pointed to his gray-stockinged feet. "I'll get my boots on, and then we can go."

She nodded, shifting her gaze to watch the skaters for a few more minutes. A part of her longed to rush onto the rink and laugh and chase with abandon, but another part of her only wanted to go home. With a sigh, she turned from the wall and stood beside the bench where Graham pulled his boots over his socks. When he'd tugged his pant legs back over the boots, he looked up at her. A sad smile played around the corners of his mouth.

"This wasn't much fun for you, was it?"

Trina's chin trembled as she fought tears.

He rose, taking her hand. "Come on. We can talk in the car."

When the door closed behind them, sealing away the noise of the other skaters, Trina heaved a sigh of relief. She shook her head. "I never realized how loud we were. Was it always so . . . uncontrolled?"

Graham laughed, swinging her hand as he led her to his waiting vehicle. "Yes, and you were usually in the middle of the ruckus."

Did she detect a note of regret in his tone? He opened the car door for her, but she stood beside the car and peered up at him. "Are you upset about leaving early?"

"No." The answer came quickly. "Time alone with you is precious, so I don't mind heading out." He put his hand on her back, giving a gentle nudge. "Slide in there."

When he was behind the steering wheel, he sent her a sympathetic look. "I noticed most people avoided you tonight. I'm sorry. I guess they're not comfortable with the direction you're taking, and they don't know what to say. So they say nothing."

Trina nodded. Her friends, with the exception of Darcy, had been distant. But, she acknowledged, she'd distanced herself, too.

She couldn't blame them entirely. "I know. I understand them. I just wish I understood *me.*" Shifting her gaze, she stared at the building that housed the skating rink. All the times Mama made her stay behind, she'd longed for the opportunity to go. Now she could go, and she longed to be away. With a soft laugh, she added, "I must be going through one of those 'stages' Mama used to complain about. I don't know what I want."

"Yes, you do." Graham gave her hand a tug, bringing her focus to him. "You want to serve God by taking care of animals. And you want me to be your support system." His smile grew. "Well, you're getting what you want. So let's see a smile on your face."

Obediently, Trina offered a smile, but she suspected it lacked luster.

Her suspicion was confirmed when Graham snorted. "That's a pretty poor excuse for a smile. I guess I'll just have to buy you a double-dip chocolate ice cream cone. That always perks you up."

After Graham purchased two double-dip chocolate cones at a dairy store's drive-through window, he aimed the car toward the highway and home. Trina kept her window up while she ate her cone to keep the dancing tails of her cap from landing in the chocolate, but the moment she finished, she rolled it all the way down and put one hand out.

The pressure of the cooling evening air against her palm sent a tremor clear to her shoulder. She experienced a sense of strength, keeping her hand braced while the coursing wind tried to push it back. If she could hold that wind at bay, surely she could overcome the difficulties facing her as she moved toward her dream.

"Trina?"

She pulled her arm inside and turned to face Graham.

"I'm glad we have this time alone. I need to talk to you about something."

His serious tone sent her heart pattering. She scooted to the center of the seat, away from the wind's whistle, so she could hear clearly. "Okay."

"You were talking about not having enough money to finish your degree."

She nodded. In her daily prayers, she had petitioned God to help make a way to cover all of the expenses.

"I think I know how you can do it."

Trina's eyes flew wide. "You do?"

"Mm-hmm." His gaze flitted sideways, a twinkle in his blue eyes. "You've never been upstairs in my folks' house, but when Dad built it, he made the second floor kind of like an apartment. My grandmother was living with them when he and Mom got married, and he wanted her to have her own space that felt like a separate house."

Trina nodded to let him know she was paying attention, but she couldn't figure out why he was telling her about his parents' house.

"Well, Grandmother died when I was still small, so Mom and Dad moved me up there after Chuck was born. Chuck has those rooms now, but there's the second bedroom downstairs still, which he could move into again." Graham removed one hand from the steering wheel and placed it over hers. "Which leaves the upstairs open."

Trina shook her head. "But what does that have to do with paying for college?"

His hand tightened. "Just listen, okay?" Another quick glance combined with a wink held her silent. "I built my house for us to live in when we got married, but we don't have to have our own house if we live in the upstairs at my folks'. If I sell my house, then —"

"No!" Trina jerked her hand free, pressing it to her chest. "I can't let you do that!"

Graham's lips turned downward. "Why not? As your husband, it should be my responsibility to help pay for your needs. And education is one of your needs."

"But, Graham! I —" And then it occurred to her that he'd referred to himself as her husband. She gulped. "Are you wanting to be married right away, then? Even before I finish school?"

He shrugged with one shoulder, the gesture boyishly appealing. "Well, if you don't have a whole house to care for — if we live with my folks — it would eliminate one responsibility, giving you more time to study. And it would also mean you wouldn't need to go off to college by yourself. I would go with you, get a job, and support you while you finished your schooling."

Trina's mind whirled. She had worried about going off alone, had fretted over putting off their wedding for so long, but now that another option was available, she didn't know what to think.

"Your parents said it would be all right for us to live with them?"

Graham smiled. "Mom's never had a daughter, so she was especially thrilled to think you might live with them for a while."

"And your dad? He didn't mind, either?"

Graham chuckled softly. "Well, to be honest, Dad thinks I'm a little nutty, building a house and then selling it, but he didn't say I couldn't do it. He said if it was what we wanted, he'd be okay with the decision."

"And Chuck isn't unhappy about losing his room?" Trina thought about how Tony would feel if he were kicked out of his bedroom. There would certainly be resentment. She didn't want to live with that.

"Chuck is fine. He's only been up there a year or so — and he's young enough to think it'd be neat to have me home again." He shot her a serious look. "It wouldn't be permanent — just until you have your degree. Then I'd build us another house."

Trina chewed her lower lip, her mind racing. "But would anyone buy your house?"

"There is someone interested." For a moment Graham didn't answer, his fingers curling briefly around her hand before slipping away to grasp the steering wheel. "Walt. For him and Michelle. They're getting married in early February, you know."

Although the words were delivered on a light note, Trina sensed an element of sorrow. She imagined Michelle working in the kitchen Graham had designed for her, and she understood the undertone. A lump filled her throat. "Oh, Graham . . ."

"It'll be all right." The glib tone didn't fool her. "After all, it's just a house. Not really a home until a family lives in it, and

280

we haven't had that chance yet. So after you've finished school, we'll build another house, and we'll move in, and it'll be home. It'll be fine."

Tears welled in Trina's eyes, and she turned her face to the window to allow the wind to dry them. Her face aimed away from Graham, she said on a sigh, "You're giving up so much for me."

His fingers cupped her chin, bringing her face around. "I'm not giving up anything I don't want to — nothing I can't live without. You're more important than ten houses — you know that."

His hand found hers, and she clung to it, welcoming the contact. "Thank you, Graham."

"So . . . if you agree . . . then we need to talk to the deacons. Get published. And start planning a wedding."

"A wedding . . ." Trina shook her head, wonder filling her. Soon she'd be Mrs. Graham Ortmann *and* a veterinarian. How could her heart hold so much happiness at once?

TWENTY-ONE

The first Sunday in October, the acting minister published Graham and Trina to the congregation, making known their intention to become husband and wife. Although Trina noted the well-wishing didn't seem quite as exuberant for her as it had for Michelle only a few weeks earlier, she managed to swallow the prick of disappointment. Changes were hard for many in the fellowship, and she would need to be patient until they accepted this new road on which she was embarking.

Mama, in preparation for the announcement, had invited Graham's immediate family plus Trina's grandparents, aunts, uncles, and cousins to dinner at the café. Dad had grumbled a bit about opening the café on a Sunday, but Mama pointed out there wasn't enough room at the house. Plus she wasn't serving paying customers — she was treating the family to a celebration. So

Dad nodded and agreed.

Nearly all of the tables and booths were filled, and when Trina tried to help serve, the ladies shooed her from the kitchen. "Go sit," Aunt Marie said, taking her by the shoulders and giving a gentle shove. "Soon enough you'll be serving Sunday dinner to your own family. For now, let us spoil you a little bit."

So Trina joined Graham's family, Dad, and Tony at the table in the middle of the dining room and allowed the others to wait on her. Mama had prepared all of Trina's favorites — meat loaf, mashed potatoes with lots of butter and fresh chives, steamed whole green beans flavored with slivered almonds, crusty rolls, and lime Jell-O holding together chopped apples, pecans, and celery. Filling her plate, Trina wondered if she'd have room for the German chocolate cake Mama had baked for dessert.

Conversation around the many tables and booths filled the café with happy noise, and Trina missed Mrs. Ortmann's comment. Trina leaned closer, raising her eyebrows in a silent query for her to repeat the words.

"Has Dr. Groening agreed to sell you the clinic when he retires?"

Trina stifled a sigh. "No, but he hasn't come right out and said he won't, either."

Trina recalled the lengthy discussion concerning the future of the clinic. While she understood the doctor's reluctance to commit to another five years of work, she still wished for the security of knowing the clinic would be there waiting for her. "He's sixty-eight years old already, and he isn't sure he wants to continue for five more years."

Mrs. Ortmann nodded, sympathy softening her expression. "I don't suppose a person can blame him. He's taken care of animals in our community for many, many years. He's earned a break."

Trina agreed wholeheartedly. Dr. Groening had been a dedicated servant and was well liked by all of the area residents — Amish, Mennonite, and worldly. She would have some big shoes to fill when she took over the clinic.

Graham's father inserted, "I can't imagine there's anyone else around here who would buy the place. I haven't heard of any young people in the nearby communities planning to go to veterinary school."

Trina's heart tripped hopefully. "I haven't, either. Even though I'd prefer a commitment from him to let me take over the clinic, I have to trust God will work things out. After all" — she flashed Graham a smile — "He's worked everything else out."

Tony reached to the middle of the table for another roll. "And who knows? If Trina makes good, maybe the bishop will say it's okay for others of us to go to school. I think it might be fun to go to college, too."

Trina put her hand on Tony's arm. "I'm not doing this for fun, Tony. If God hadn't put the desire in my heart, I wouldn't be pursuing it." Her brother's cheeks flushed even though Trina kept her voice gentle. "You need to pray about your future and follow the plan God has for you instead of looking for fun."

Dad harrumphed under his breath, the sound barely discernible.

Trina hung her head, battling tears. The celebratory mood darkened with her father's reaction. Why couldn't he see she hadn't set out to hurt him by following her heart? Why couldn't he allow her to follow God's leading without making her feel guilty?

Graham's warm hand on her shoulder brought her head up. Graham leaned forward to address her father. "Mr. Muller, I know you still harbor concerns about Trina going to college."

Dad's brow furrowed into a scowl. "You're right."

"I want you to know I was very concerned, too, but prayer gave my heart peace. I will continue to pray for your peace."

Silence fell around the table, although talking went on animatedly at the other tables. Everyone looked at Dad, who kept his gaze on his plate. Suddenly he pushed his chair back and dropped his napkin on top of his uneaten food. "If you'll excuse me." He strode from the restaurant. Mama jumped up and followed him.

A knot formed in Trina's throat, and she swallowed hard, willing herself not to cry. Too frequently tears had been her companion of late. She did not want to cry today — not on the day she was published to the man she loved. With effort, she lifted her chin and forced a bright smile. "Tony, pass the green beans, please. Mama outdid herself today — everything is so yummy!"

To her gratitude, the others followed suit by talking again, filling the uncomfortable silence with cheerful chatter. In minutes, Mama returned, sat down, and sent Trina an apologetic look. Trina shrugged, offering a silent reply, and they finished their meal without commenting on her father's absence.

When everyone had finished, Tony and their cousins Andrew and Jacob and their wives volunteered to wash dishes and put the café back in order. Graham gave Trina a gentle hug good-bye at the door.

"Do you want me to come over to the house with you?"

She knew he was asking if she would need support in facing her father, and her heart swelled with gratefulness for this understanding man. But she shook her head. "No. I'm going to have a talk with Dad — somehow I must make him understand why I have to follow my heart — but it needs to be between the two of us. In fact . . ." She scowled, glancing past Graham to her mother, where she chatted with Uncle Henry and Aunt Marie. "I'm going to see if Mama will leave us alone and let us work this out for ourselves. She means well, but she tends to interfere."

Graham smiled, releasing a light chuckle. "Your mother interfering? I can't imagine that."

Trina laughed, recognizing the teasing. "Yes, we all know her well! But I love her anyway. And since this whole thing started, she's become such a surprising support. I feel as though I finally have the mother I always wanted. I'll never complain about her again."

Graham quirked one brow.

She laughed again. "And someday you'll probably need to remind me I said that. But for now . . ." With a quick glance around, she rose up on tiptoe and planted a quick kiss on Graham's smooth cheek. "I'll go talk to Dad. Pray for me?"

"Of course." He squeezed her hand.

Mama willingly agreed to give Trina and her father some alone time, and she went to Uncle Henry's. Trina headed home, praying all the way for a reconciliation of her relationship with her father. When she entered the house, she found Dad in the living room on the sofa. A newspaper lay in his lap, but his eyes were closed, his head back.

Trina cleared her throat, and Dad jumped. He opened his eyes and peered around, focusing on her. Immediately a frown formed on his face.

"Trina." The single word managed to convey disapproval.

"Dad." Trina sat down at the other end of the sofa.

He straightened in the seat, lifting the paper. "Is the party over?"

"Yes."

"Where are your brother and mother?"

"Tony's cleaning up the café, and Mama went over to Uncle Henry's."

Dad's eyebrows rose. "Oh?"

"I asked her to."

His brows came down. "Oh."

Trina scooted a little closer. "Dad, can we talk?"

Dad shook the paper, turning his frowning gaze to the printed pages. "About what?"

Trina reached out and pushed the newspaper back into his lap. "About me. And college. And you." Despite her determination not to let emotion get in the way, tears pricked her eyes. "Please, Dad. You're tearing me in two."

Dad set his jaw, his eyes straight ahead. "You obviously don't need my approval, Trina. You're going on without it, so I don't see why —"

"Because I love you." Trina spoke quietly, her gaze never wavering from her father's face even if he refused to return it. "Because your approval is important to me. You were so supportive when I asked to work for Dr. Groening. I know I should have been completely honest about why I wanted to work for him, but I've asked you to forgive me for that. I guess I'm asking again, because until you truly forgive me, I don't think we'll ever be able to get past your anger."

"I'm not angry!"

In spite of herself, Trina smiled. "Your tone says otherwise."

"Trina . . ." Dad sighed, dropping his head

as if he carried a great burden. "It comes out as anger, but I'm not as much angry as worried. Worried for you. Worried for Tony. Worried for the fellowship as a whole."

Trina tipped her head. "Why?" Finally Dad looked at her. She saw the concern in his eyes, and her heart melted, her frustration with him washing away. "Please tell me why."

"You're young, Trina. You haven't seen what change can do to the community. When I was just a young boy and my father was a deacon, the fellowship split when the deacons agreed to allow members to have electricity in their homes. Those who disagreed with the decision moved to southeast Kansas — among them, some cousins I miss to this day. My life was never the same. Relationships were never the same."

Dad flipped one hand outward, grimacing. "Oh, over time, the furor settled down, but there was always a hole where those people used to be. And that hole has never been filled." He snorted. "The benefit of electricity can't take the place of *people* in a person's heart."

Trina nodded. Being able to pursue her dream had created a rift in several relationships. Even though she hadn't been separated from those people physically, there was an emotional separation that was just as wide. "I understand."

"I don't think you do." Dad leaned his elbows on his knees. He linked his fingers then stared at his joined hands. "What you're doing — going to college — has the potential to divide the fellowship again. Already I've heard rumblings that one of our members plans to leave with his children. Others could follow. Even if it doesn't divide the entire fellowship, it's dividing our family. Things haven't been the same under this roof ever since you woke your mother and me up in the middle of the night."

Trina could have argued it was her father's choice to divide the family — with his acceptance, things could return to normal. But she kept her thought to herself, allowing him to fully express his views without interruption.

"Now your brother is talking about college." He blew out a noisy breath. "What would he do in college? He wants to be a farmer, like me. Like his grandfathers. All college would do for him is to take him away from the fellowship and put him with worldly people who could distort his faith. No good could come of that."

Dad angled his head to peer at her. His lowered brows turned his eyes into slits of distrust. "By giving you permission to attend college, the deacons have opened the door for all of our young people to leave the community. Some will do it just because they can, not because — as you've claimed — God put a desire in their hearts. And some will get caught up in the world and never come back. Leaving holes, Trina."

Trina swallowed, seeking words to offer reassurance. She wanted to promise that what her father feared wouldn't come to pass, yet she knew words would be futile. And she couldn't make promises that might not be able to be kept. How could she predict what might happen in the future?

"I wish I could say you're wrong, Dad, and that only good will come of my being allowed to become a veterinarian. But I don't know what others will do. I keep praying things will be okay, that everyone will accept it as God's will. Some will, eventually, and others may not. All I know for sure is I can't ignore it. When I wasn't preparing to walk where God called, I was miserable."

Dad's head slowly bobbed in a single nod.

"I sure don't want to make others feel miserable — especially you, because I love you so much — and a part of me still aches because of the unhappiness I've created. But now that I'm studying again, I feel . . ." She sought a word to describe what following her dream meant, and she settled on one: "Whole. I *have* to do what God asks me to do. Can you try to understand that?"

Dad drew in a deep, slow breath and held it for several long seconds. The breath expelled in a rush, and he puckered his lips into a thoughtful scowl, staring straight ahead. Finally he looked at her and shook his head. "No guarantees, Trina, but I'll try to understand. And I'll try not to let my worries turn into anger."

Trina squeezed his knee. "Thank you. I can promise one thing, Dad. I won't be pulled into the world permanently. When I'm done with college, I'm coming back. I want to be a veterinarian right here in Sommerfeld. My heart is in this community, in this fellowship, in this family. That won't change."

Dad pushed to his feet. He looked down at her, his face resigned. "All right." He glanced toward the window. "It's a pretty day. I think I'll take a walk."

"Do you want me to come with you?"

"No." He softened the negative reply with a sad smile. "Sometimes it's good for a man to be alone with his thoughts."

"Okay." Trina rose and stepped up to hug her father, wrapping her arms around his middle and pressing her face into the familiar curve of his shoulder. "I love you, Dad."

His hands chafed her upper arms, and then he set her aside. "I love you, too, daughter."

Trina's heart thrilled to the words. She watched him stride out the door with his hands in his pockets and his head hanging low. His dejected pose brought a rush of pity to the surface, and she closed her eyes. *Lord, please give Dad the same peace You gave me. Not so I can do what I want to, but so he can rest in You.*

Although Dad never mentioned where he'd gone or what he'd done on his walk, the next week was peaceful in the house. The blanket of anger was gone, replaced by a respectful if resigned acceptance far preferable to the gloom of previous days. Trina rejoiced constantly in the change and trusted full acceptance would one day come when her father realized she intended to keep her promise of remaining rooted in the fellowship.

She missed Graham tremendously in the evenings, since she had to spend her after-work hours studying. But she consoled herself with the knowledge that soon she would be his wife. They would reside together in the upstairs of his parents' home, and she would study at a table in the kitchen, where Graham would sit on the opposite side and read a book each evening. Even if they were quiet together, they would be together.

They enjoyed their brief minutes when Graham transported her to and from Dr. Groening's clinic each day. Graham began stealing kisses as he let her out of the car, and those tender moments made her long for the day when they could express their affection openly within the privacy of their own rooms.

On Friday, Graham's kiss lengthened, and Trina giggled as she gently pushed him away. "I have to go in."

He groaned, grinning. "I know. How many more days?"

"One hundred and twenty." They had chosen the second Saturday in February as their wedding day, one week after Walt and Michelle's.

"Then I need one more kiss to make it that long."

She laughed but obliged, then scooted across the seat. "I'll see you after work."

"I love you! Have a good day!" he called as he pulled away.

Still smiling, basking in the warmth of

Graham's love, Trina bounded up the stairs and entered the clinic. "Good morning, Mrs. Penner. Do you have —" She stopped when she noticed a tall, well-dressed man leaning on the counter. As she spoke, he straightened and turned to face her, a smile lighting his narrow face.

"Oh!" Trina smoothed her hands over her work apron. "I'm sorry. I didn't realize anyone else was here already. I'll just go get started —"

"Trina, wait." Mrs. Penner's voice stopped Trina from dashing to the back room. "I want you to meet Marc Royer."

Trina offered a shy nod at the tall stranger. He held out his hand, and Trina took it, giving it a slight shake. Then she grabbed her apron again. She couldn't explain why, but the man intimidated her.

Mrs. Penner went on. "Marc was born in Hillsboro, but his family moved away when he was in junior high."

Trina finally found her voice. "Are you visiting friends?"

Marc Royer flicked his smile to Mrs. Penner then back to Trina. "Not exactly. I'm here to shadow Dr. Groening."

Confused, Trina looked from one to the other. " 'Shadow'?"

"Follow him around today." Mrs. Penner

beamed. "Marc graduated last May as a doctor of veterinary medicine and has come back to his hometown in the hopes of opening a practice."

Trina's dreams crumbled at her feet.

TWENTY-TWO

Trina stumbled through the day, hardly able to function. If that man — Marc Royer — already had his degree, then surely Dr. Groening would choose to let him purchase the clinic. He would have no need to wait five years for Trina.

Oh God, her thoughts groaned, *what am I to do? Why did he have to come now?*

She managed to complete her tasks with efficiency, keeping her fears to herself until Graham showed up at the end of the day. The moment she slammed the passenger door closed, she covered her face with her hands and let loose a torrent of confused tears.

"Trina!" Graham slid across the seat and embraced her, pulling her head into the curve of his neck. "What is it? What's wrong?" Trina took great, shuddering breaths to bring herself under control. But when she looked into his worried face, she fell apart again.

He gently set her in her seat and said, "I'll get you home."

All the way, Trina stared at the landscape, tears continuing to fall in torrents down her cheeks. Why, why, why did it have to be so hard for her to achieve her dream? She tortured herself with the question that had no answer.

When Graham pulled in front of her house, he put the car in PARK, turned off the ignition, and shifted on the seat to face her. "Ready to tell me what happened today?"

Trina sniffed hard and nodded. She shared, haltingly, about Marc Royer's arrival at the clinic, his educational background, his goals. On a sob, she finished, "So where does that leave me? The clinic won't be available to me when I finish my schooling."

Graham pulled his lips to the side, looking at her in silence. Finally, he asked, "Do you have to take over Dr. Groening's clinic?"

Trina huffed, throwing her hands outward. "Graham! It makes so much sense! He has the building, the equipment. People are used to going there. It would have been so perfect! But now . . ."

"But now maybe God has something else in mind." Graham caught her hand and carried it to his lips, pressing a kiss to her knuckles. "When God closes a door, there's usually a reason. Can't you trust Him with this?"

"That's easy for you to say." Trina's voice sounded hollow from her stuffed-up nose. She snuffled again and shook her head, turning to stare out the window. "You didn't just get the rug pulled out from under your feet. All my plans . . ."

"All *your* plans?"

Trina recognized the emphasis. She clamped her teeth together and refused to answer.

Graham lowered their joined hands to the seat. "Trina, you haven't been in charge of this from the beginning. Why did you choose to pursue becoming a vet? Because God led you to. Don't turn it into *your* plans now, or nothing will work right. You know that."

Shamed, she knew he was right. But the pain of finding a degreed doctor ready and able to assume responsibility for the clinic was still too fresh. She stared out the window and refused to answer.

After a long while, Graham spoke in a reasonable tone. "Look at the obstacles you've had to overcome to get this far. You had to convince me and your family that it was right, you had to convince the fellowship leaders it was right, you had to prepare to be accepted into a college. Look at everything you've accomplished so far."

"Look at how many mountains I had to climb already," she shot back.

"All of which God helped you climb," he returned calmly.

Her frustration grew. Why did he have to be sensible? "Maybe I'm *tired* of climbing, Graham!"

"Then maybe you aren't cut out to be a veterinarian."

At his soft statement, Trina whirled to face him, her mouth dropping open. "What?"

He met her gaze squarely. No hint of a smile showed on his lips. "If you get a case with an animal that's hard to solve — an illness you can't figure out at first — will you just quit and let the animal die?"

"Of course not!" How dare he even suggest something like that?

"What you're facing right now isn't much different, Trina. It's a challenge. So this Marc somebody —"

"Royer."

"— Royer is here, ready to take over. Sure, it works better for Dr. Groening, so he'll probably let him take over. But that doesn't mean there will never be room for you. It just means you've got some competition. A challenge. The question is, are you going to meet it or be defeated by it?"

Trina thought about Graham's words. She wanted to rise to the challenge, to let everyone know nothing or nobody would hold her back from walking where God directed her to walk, but at the moment she felt spent. She didn't have the energy to form a response, let alone rise to a challenge.

And then her greatest fear struck — the one that had festered in the far corner of her mind all day. The one she hadn't wanted to bring out and examine but knew must be addressed. She swallowed, took a breath, and whispered, "But . . . what if this is God's way of telling me I've been going the wrong way?"

Graham lowered his brows, his expression thoughtful. "Are you thinking He doesn't want you to be a veterinarian, after all?"

"Do you think it might be possible?" Trina held her breath, thoughts tumbling through her mind. What if this whole idea was her own fanciful flight rather than God's will? If she gave up the dream, things would be much simpler. Her father could relax, the fellowship would return to normal, Graham wouldn't have to sell his house. . . .

She stared at him, waiting, while her heart beat in fear — or hope? — that he would agree with her statement.

Suddenly he shook his head, his fingers clamping hard around her hand. "I don't believe that, Trina. I've had too much peace about it to think it's wrong. And I've seen too much evidence of growth and peace in you to think it's wrong. You're meant to be given the work of your hands as a caregiver for animals."

Trina released her breath on a lengthy sigh. Having his confirmation helped eliminate the mighty worry. Yet another one remained, nearly as sizable as the first. "But do you think I'll still be able to be a veterinarian in Sommerfeld? In all the years Dr. Groening has practiced veterinary medicine, he's handled it alone. If Marc Royer takes his place, then —"

"Then we'll figure something out." Graham rested his head briefly against the seat. When he looked at her again, conviction burned in his eyes. "God never said we wouldn't face hardship in life. He only promised to walk with us. He's been your companion along this journey so far. He's even managed to convince several people to walk along beside you as your encouragers. I don't know why this other man has shown up now, but I do know you can't quit. You *can't* quit, Trina."

"You can't quit, Trina." Those words carried Trina through the week. She deliberately called upon them as she studied and completed assignments. She pulled them out and let them be her encouragement when faced with an unpleasant task at the clinic. She whispered them to herself when Marc Royer returned for a second day of shadowing Dr. Groening. And she nearly chanted them aloud when Dr. Groening took her aside on Friday to talk.

By the look on his face, she knew what he was going to say before he opened his mouth. "Trina, I know you hoped to be able to take over the clinic when you get through school, and it pains me to disappoint you, but —"

Trina nodded. "You're going to sell it to Marc Royer."

Dr. Groening sighed, sympathy in his lined eyes. "Yes. After the first of the year, we'll make it official. In the meantime, he'll be working with me, familiarizing himself with the area and gaining the trust of the folks who live around here."

Trina crossed her arms, trying to press away the ache that filled her middle. "But there must be other places he could work — other cities. Why here?" *Why my town?*

"Since he lived in Hillsboro when he was a youngster, he feels at home in this area. He's eager to stay."

Trina blinked hard, determined not to cry. But the doctor must have seen the presence of tears, because he put his warm hand on her shoulder.

"Your job is secure. Even Marc acknowledges your assistance is needed. As long as you want to, you can still help out here. And when you have your degree, maybe you and Marc can work together — a partnership."

Heat flooded Trina's face. She couldn't imagine joining in a partnership with a man. Especially a man who was not Mennonite. She didn't answer.

The older doctor sighed, lowering his gaze for a moment. "But if you decide you don't want to work here —"

"I need the job." If she was to pay for college, she had to work. Graham was giving up his house for her education — the least she could do was contribute.

"Good. Well, then . . ." Dr. Groening stepped back and slipped his hands into the pockets of his faded blue scrub top. "I just hope you understand this has nothing to do with a lack of confidence in you. I've seen you with animals, Trina. You'll make a fine doctor one day. I only wish you were further along in your studies. Maybe then . . ."

Trina nodded, forcing a smile. "It's all right, Dr. Groening. I understand. And I appreciate your kind words. Whether I end up practicing in Sommerfeld or not, I will still be a veterinarian. Graham and I agree it's what I'm supposed to do."

But, God, her thoughts continued as she headed for the door to meet Graham for the ride home, *I wish You'd let me know where I'm meant to serve as a veterinarian. I don't think Dad will ever forgive me if I leave another hole where a person used to be.*

Graham flicked the edges of the Louis L'Amour western he'd brought along to keep himself occupied while Trina took her midsemester exams. He wished he'd brought a second book, too. Next time he'd know to plan for more than two hours of waiting.

The chair, although padded, boasted a straight back that kept him uncomfortably upright. If he slouched, the slickness of the vinyl cover made him feel as though he might slide right off onto the tiled floor. An action like that would certainly capture attention. And he was conspicuous enough already.

Perched in a seating area where two bustling hallways converged, he was in a prime location to be noticed. Normally when he ventured away from Sommerfeld, he was in a group. Being alone in worldly surroundings was new and, he decided with a tug at his collar, less than pleasant. No one was rude to him, but he was painfully aware of the curious glances, the muffled giggles, the whispered comments — "What's up with that?" and "Dude, call the fashion police." When with his friends, he could focus on them and ignore gawkers. But today he didn't have that privilege.

A door down the left hallway opened, and people spilled out. Graham glanced up, his heart leaping with anticipation — was Trina coming? But to his dismay, he realized the classroom door through which she had disappeared was farther down. Stifling a frustrated huff of breath, he opened the novel and began reading it for the second time.

He was just starting the fourth chapter when another *click* and several voices pulled his attention away from the book. This time, he spotted Trina among the group milling in the hallway. The other students made a berth around her, making it easy for her to rush toward him. He rose, reaching for her sweater, which she'd left on the chair beside him, and smiled as she approached.

"All done?" he asked as he draped the sweater over her shoulders. Two girls in shirts that didn't quite meet the waistlines of their very tight blue jeans walked by, their heads swiveling to stare. Graham kept his gaze pinned to Trina's face.

"All done. We can go."

Graham almost gave an exultant shout. He deliberately ignored the other people who moved around them as they made their way to the parking lot. "So how do you think you did?"

Trina hunched her shoulders with a nervous giggle. "I hope okay, but I won't know for sure until they post the grades online." She stopped, gave a quick glance around, then rose up on tiptoe to whisper, "It felt funny to be in there. I've never been with so many worldly people by myself."

Graham nodded. He understood exactly. "But you did it," he praised. And he had, too. If they were going to have to live out on their own, away from Sommerfeld, while she finished college, they might as well get used to it.

She sighed, swinging their joined hands as

they began moving again. "People are so funny. They look at my clothes and my cap. They look and look, but they don't say anything. They look, but I don't think they really see *me*." She frowned. "Maybe that's why I like animals so much. They don't much care what you look like — they just respond to how you treat them."

Graham searched for words to encourage her and make her feel less uncomfortable, but none came. They reached his car, and he opened the door for her. On his own side of the vehicle, he took care not to let his door bump the side of the fancy red sports car parked very close to his car.

Once behind the steering wheel, he finally responded to her statement. "I think, once they get used to seeing you on campus, they'll look beyond your clothes to Trina." Wondering how he would cope, he asked, "But what about you? Will you get used to being around them?"

She chewed her lower lip, her thoughtful gaze aimed in his direction. "I suppose over time you can get used to anything."

At that moment, a young man in baggy jeans, an untucked plaid shirt, and flat rubber shoes that whacked against his bare soles approached the car. The man halted at the hood of Graham's car, lifted silverlensed sunglasses to the top of his head, and let his gaze rove over every inch of Graham's fellowship-approved dark blue sedan. Graham felt his face grow hot as the man's face twisted into a smirk.

Giving the hood a pat, the man called, "Nice wheels, dude. Did you inherit this from your gramma?"

Graham pinched his lips tight and started the engine, backing out of the space. The other man laughingly slipped his sunglasses into place, aimed a little black box at his car, then climbed behind the wheel. Graham's face continued to burn as he left the parking lot, watching carefully for traffic. There seemed to be more drivers on this campus than on Main Street in Sommerfeld on its busiest shopping day.

When they were finally away from the campus and heading toward the highway, Graham puffed his cheeks and blew out a breath, relaxing his tense shoulders. "Tell me again how a person can get used to anything given time."

Trina slid her hand across the seat, and he grabbed it. The squeeze of her fingers let him know she felt bad about how the college student had behaved. He glanced at her and saw apprehension in her expression. He couldn't let her worry about his feelings — she needed assurance they would make it just fine in the world while she finished her schooling. So he pushed his lips into a smile and forced a light laugh.

"I think next time I'll just wear my work clothes instead of my Sunday suit. The students don't seem to wear formal attire." He knew his statement would let her know he was willing to go there again.

A smile lit her eyes. "Thank you, Graham."

Graham winked in reply then turned his attention to driving. He would go out again. And again. He would continue going until the stares and comments didn't bother him anymore. *Lord, let that day come quickly!*

Twenty-Three

Over the next two weeks, as October slowly melted away, Graham took every opportunity he could find to drive into one of the larger towns nearby — Newton or McPherson and once all the way to Hutchinson. Always by himself. Always wearing his distinctive Mennonite suit. He chose the busiest stores and walked around, sometimes pushing a cart, always meeting others' gazes, forcing a smile and nod if someone maintained eye contact long enough to see it.

These excursions used up a lot of gasoline, time, and energy, but Graham decided it was his form of education. Trina was learning to be a veterinarian; he was learning to feel comfortable outside of Sommerfeld. The time would come when the two of them — just them, no crowd of friends — would leave their secure Mennonite community. He would work among the worldly. Shop among the worldly. Reside in an apartment next door to the worldly. And he refused to spend that time feeling misplaced and uncomfortable.

It was simply a matter of adjusting, he told himself as he pushed a squeaky metal cart around a large discount store on the outside edge of McPherson. And he would adjust. For Trina's sake. If he was comfortable, then she would be comfortable. He was determined she *would* be comfortable. Because if she wasn't, she wouldn't be able to focus on her studies. So he would make sure everything flowed smoothly for his Trina.

He dropped two cans of honey-roasted peanuts — his favorite snack — into the cart, his heart lifting with the thought of Trina. Fewer than fifteen weeks and she would be *his Trina* in every way. Already they were best friends, but soon they would be husband and wife. Nothing could be better, he decided. He envied his friend Walt, who had seven fewer days than Graham to wait.

Mom couldn't wait, either. In her delight at having another woman under her roof, she had been busy in the upstairs of his childhood home, cleaning and hanging new curtains and repairing the rag rugs that had become torn from energetic boys using them to slide across the linoleum floor.

Which reminded him, Mom wanted him to pick up a spool of upholstery thread since she'd used hers up on those rugs.

He turned the cart toward the fabric department, and when he rounded a display of bolts of cloth, his cart banged into someone else's. "Please excuse me!"

The woman gave a start, dropping the bolt she'd just pulled from the shelf. To Graham's surprise, he knew the woman — Dr. Groening's wife. He rushed around the cart and retrieved the dropped bolt.

"Thank you," she said as she took the cloth from his hands. Then her expression turned puzzled. "Do I know you?"

Graham nodded. "We've seen each other before at the café in Sommerfeld. I'm Graham Ortmann. My fiancée, Trina Muller, works at the clinic with your husband."

"Of course! Trina!" The woman smiled broadly, her eyes twinkling. "What a sweet girl. But engaged . . . I didn't realize she was engaged."

Graham offered another shy nod.

"Well, congratulations." Mrs. Groening extended her hand, and Graham shook it. "Josiah thinks the world of Trina. He felt so bad about not being able to let her buy the clinic."

Graham swallowed. "I know. And she

understands. We don't hold a grudge."

The woman pressed a wrinkled hand to the bodice of her sweater. "That's a great relief. Even Marc was concerned about taking over, knowing of Trina's interest." She tipped her head. "Isn't it odd that two people would want to establish themselves as veterinarians in the same small circle of communities? I would think it would be more likely to have to hunt for someone, yet two step up, ready and willing to take Josiah's place."

With a shake of her head, she smiled again. "It has certainly made things easier for us. Joe was ready to retire two years ago, but he couldn't because he wouldn't leave people without care for their animals. Now it isn't a concern. We're very grateful."

"I'm glad it's worked out for you."

"Well!" The woman released another light laugh. "I've kept you here too long already. I'm sure you have other things to do than visit with me. It was nice seeing you, Graham, and please give Trina my sincerest congratulations. I wish you both much happiness."

"Thank you, ma'am." Graham moved on, but his thoughts lingered over Mrs. Groening's comment about two people interested in taking over the veterinary clinic. Trina's keen disappointment in not being able to assume the Groening Clinic made his heart ache, but he couldn't help but believe God had something special planned in its stead. *Lord,* he silently prayed as he pushed the cart down another long aisle, *thank You for the opportunities You've already given Trina. Guide her in where to use her degree. And, Lord, please, if it be Your will, let us remain in Sommerfeld.*

Beth leaned over Trina's shoulder and moved the mouse on the pad, bringing the cursor on top of a word underlined with a red squiggle. "See that funny line? That means you've spelled the word wrong. Now look. If you right-click on the mouse, the correct spelling will come up, and you can change it."

Trina shook her head, tossing her ribbons over her shoulders. "Well, why didn't you tell me that before now? I wouldn't have gotten so many poor marks on the English papers!"

Beth laughed, bumping Trina's shoulder. "You didn't ask. Let me show you some-thing else." She dropped to one knee beside Trina's chair and brought up an options box. Clicking inside one small square, she activated the grammar check. "This will even tell you if you've made grammatical errors in your sentences. I usually don't use it, but I'll keep it on for you, if you would like."

"I would like that!" Trina sighed as Beth saved the change. Suddenly she grabbed Beth's hand, her face pinched into a worried scowl. "This isn't considered cheating, is it? I don't want to use something the other students don't have."

Beth snorted. Trina's naïveté was endearing, but she needed to learn the wiles of the world if she was going to venture into it. "Believe me, Katrinka, nearly all of the other students have had computers from grade school on up. They're familiar with the use of these tools. I'd be willing to bet a lot of them just surf the Net, find an essay, download it, tweak it a bit, and then turn it in as their own."

Trina's brown eyes grew round. "That's dishonest!"

"Of course it's dishonest. And if they got caught, they'd be punished — hopefully. But quite a few still take the chance."

Trina shook her head, her eyes snapping with indignation. "Well, I don't see how anyone could do that. Letting someone else do the work for you does nothing more than cheat yourself. How do you learn if you don't do the work on your own?"

"Aw, Trina . . ." Beth sat back on her haunches, warmth filling her middle. "It is so refreshing to know there are still honest, hardworking people in the world. I suspect you are going to be a terrific influence on your co-students when you're finally sitting in a classroom instead of all alone in front of a computer screen."

The indignation faded, replaced by an expression of apprehension. "Beth, can I tell you something?"

"Sure you can."

For a moment, Trina bit down on her lower lip, her gaze averted. "Sometimes I get really scared about going to those classes." She lifted her head, her dark gaze meeting Beth's. "It's so much easier here — all alone, like you said. I don't feel like anybody's watching me or judging me. I can just work and feel at peace. But when I went to El Dorado to take my tests, it was *hard.* Not just because of what was on the tests, but because I had to be with so many people who are different from me."

Beth released a short, rueful chuckle. "You aren't telling me anything I can't under-stand. Look at me!" She held her hands to her sides, glancing down at her blue jeans and long-sleeved T-shirt. "Don't you think I feel different when I walk down the streets of Sommerfeld? I don't exactly fit, you know."

Trina stared at Beth, her eyes wide. "I hadn't thought of that. When I look at you, I don't worry about your clothes. You're just Beth, my friend. That's all that matters."

"And how did that happen?" Beth tipped her head, smiling at Trina.

Trina shrugged, bunching the white ribbons on her shoulders. "I don't know."

"I do." With a smirk, Beth bounced to her feet and put her hands on her hips. "You got to know me as a person. That's how we became friends. Between friends, the outside doesn't matter nearly as much as the inside, Katrinka." She gave one of Trina's ribbons a gentle tug. "It will feel strange at first — it did for me — but you'll get acquainted with others in your classes, and pretty soon you won't feel out of place anymore."

Beth frowned, hearing her own words. Was she being completely honest with Trina? There were still times she and Sean felt out of place in Sommerfeld. They'd found a measure of acceptance, for which she was grateful, but a segment of the community either acted resigned to their presence or held them at bay, barely tolerating them.

Yet she sensed if she shared this whole

truth with Trina, it would only discourage her, so she offered another smile and said, "Give it time. It'll all work out eventually."

Trina sighed. "I hope so. I know a lot of things have already worked out, but there's still so much that must be done. Sometimes it's scary."

"New things always are." Beth caught the back of the computer chair and turned Trina to face the computer. She assumed a teasing voice as she instructed, "But you now have a new thing at your disposal that is going to make writing these papers easier, so get to it. Sean is due home this evening around nine, and I'll want you out of here by then so he and I can be alone."

Trina's cheeks flooded with pink.

Beth laughed. "There's something else you'll learn, Katrinka. It's wonderful to have all-alone time with your husband."

For a moment, Trina pressed her lips together, peering at Beth out of the corner of her eye. Then an impish grin climbed her cheeks. With a smug look, she said, "That's one lesson I don't need to learn. I already know it well."

Beth laughed again, gave Trina a quick hug, and backed away from the computer to let her work. Settling into Sean's recliner, Beth picked up a book and opened it, but

Trina's comment — *"I already know it well"* — ran through her mind, and she couldn't stop a chuckle from rumbling. That Trina . . . full of surprises. She sincerely hoped the world wouldn't squelch Trina's joyful spirit. Just to be on the safe side, she closed her eyes and handed that concern to her heavenly Father.

At a quarter to nine, Trina closed down the computer, gathered up her papers, and headed for home. Beth watched her through the front window until she turned the corner. Then she watched for Sean's return. The days were shorter, and full dark let her see the car headlights when they turned the corner a block away. She stepped out onto the porch, dancing a bit as the cold floor seeped through her socks, and waved when he turned into the driveway.

He rolled down the window and called, "Hello, beautiful!"

She danced across the grass to lean in and give him a welcome-home kiss. She missed him tremendously when he spent days away, but she had to admit the homecomings were nice.

"Mmm." He pulled back, still smiling. "Let me get this car put away, and we can continue in the house."

With a giggle, she slipped into the backseat then accompanied him as he walked across the yard to the back door. Once inside, he wrapped his arms around her and lowered his head to meet her lips. They enjoyed a lengthy welcome-home kiss before he finally pulled back, sighed, and said, "Wow, I'm hungry."

Beth created a mock scowl. "That's all you have to say?"

He tipped his head, his eyes teasing. "I'm hungry, *darling?*"

She laughed. "Okay. Supper first." She turned toward the refrigerator. "I have some leftover goulash, which I can heat up, or there's a bagged salad, or I can fix you a sandwich. Which sounds the best?" Her hand on the fridge door, she peeked at him over her shoulder.

He sat at the table, one elbow propped on its edge with his chin in his hand. He grinned. "Come here." He patted his knee.

Without hesitation, she sat. He buried his face against her hair and sighed. "I hate these days apart."

Beth coiled her arms around his neck, holding back the comment that the days apart were his choice, not hers. He could draw blueprints from here and let his father travel to the different areas to present the plans, but instead, he packed his bags and headed out at least once every other week. She wondered sometimes if he did it just to escape to places where he didn't feel as odd as a licorice whip in a jar of jelly beans. He'd never completely adjusted to Sommerfeld.

She kissed his ear and pushed off his lap, crossing to the refrigerator to remove the tub of goulash. Dumping the macaroni and ground beef into a bowl, she asked, "Did the meeting go well?"

He nodded, yawning. "Oh yeah. And if they sign, it'll mean more stained-glass work. Just across the front, but four windows at least."

Beth nodded, popping the saucer into the microwave. Just before hitting ON, she remembered to throw a napkin over the bowl. She leaned against the counter while the microwave zapped Sean's supper. "When will you know?"

"They want me to make an adjustment in the dimensions of the Sunday school classroom wing. I had made the classrooms all of comparable sizes, but they want the children's rooms larger than those for adults, so I'll need to move a few walls around. Once they get that in hand, they should make a decision." He yawned again. "And they want to see the final drawings by the end of next week."

The microwave dinged, and Beth carried the bowl to Sean. She waited while he offered his silent prayer. When he grabbed a fork from the cup in the center of the table, she said, "So you'll probably be using the computer quite a bit in the next couple of days."

"No doubt." He took a bite, chewed, and swallowed. "Why? Do you need it?"

Beth sank into the chair across from him and shrugged. "I can use the laptop. I just want to make sure there's one available for Trina to do her schoolwork."

Sean, his head lowered over his bowl, peered at her with a thoughtful expression.

"What are you thinking?"

He set down the fork for a moment. "I just wondered how long Trina will continue to make use of our computer. It isn't terribly convenient."

Beth blustered, "Well, what do you want me to do? She doesn't have any other way of completing her assignments."

Sean shook his head, his eyes twinkling. "My combatant, Beth. Must you always jump to conclusions?"

"But you made it sound like you want to take our computer away from Trina."

A grin twitched his cheek, and he smoothed his fingers over his mustache, removing the smirk. "I do."

Beth started to jump up, but Sean's hand around her wrist kept her in place.

"Stay put, my bristling beauty." His chuckle did little to alleviate Beth's frustration. "Let me finish eating, and then I'll propose a compromise I think you, Trina, and I can all accept."

Beth folded her arms across her chest and scowled. "I'll listen, but it better be good."

Twenty-Four

"Trina?"

Trina jumped, clanking together the clean test tubes cradled in her apron. She spun around from the surgery's wash sink. "Y-yes, Dr. Royer?" His very presence made her stomach quake. Even after nearly a month of working with the man, she still found him intimidating. His height, his superior manner of looking down his nose when he addressed her, and his enviable knowledge — proven by the certificates that now hung on the wall of the reception area above Dr. Groening's — left her feeling very young, very backward, and hopelessly igno-rant.

"Would you please explain the condition of the poodle in exam room one?"

Hope leaped in her breast. Was he asking her opinion? She licked her dry lips and formed an answer. "He hurt his leg — cut it on something. It was quite jagged in appearance and obviously requires stitches."

She waited for him to affirm her assessment, but the man folded his arms across his chest, his expression severe. "I am well aware of the injury and its required treatment, Trina. My question concerns the bandage on his leg. A bandage, his owner tells me, *you* applied."

Her heart pounded like a bass drum as trepidation made her knees go weak. "Yes, I — I applied a bandage. You were busy in another room, and the dog was bleeding badly. His owner was very upset. So I cleaned the wound with an antibacterial wash and bandaged it in readiness for your attention." She swallowed, fear rising as he continued to glare at her. Had she injured the dog somehow? Her hands pressed to her heart, she rasped, "The dog . . . did I do something wrong?"

Dr. Royer took a step forward. His great height coupled with his look of fury made Trina shrink backward. "Yes, you did something wrong. You have no business providing medical attention to any animal."

Trina opened her mouth to explain she had performed a similar treatment for numerous animals in Sommerfeld, but Dr. Royer forged on in a scathing tone.

"You crossed the line, Trina, and I won't

tolerate it. You are not a veterinarian or even a certified assistant. I will not be held liable for your rash actions. You are never — I repeat, *never* — to put your hands on an animal in this clinic for the purpose of providing medical care."

"But I only wanted to help the little dog," Trina protested weakly.

"Help all the dogs you want to in your neighborhood at home, if people are willing to bring their pets to you." He pointed his finger at her, his brows low. "But at the clinic, you will leave the care of the animals to me. Do you understand?"

Too stunned to do anything else, Trina nodded.

"Good." He took a step back, his gaze sweeping the operating room. "Finish your cleaning in here, and then shelve the shipment of pet food that arrived this morning. As soon as I've stitched the poodle's leg, I'm going in to Hillsboro. Mrs. Penner knows to contact Dr. Groening if there is an emergency." His voice rose, carrying, she was sure, to the examination room where the lady and her poodle awaited his attention. "Should someone come in requiring attention, you are *not* to try to handle it."

"A–all right," she replied, blinking back tears of humiliation.

He strode out of the small laboratory on long legs that covered twice the distance in half the time as those of most people Trina knew. She sank against the sink's edge, her chest aching with the desire to cry. How Dr. Royer's attack stung. She'd only wanted to help. Dr. Groening never would have spoken to her so harshly, even if it was deserved. But since his decision to sell the clinic to Dr. Royer, the elderly vet had spent less time at the clinic.

Unwilling to suffer another rebuke, she focused on completing her assigned tasks to the best of her ability. When the last bag of cat food was neatly on the shelf, she wandered to the reception area and leaned her elbows on the counter, peering over its top to Mrs. Penner. "What is Dr. Royer doing in Hillsboro?" She supposed it wasn't her business, yet she couldn't deny being curious.

"I'm not sure. He doesn't tell me things the way Dr. Groening always has."

Trina wondered if that bothered the receptionist. It must be different for her to work for this new young doctor after spending so many years with the gentle, laid-back Dr. Groening.

Mrs. Penner tapped her lips with one finger, looking hard at Trina. "You don't like him much, do you?"

Trina jerked upright. "Who?"

"Dr. Royer."

Heat filled Trina's face. "What — what makes you say that?"

The older woman laughed softly. "How much do you think you hide with those big eyes of yours?"

Trina hid her cheeks with her hands. "I'm so sorry . . ."

Mrs. Penner offered a flippant wave. "Oh, honey, don't apologize. He hasn't given you much reason to like him, has he? Waltzes in, takes over, talks to you as if you don't have a brain in your head . . . and the way he hollered at you today . . ." She shook her head, sympathy in her eyes. "You have every reason to dislike him."

Trina stared in silence at the older woman.

Mrs. Penner went on in a thoughtful tone. "I think because he's newly graduated he feels pretty full of himself — conceited. He had a tendency toward that when he was a boy because he stood a good six inches taller than any of his classmates." Her eyebrows flew high. "That's not an excuse, mind you, but it's a reason. In his mind, I suppose, 'bigger' equated with 'better.' " With a rueful sigh, she added, "All that being said, don't let him bother you, Trina.

You're a smart girl — Dr. Groening thinks so, and I do, too — and you do a good job. You keep doing that job. The people here appreciate you."

Trina's face still felt hot, but now pleasure rather than embarrassment created the warmth. She couldn't remember the last time anyone had complimented her so blatantly. She swallowed hard and managed to reply. "Thank you, Mrs. Penner. I — I appreciate your kind words."

Another wave of her hand dismissed Trina's words. Propping her chin in her hands, Mrs. Penner grinned up at Trina. "So . . . tell me about your wedding plans. How are you balancing preparing for a wedding with your work here and all your studying?"

Trina laughed. Mrs. Penner obviously didn't know Mama. "I don't have to do a thing in preparing for my wedding — my mother has it under control. The ceremony will be at the café since our house isn't big enough to accommodate all of the guests. She already has one of my aunts sewing my dress, another aunt making and freezing cookies, and Mama will prepare the fine dinner for afterward." She laughed, shaking her head. "She won't let anyone else bring anything for the dinner — she says she'll do it all herself."

"What colors are you using?"

Trina blinked twice. "Colors?"

"Yes. Don't you have a color theme, like lavender and mint, and particular flowers picked out to go with the theme?"

Trina remembered peeking in a bride's magazine once in McPherson. Those pictures were nothing like a Mennonite service. With a shake of her head, she explained, "No, ma'am. Weddings are pretty simple affairs. People come dressed in their Sunday worship clothing, and only the bride has a special dress."

She closed her eyes for a moment, imagining the moment she would stand beside Graham in her pale blue dress, holding a white Bible. Her heart picked up its tempo at the thought of Graham in his black suit and tie, his blue eyes shining with love for her.

"And why aren't you getting married in the church?"

Trina popped her eyes open. "We only use the meetinghouse for worship, although I've heard some Mennonite groups elsewhere have begun holding weddings in their meetinghouse. But mostly weddings are in the bride's home or a community building. Since Sommerfeld doesn't have a community building, Mama says the café will do."

"I see." The woman pursed her lips thoughtfully. "I guess I didn't realize a Mennonite wedding would be different from those performed in my home church. Do you have bridal showers? A party where people bring you gifts?"

Trina shook her head, smiling. "That sounds nice, but no. But people will bring gifts for our new home to the wedding. Mama doesn't know I know, but my cousins are working on a quilt for our . . . bed." Heat flamed her cheeks again. She hurried on. "My cousin Andrew's wife, Livvy, is especially talented with quilting, and she's helping, so I'm eager to see it."

"And where are you and Graham planning to live? Do you have a house in Sommerfeld all picked out?"

Guilt pricked Trina's conscience. She still felt bad about Graham selling his house to Walt, yet she knew he wouldn't have done it had he not prayed about it and believed it was the right thing to do. "No. We'll live with Graham's parents — until I go away to finish my college. While I finish up, I imagine we'll rent an apartment near the campus, and Graham will find a job. Then we'll probably live with his parents again until we can save enough money to pay for another house." She realized she was sharing plans that would take her several years down the road. Drawing a deep breath, she admitted, "It's all a little frightening but exciting, too."

"Starting out always is," Mrs. Penner agreed, sounding like Beth. "But you know something, Trina? You are a very blessed young lady. Just from listening to you now, I can tell you have family and friends who think a great deal of you and want to help you out. You have a young man willing to help you pursue an education beyond what I've heard the Mennonites usually allow. And you are going to have knowledge that will benefit you as well as give you an opportunity to bless the community wherever you and Graham decide to settle down. You have much for which to be thankful."

Trina nodded, her chest expanding with gratitude for each of the things Mrs. Penner had mentioned. "You're right." She needed to do a better job of thanking God for all of the doors He was making available to her, including working here at the clinic. Even if Dr. Royer was difficult, she could still learn from him if she set aside her personal antagonism toward the man. She made a private vow to give God His deserved appreciation the next time she prayed.

The crunch of tires on gravel intruded, and Trina dashed to the window to peek out. "There's Graham! Five o'clock already." She hurried to her time card and scribbled the time then flashed Mrs. Penner a smile. "I'll see you on Monday. Have a good weekend."

"You, too, Trina. Good-bye."

Trina trotted out the door and down the steps to Graham's car. The moment she slid into her seat, she leaned over and placed a kiss on Graham's cheek.

He drew back in surprise, a smile on his face. "What was that for?"

"A thank-you kiss," she said with a grin, "for being such a wonderful, supportive blessing in my life."

He chuckled as he put the car in DRIVE and aimed it toward the highway. "Well, you must have had a good day."

Trina thought about her encounter with Dr. Royer and how he made her feel inept. She wouldn't call all of it a good day, but Mrs. Penner's comments had changed her attitude. Her focus needed to be on the positive things happening rather than the negative. "It has been a good day. And the best part is right now because I'm with you."

Graham reached his arm out to capture Trina's shoulders and pull her close. He glanced down at her, smiling, and she smiled right back, tipping her chin upward to graze the underside of his jaw with her lips. He chuckled, and she shifted to rest her head on his shoulder. But when she looked forward, her heart leaped into her throat.

A truck, its driver appearing to dig under the dash for something, crossed the center line, the grill aiming directly at Graham's car. Trina screamed, "Graham!"

Graham jerked his gaze forward, and his elbow slammed into Trina's head as he flung his arm free to jam the heel of his hand against the horn. A discordant *ho–o–onk!* sounded. The other driver looked up, and Trina clearly saw his panicked face. But instead of turning away from them, the truck lurched directly into their path.

"God, help us!" Graham cried out. He yanked the wheel to the right then threw himself across Trina. The impact of the truck slamming into the driver's side brought Trina out of the seat. The sickening crunch of metal against metal echoed through her head, and she opened her mouth to scream again as the car spun around.

Trina's stomach turned inside out as the car slid into the ditch then flipped onto its side. She felt herself being tossed like a tumbleweed as the car turned again, rolling to its top, and she closed her eyes, battling nausea. Another wild turn, and finally the car stopped, bouncing on its tires, with Trina crumpled onto the floorboard.

For a moment she simply lay, stunned, but then she realized Graham was no longer in the vehicle with her. She pushed to her knees, calling, "Graham! Graham!" She continued screaming his name as she banged her hands uselessly against the passenger's door.

Frantic, she grabbed the dash and pulled herself upright, peering through the shattered windshield. A strong odor permeated the area, burning her throat. She buried her face against her shoulder for a moment and coughed. Then she forced her gaze back to the window. The shattered glass distorted her vision, turning the world into tiny pieces, like a jigsaw puzzle with its parts lined up but not connected. She squinted, her heart pounding, her dry throat rasping one word over and over: "Graham . . . Graham . . ."

And finally she spotted him — lying in a heap in the ditch just a few feet away from the car. "Graham!" She pounded her fists, desperate to get to him. "Graham! Graham!

Graham!"

The world became a sickening, disjointed dream. Cars stopping. People running from every direction. Voices calling.

"Has anyone called 911?"

"There's a girl in that car! We need to get her out in case the gas tank catches fire!"

"Is the man in the pickup okay?"

"Don't try to move anybody — wait for an ambulance!"

Frantic, bustling activity everywhere. And Trina, her heart pounding, shut it all out. With her bleeding hands curled over the dash, she stared, grunting with displeasure when milling people temporarily blocked her vision. Trapped like a bug in a jar, she kept her gaze pinned to Graham, praying silently, *Please, oh, please be all right.*

But not once did she see him move.

Twenty-Five

Around, and around, and around. Trina spun like the clothes in a washer drum. She reached out to grab something . . . anything . . . to make the spinning stop, and her hand connected with something solid.

Pain stabbed, bringing her eyes open. She blinked, uncertain, peering into a dim, unfamiliar room. She lay in a tall, narrow bed. Something trailed from one hand, and the other — the one she'd flung outward — was wrapped in a bandage. It throbbed. She cradled it against her chest. Soft beeps interrupted the silence. A lump shifted in the chair beside the bed, and Trina squinted, trying to make sense of the strange surroundings.

By increments, remembrance dawned. She was in a hospital room. An ambulance had brought her here after the emergency workers had extracted her from Graham's car. The doctor — young, with kind eyes — had insisted she stay overnight for observation. Mama was in the chair because she refused to leave with Dad.

Now, her gaze on her mother, she whispered, "Mama?"

Mama shifted again, groaning slightly. Then she sat straight up, twisting around to face Trina. "Trina, you're awake? The doctor said the sedative would make you sleep all night."

So that's why she felt so groggy. It took great effort to hold her eyelids open. But her memory only retained bits and pieces. She needed the whole picture. "What happened to Graham?" Her tongue felt thick, clumsy, and her words sounded slurred. For a moment, she wasn't sure Mama understood.

But then Mama answered. "Graham . . . isn't here."

Trina's heart leaped in her chest. "Where — where is he? He isn't —" A picture of him sprawled on the ground, unmoving, filled Trina's head. She squeezed her eyes shut. *Oh, please don't say it. Don't say it!*

A warm hand smoothed Trina's tangled hair away from her face, and Trina opened her eyes. Mama leaned over the bed, her tired face sad. "He's in Wichita, Trina. They needed him to be where there were surgeons who could better take care of him. They think he fractured his spine."

Trina swallowed, her mind scrabbling to grasp the possible consequences of such an injury. The most severe lodged in her brain and refused to leave. "Oh, Mama . . ."

"Now, it's too soon to worry," Mama soothed, her hand stroking, the touch comforting. "You just sleep and let the doctors take care of Graham. Trust, Trina. Just trust."

Despite the fear that pressed upward, her eyelids were too heavy to hold open. They drifted shut, sending Trina back into the dark world of sleep.

"She's going to be fine." The doctor sent Trina a smile then turned to face Mama, who hovered on the opposite side of the bed. "She does have some bruised ribs, and her wrist is sprained, but fortunately there are no broken bones. Over the next few days, you'll probably see lots of black and blue places pop up, but considering the way she was thrown around, that's to be expected. It's miraculous, really, that her injuries aren't more severe."

Like Graham's, Trina's thoughts continued. "So I can go?" she asked.

"Yes, I'll prepare your release papers right

now." The doctor put his hand on Trina's shoulder. "But I want you to take it easy for a few days. Take a week off from work. Don't just lie around — your muscles will stiffen up if you do that — but don't overdo, either." He shifted his gaze to Mama. "I'll want to see her again in a week, just as a follow-up. I ordered a prescription painkiller to help her sleep. You can pick it up in the pharmacy on your way out, as well as a list of dos and don'ts to follow while she's recovering."

"Thank you," Mama said, and the doctor left.

Trina immediately grabbed the rail of the bed and pulled herself upright, throwing her legs over the side. A sharp pain stabbed her left side, but she ignored it and rose to her feet. "Help me dress, please."

Dizziness struck, and she clung to the bed rail while Mama retrieved her dress from a small cubby in the corner. She helped Trina remove the hospital gown and slip back into her clothes. Her dress was dirty and torn, but Trina didn't care. She sat on a chair and let Mama put her socks and shoes on her feet. Then, fully dressed, she said, "I want to go see Graham."

Mama, still on her knee in front of Trina, shook her head. "No. You heard the doctor.

He said —"

"He said to take it easy, but he didn't say I couldn't ride in a car." Memories of her last car ride struck, and for a moment, her resolve faltered. Then she thought of everything Graham had done to make her dream of becoming a veterinarian come true. She shook her head, dispelling the unpleasant memories. "I need to see him, Mama. I need to talk to him — to find out for myself how he's doing."

"His mother promised to call and leave word with your dad," Mama said. "We'll get all the information we need from Mrs. Ortmann. Besides, you can't do him any good in Wichita."

"But it will do *me* good," Trina insisted, imploring her mother with her eyes. When she was growing up, she never begged her parents — she always accepted their no. But Graham was worth begging for. Graham was worth everything.

Mama grimaced. "Trina, we're both filthy."

For the first time, Trina noticed Mama's scraggly hair and rumpled clothing. Dark circles rimmed her eyes, sending a silent message of Mama's restless night. Tears welled in Trina's eyes as she realized the selfishness of her request, yet she couldn't set the desire aside. "Mama, *please.*"

Mama turned stubborn, setting her mouth in a firm line. "Not today, Trina. We'll go home, talk to your dad — find out the news on Graham. But we won't be traveling to Wichita."

It was all Trina could do to keep from dissolving into a tantrum, but she managed a stiff nod. "Tomorrow, then?" Tomorrow was Sunday, a day of rest.

Mama sighed, her head sagging as if her neck muscles were incapable of holding it up. "We'll see."

Not a promise, but not an outright denial, either. Trina could accept it. For now.

Mama headed for the door. "I'm going to go call your father and tell him to come pick us up. You stay there in the chair and rest. I'll be right back."

Dad joined ranks with Mama in keeping Trina home to recover rather than taking her to Wichita to see Graham. Beth, Andrew, and Uncle Henry all volunteered to make the drive, and her parents still said no. Dad insisted Mrs. Ortmann could keep them apprised of Graham's progress without their visiting. Trina resented the decision, but she could do little but obey since she had no vehicle of her own and no driver's license.

Sunday after service, many people approached Trina to let her know they were praying for both her and Graham and to express their happiness that the couple had survived the accident. Trina's family went to Uncle Henry and Aunt Marie's house for lunch. When they'd finished eating, Trina and Tony walked next door to Uncle Henry's repair garage to see Graham's car. A tow truck had hauled it there, but looking at it, Trina had to wonder why it hadn't been taken straight to a junkyard. She was no expert on vehicles, but even she could see the car wasn't salvageable.

Another thing Graham had to give up.

Tony ran his hand over the crumpled hood. "Whew, Trina. It's hard to believe you were in that thing and walked away from it." He stared at her with wide brown eyes. "You could have been killed!"

"That's what the doctor said," Trina said. She walked to the driver's door and placed her uninjured hand on the window frame. The firemen had broken all the glass out when they pried the door open to rescue her, and bits of glass sparkled on the seat. Trina shivered, remembering the fear of the moments when the car went rolling from top to bottom. She pushed the memory away and said, "I don't know how Graham will buy another car."

Tony perked up. "I do. I heard the folks and Uncle Henry talking. This one is going to be claimed as totaled, and the insurance company will give him a check for its value. It should be enough to buy another used car."

Trina was pleased it would be replaced, yet she knew it wouldn't be the same. Graham's grandparents had given him this car as a gift — it meant a great deal to him. Something else occurred to her. "But won't he need to use the money from the car insurance to pay for his doctor bills?"

Tony shook his head. "That pickup driver — the one who hit you? The police said the accident was his fault, so his insurance is covering all the hospital expenses. Even yours."

Trina nodded slowly. At least there would be no concerns about paying the bills. Almost three years ago, when Aunt Marie's twins had come early, requiring surgery for Aunt Marie and a long hospital stay for the babies, the community had rallied around to help pay the bills. Even with the contributions, Aunt Marie and Uncle Henry still made monthly payments to the hospital and probably would for many more years. If Graham needed surgery and a long stay in the hospital, his bills would probably be just as big as Aunt Marie's had been.

"I wish I could see him."

Somehow Tony understood she meant Graham and not the truck driver. He nodded, his eyes sad. "I know."

"It was all my fault." She whispered the worry that had plagued her ever since she'd glimpsed Graham lying in the ditch.

Tony's brows came down. "No, it wasn't."

"It was." Trina gulped. "Graham only had one hand on the steering wheel because I — I was snuggling up to his side, and he put his arm around me. If I'd stayed on my own side of the seat, then —"

"Trina, that's dumb." Tony's voice sounded like Dad's, although Dad never used the word *dumb.* "The police said the pickup truck driver was messing around with the CD player in his cab and not paying attention. That's why he crossed into your lane. Then, instead of hitting his brakes, he panicked and pushed down on the gas pedal. He made a mistake and ran into you."

Trina considered Tony's words. She remembered seeing that the driver's head was down, as if looking at something below the dash. But still, if Graham would have had both hands free, maybe he could have gotten out of the way. If only she could see him and apologize to him! If she knew he was going to be all right, maybe she could set this worry and guilt aside.

"Trina," Tony said, his voice fervent, "it wasn't your fault. It's just something that happened — an accident. Don't feel bad, huh?"

Suddenly she realized she didn't know whether the truck's driver was injured, and a different sort of guilt struck. "Was the other driver hurt?"

Tony made a face. "According to Dad, he had some bumps and bruises — kind of like you. But nothing serious."

A part of Trina was relieved by the news but a tiny bit rankled at the unfairness of the situation. Graham hadn't been in the wrong. She and the pickup truck driver had been in the wrong. They were the ones who should be suffering. Pressing her forehead to the top of the window frame, she closed her eyes and prayed again for forgiveness for her part in the accident.

"Let's go back over to Uncle Henry's," Tony suggested, touching her arm. "You've been up long enough now."

Trina wanted to snap at her brother that she already had enough people telling her what she should and shouldn't do — he didn't need to add to it! But she knew her brother only wanted to help, so she held the words inside and nodded.

That evening, after supper, Trina asked, "Will someone drive me to Wichita tomorrow so I can see Graham?"

Mama and Dad exchanged looks across the table.

Before they could refuse, Trina spoke again. "He's going to wonder why I haven't come. He may worry that I'm really hurt and I'm not able to come. Worrying can't be good for him — not if he's seriously injured." She looked at her mother. "You aren't working tomorrow, Mama. Please, won't you find someone to drive us to Wichita?"

Mama sighed. "Trina, there isn't anything we can do for Graham right now except pray, and praying can be done from home. Remember how crowded the waiting room got when we all spent time at the hospital with your aunt Marie? We'd only be in the way over there."

"But I promise not to bother anyone. I just want to see him, to talk to him, to make sure he's okay and let him know I'm okay."

Another lengthy silence followed while Mama and Dad poked at their nearly empty plates and refused to answer.

Trina bounced her gaze back and forth between her parents, taking in their firm, unmoving faces. A fierce fear struck, and she dropped her fork with a clatter. "What are you trying to keep from me? Why don't you want me to see Graham?"

"That isn't it at all, Trina," Dad blustered. "Of course we want you to be able to see Graham, but —"

Mama interrupted. "We've told you everything we know about Graham."

"Tell me again." Surely she'd missed something. There had to be some reason her parents wouldn't take her — some tidbit of information that would explain everything.

Dad lifted his face to the ceiling for a moment, as if gathering strength, then faced Trina. "Graham's spine was fractured. When he's stabilized and they are certain he has no internal bleeding, they plan to operate. Until then, they are keeping him in a drug-induced coma so he doesn't move around and cause further injury to the spine. That's all we know, Trina."

"If he's not awake, he won't know you aren't there," Mama added, putting her hand over Trina's.

Trina jerked her hand free. "But *I'll* know! And I need to see him. For myself — I need to see for myself that he is alive. Why won't you let me see him?"

Tony, normally silent during family discussions, cleared his throat. "I think you should let her go. She's really worrying about him. It would do her good."

Much to Trina's surprise, neither parent reprimanded Tony for interfering. For long moments Mama and Dad looked at each other, and Trina sensed they were silently communicating with each other. Hoping they were deciding to let her go to Wichita, she remained quiet, too, her breath coming in little spurts while she waited for them to reach the conclusion.

Finally, Dad put both hands flat on the tabletop and faced Trina. "Daughter, we didn't want to tell you this because we feared it would hurt you. But you don't leave us much choice." His voice sounded low, gruff, heavy with pain.

Trina's heart turned a somersault in her chest. "W–what is it?"

Dad pinched his lips together, his forehead creasing into a knot. "When Graham's mother called the first time — when they'd just gotten Graham settled in the room at Wichita — she had a message for you from Graham."

"Well?" Trina thought she might explode

from impatience. "What? What did he say?"

Her father's head lowered, giving her a view of his thinning scalp. His shoulders heaved in a sigh. Then, his face still aimed downward, he said, "She said that Graham said to tell you not to come."

TWENTY-SIX

Wednesday morning after breakfast, Dad and Tony headed to their jobs as usual, and Mama walked to the café. She had chosen to keep it closed Tuesday and spend the day with Trina, but she said people needed a return to normalcy, so she'd better go back. However, right before leaving, she instructed Trina to take it easy. Trina couldn't remember her mother ever leaving her alone without a list of chores to occupy her time. At first, it seemed like freedom. But in short order, restlessness struck. Sitting and doing nothing made the time crawl by.

Her schoolbooks sat on the table in her room, yet she couldn't open them. Her focus was too far away — one hundred and ten miles away, to be exact. She knew whatever assignments on which she tried to work would only be done poorly. *Why would Graham ask me to stay away?* The question plagued her constantly, but she could find no answer.

She tried reading her Bible and praying, seeking peace, but even talking to God turned into a frustrating question session without answers. So with nothing else to do, she paced the living room, pausing at the window at each turn to stare out at the late October morning. It almost surprised her to see the multicolored leaves on the trees. Fall had sneaked up on her this year.

Staring unseeingly across the yard, she thought about the hours she'd spent in her bedroom or at Beth's computer, working on her college classes. Even though she knew it was God's call on her heart and something Graham encouraged, she now discovered a small prick of resentment. She'd missed watching summer give way to fall. She'd missed hours and hours of time with Graham. Those lost hours multiplied in value when faced with the prospect of not having time with him again.

She thumped the window casing with her fist. "I've got to think about something else!" Stewing over the strange message wouldn't change it. She'd not be able to make sense of it until she talked to Graham, and she might not be able to talk to Graham for several more days. According to his mother, the doctors would keep him in the drug-induced sleep until the swelling completely subsided. Then they would try to repair the damaged vertebrae.

How she wished the doctors could say for sure what the end result would be after the surgery. Whether Graham would have full use of his legs. If he couldn't, it would change everything.

But what would it matter if he no longer wanted her around?

Turning from the window, she flumped onto the sofa and ran her fingers over the elastic bandage that held the splint on her left wrist. Typing would be even more of a challenge now that she was one-handed. How would she keep up with her classes? Or should she even continue her classes?

"Oh, dear heavenly Father," Trina groaned, rubbing her hand down her cheek and discovering tears, "what am I supposed to do now? I'm so confused. Why does it seem there's always something in the way of my becoming a doctor for animals?"

Just as she finished the thought, a knock at the door sounded. She quickly wiped away the remainder of tears and opened the door. Andrew stood on the porch, a serious look on his face.

"Hi. Can I come in?"

"Sure." Trina stepped back as he moved

through the opening then closed the door behind him. "Aren't you working today?"

"Beth is sending me on an errand."

Trina sat back on the sofa, peering up at her cousin. Andrew had been very honest in his feelings about her pursuing veterinary science. Even though he had stopped openly discouraging her, his silence on the subject had spoken loudly about his continued disapproval. They hadn't had time alone for several weeks, and to Trina's regret, she realized she felt uncomfortable in his presence. The discomfort held her tongue.

"I'm taking a couple of stained-glass projects for consignment to the Fox Gallery in Wichita. The drive gets long all by myself, so I thought I'd see if you might want to go to give me some company."

Trina's heart skipped a beat. *Wichita.* Then maybe she could go by the hospital and see Graham. Immediately the anticipation plunged. Graham had said not to come. She sighed. "Mama and Dad probably won't let me."

Andrew worked the toe of his boot against the carpet, his brow furrowed. "I stopped by the café before coming over here. Aunt Deborah said it was okay."

Trina's jaw dropped. "Really?" But then, Mama had given permission to go to the

356

gallery, not the hospital.

"And while I'm in town, I plan to go by St. Francis and take some cards and food to the Ortmanns. I figured you'd probably like to check on them, too."

Trina bounced to her feet, cringing as pain caught her ribs. "Did you tell Mama all of this?"

"I wouldn't be asking you otherwise. I don't want to sneak behind her back."

Recognizing the hidden message, Trina nodded. "I wouldn't ask you to. That's why I wanted to make sure."

A slight smile finally tipped up the corners of Andrew's mouth. "So do you want to go or not?"

"I want to go!" She started for the bedroom then turned back. Tipping her head, she sent him a curious look. "How did you convince her? She and Dad told me I couldn't go."

Andrew raised his shoulders in a slow shrug. "I just told her being kept away from Graham when he needs you most isn't fair to you or to Graham."

Trina stared, amazed that Mama had listened. "Thank you."

Andrew nodded then pointed at her feet. "Go put your shoes on, and we can go."

Trina scampered for her bedroom.

■ ■ ■ ■

Trina greeted Graham's mother with a hug that turned lengthy. The older woman clung, pressing her cheek to Trina's.

"Oh, Trina, it's good to see you. I've been so worried about you." Mrs. Ortmann pulled back and grasped Trina's shoulders. "How are you? Are you recovered from the accident?"

"I'm all right. Just bruises, that's all."

"Good. I'm so grateful." She gave Trina another gentle hug before guiding her to a vinyl settee. It squeaked with their weight when they sat down. The waiting room was small, with windows that looked out on a courtyard. Crumpled candy wrappers, empty soda bottles, and fast-food cartons gave mute evidence of a long stay.

"Are you comfortable here?" Trina wiggled on the stiff cushion. "Is there anything else you need?"

"The hospital staff has been wonderful," Mrs. Ortmann said. "They bring us blankets and pillows each night, and of course we have visitors from Sommerfeld who bring us food. We're doing okay."

Trina gestured toward Andrew, who stood in the crack of space between the window and a small table. "Andrew brought a box of snack things — crackers, fruit, candy, and granola bars."

"That's kind of you," the older woman said, flashing a tired smile in Andrew's direction. "Ed and Chuck went down to the cafeteria to get some lunch a few minutes ago, but we try to stay here in the room as much as possible. Just in case someone comes with news. We aren't allowed much time with Graham — not while he remains in the intensive care unit."

Trina took Mrs. Ortmann's hands. "What is the latest news? Mama said they're still keeping him in a coma."

"That's right." The woman's chin quivered. "He looks so pale and weak, but I suppose that's to be expected. The not knowing is the hardest part. Until they do the surgery, we won't know for sure the severity of the injury. It could be that they'll be able to fix his spine and everything will be all right. It could be that there was spinal cord damage, and he won't be all right. It's nearly driven me mad, wondering."

Trina swallowed hard. "I'm so sorry."

Mrs. Ortmann pressed her lips together tightly and lifted her chin. "Well, if they follow through as planned, they'll do surgery tomorrow. Then we should know what we're facing. That will help."

Trina nodded, her head down. Several minutes ticked by before Mrs. Ortmann drew in a deep breath and tugged Trina's hands.

"So have you been doing what Graham said?"

Trina jerked her gaze up, her brow crunching. What a funny question. Obviously she'd stayed away. Trina didn't know how to answer.

Mrs. Ortmann's expression turned puzzled. "Your father did give you the message, didn't he?"

A band of hurt wrapped around Trina's chest. "Yes. He told me."

"Good." A smile quavered on the woman's face. "Graham was so worried you'd fall behind because of him."

That statement made no sense. Trina shook her head, her ribbons grazing the underside of her jaw. "Mrs. Ortmann, I'm sorry, but —"

She squeezed Trina's hands hard. "You were the last thing he thought about before they put him under." Tears appeared in the corners of her eyes. "I'm so glad you're studying. Graham will feel so bad if this accident has kept you from doing your work."

Trina's heart thudded hard in her chest.

Studying? Dad hadn't mentioned studying — only staying away. "Mrs. Ortmann, I don't know what you're talking about. My father told me Graham said I shouldn't come here."

The woman's eyes flew wide. "Well, he did — but somehow you only got part of the message." She clapped her hand over her mouth. "Oh my! I hope . . ." Capturing Trina's hand again, she leaned close, her face pursing into a look of worry. "I was so upset that night, Trina — there were people coming and going, so much activity, so much concern. I may have mixed up my words and left your father with the idea that Graham didn't want you here.

"It is true that's what he wanted, but not because he didn't want to see you." She shook her head. "He only wanted you to keep studying — not to let the accident interfere with your work. Do you understand?"

Trina understood. And she'd let Graham down by not picking up her books this week. She would make it up, though. Then she looked at her bandaged wrist and . groaned. She held up the injured hand. "I want to study, Mrs. Ortmann, but I don't know how I'll submit my assignments. I can barely type with two *good* hands. I don't know how I'll do it with one."

"Oh, honey." Mrs. Ortmann offered a brief, sympathetic hug. "Can you contact your teachers? Let them know you've been hurt and ask if they'll let you turn things in late? Or maybe you could talk into one of those machines . . . what are they called?"

Andrew inserted, "A tape recorder?"

"Yes!" The older woman turned to Trina, eagerness lighting her eyes. "You could *say* your assignments and send them in."

"I don't know." Trina had never operated a tape recorder. But then, until she'd started college, she'd never used a computer, either. Yet she'd managed to master it well enough to keep up. "I — I guess I could try, though."

"Of course you can!" Mrs. Ortmann beamed. "And as soon as Graham comes out of surgery, I'll let him know how you're doing and that you aren't falling behind. If he knows you're moving forward just like you two planned, it will give his heart a lift. It will give him a reason —" Her chin crumpled, tears spurting into her eyes. "A reason to try to get well."

"I'll do my best," Trina promised.

The door to the little room opened. Mr. Ortmann and Chuck came in, carrying a tray of food.

Trina rose, looking at Andrew. "We should get out of the way so you can eat." She gave Mrs. Ortmann another hug, shook Mr. Ortmann's hand, and tweaked Chuck's ear. After their good-byes, she and Andrew headed back to the lobby.

"I'm sorry you didn't get to see Graham," Andrew said.

"Me, too." Trina's heart felt heavy with desire to see him, talk to him, touch him, and assure herself he was alive. "But maybe Mama and Dad will let me come back after he's had his surgery and he's no longer in the coma."

"I'll bring you if they can't," Andrew offered.

Trina held his elbow as they crossed the parking lot. "Thank you. But won't Beth need you at the gallery?"

"Beth knows I'll make up the hours." Andrew opened the car door for her. "Besides, Graham is practically family. She'll understand."

When Andrew started the car and headed into traffic, Trina said, "What do you think of Mrs. Ortmann's suggestion about doing my assignments on a tape recorder?"

"I think it's better than not doing them." Andrew glanced at her. "What would be easier — typing with one hand or speaking into a tape recorder?"

Trina laughed. "I don't know. I haven't tried either one of those things."

Andrew grinned. "Well, I guess you won't know until you try."

Trina sighed, her laughter fading. "Andrew, I'm worried about how things will be when Graham gets out of the hospital." It felt good to share her concern with Andrew, the way she would have before he got so angry with her. She let all of the fears of the past days spill out in a rush. "If he can't walk, how will we live in the upstairs of his parents' house? Will he need me to stay home and take care of him? Will he still want to marry me? What kind of job will he be able to do? I could provide for him if I become a veterinarian, but how can I leave him to go to school if he needs me to care for him?"

Andrew held up his hand, shaking his head. "Slow down, Trina. Seems to me you're borrowing trouble."

Despite herself, she smiled. He sounded just like the old, patient, big-brother Andrew she knew and loved.

He went on. "We don't even know yet how severely he's injured. Sure, it will take him awhile to recover — he'll be having major surgery. But he could very well walk out of the hospital. I say put off all those questions until we get word from the doctor concerning how badly Graham is injured. You'll make yourself sick worrying."

Trina sighed. "I know you're right, but it's hard."

"Put it in God's hands, Trina. Just like you've done with everything you needed to accomplish to become a college student." Andrew bumped her elbow, winking. "He took care of you, right? Now trust Him to take care of Graham."

Twenty-Seven

"You have to push RECORD and PLAY at the same time, Katrinka, remember?" Beth pointed to the two side-by-side buttons on the 1980s cassette tape recorder. "If you don't push them both, it doesn't record."

Trina's face fell. "You mean this whole morning's work didn't record?"

Beth shook her head. When Andrew had returned Wednesday and mentioned the possibility of Trina's using a tape recorder, Beth had taken it upon herself to locate one. She'd visited three pawnshops before finding one in good working condition with a built-in microphone. But finding it proved to be easier than teaching Trina to use it.

Twice now, Trina had neglected to push the right buttons to record, and once she'd accidentally overwritten everything by hitting both buttons when she meant to listen to what she'd recorded previously. Although they'd both laughed at the puzzled "Why am I not hearing anything? Where's the assignment? Oh, what did I do wrong *now?*" that took the place of the work intended to be there, Beth didn't want a repeat. It took too much time to replace the errors, and Trina was already playing catch-up thanks to the accident.

"I'm sorry, but no. Look carefully and make sure both buttons are all the way down before you start talking."

Tears glittered briefly in Trina's eyes; then she blinked them away. "All right. So before I start working on my history paper, I'll try again to record the grammar assignments."

Beth smiled at the determined set to Trina's jaw. "Both buttons!" she said before turning back to the computer. She listened to Trina go through the grammar exercises, her voice steady and enunciation precise. It was good to keep Trina busy today — Graham's surgery had been scheduled for eight o'clock that morning. His mother had promised to call as soon as he was out. Beth intended to keep Trina too occupied to watch the clock, even if it meant spending the whole day away from the studio. Andrew was capable of running things over there, and she could do whatever planning she needed to do on her home computer.

Computer. She smiled, sending a secretive

glance over her shoulder at Trina. Wouldn't Trina be surprised when she found out what Beth had hidden in the bedroom? The shipment had arrived late yesterday afternoon, and Beth's eyes had filled with tears when she realized how perfect the timing was of its arrival. God had met a need before Trina knew it would exist.

Regardless of how the surgery turned out, Graham would need attention for several weeks. If she knew Trina, the girl wouldn't want to leave him alone in the evenings. Thanks to Sean's "compromise," it wouldn't be necessary for her to come to Beth's or the studio to use a computer again.

Although Beth suggested a desktop, Sean insisted on purchasing a laptop — something Trina could carry to class with her, if need be. It wasn't a top-of-the-line model, but it had adequate memory, wireless Internet capabilities, and several programs including word processing, budget helps, and spreadsheet templates that could come in handy when Trina was charting the care given to furry critters later down the line. When Sean returned from his latest trip, they would present the laptop to Trina together. Although Beth itched to do it now, it had been Sean's idea in the first place, so he should be involved.

Beth suspected Trina would argue about taking the gift, but Beth could be stubborn, too. She'd make Trina understand how much she'd need that computer, especially when she and Graham left Sommerfeld. Suddenly a wave of sadness struck. Of all the people in Sommerfeld — other than Mom and Henry, of course — Trina was her favorite. The town wouldn't be the same without her.

But she'd be back, Beth reminded herself, turning her attention to the computer screen. With that new veterinarian taking over Dr. Groening's clinic, maybe Trina could establish her own clinic right here in Sommerfeld. It would be harder starting from scratch, but she had a rapport with the community that would encourage people to come to her. Beth suspected Trina had the gumption it would take to make a brand-new veterinary clinic run success-fully, and it would be fun to watch it all happen.

Trina's voice stopped, and a *click* signaled she'd turned off the machine. Beth swiveled in her seat. "All done?"

"With the English," Trina reported with a sigh. "Now on to the —"

The telephone rang, and both women jumped, spinning toward the sound.

"It's probably about Graham." Trina rose from the table, straining toward the telephone.

Beth snatched it up on the second ring. "Hello?"

"Hello, Beth." Deborah Muller's voice. "We just got the call from Mrs. Ortmann. May I talk to Trina?"

Beth's hand trembled as she held the phone to Trina. "It's your mom. She has news on Graham."

Trina dashed around the table and snatched the receiver from Beth's hand. Beth leaned close to listen, too. Trina rasped, "Yes? How is he?"

"The doctor said they successfully replaced the damaged vertebrae with a piece of cadaver bone." Relief carried clearly through the line. "There was a bone sliver dangerously close to the spinal cord, but it didn't appear to have punctured the cord. The doctor felt confident Graham will eventually regain use of his legs."

Beth let out a war whoop, and Trina burst into tears. Trina shoved the receiver into Beth's hands and sank down at the table, burying her face in her arms. Beth asked all the questions she knew Trina would want answered: How long would Graham be in the hospital? Would he require rehabilitation? When might he be able to return to work? Would they be able to proceed as planned for their wedding?

To Beth's surprise, Deborah responded to each question without a hint of impatience. And when Beth ran out of questions, Deborah said, "Thank you, Beth, for helping Trina and keeping her busy this morning. We appreciate you." The line went dead before Beth could reply.

She placed the receiver back in its cradle, shaking her head in wonder. Funny how conflict brought people together . . .

Sitting next to Trina, she put her arm around the younger woman's heaving shoulders.

"I–I'm so sorry." Her face still hidden against her arms, Trina's voice came out muffled and broken. "I d–don't know w–why I'm crying now."

Beth chuckled, rubbing Trina's shoulders. "Go ahead and cry. I would imagine there's a lot of pent-up worry behind the tears. When you're done, I'll tell you everything your mom said about Graham, and then we'll walk over to the café and have some lunch to celebrate a successful surgery."

A half hour later, Trina splashed her face with cold water, and the two women headed to the café. The dining room was full of excited, chattering Sommerfeld residents, all seeming to discuss Graham's surgery. Trina got pulled into the conversations, so Beth sneaked into the kitchen to find Deborah.

"It's wonderful news about Graham's legs," Beth said by way of greeting.

Deborah used her apron to wipe her brow and nodded. "An answer to prayer."

Beth agreed. "But I've been wondering. Rehabilitation could take several months. Who knows how long it will be before Graham is able to work? I know Trina is going back to Groening's clinic on Monday, so she'll have a little income, but how will they get by?"

Deborah smiled, the lines around her eyes tired. "Beth, haven't you figured out by now that Mennonites take care of the needs of their people?" Not a hint of sarcasm colored her tone. "It's kind of you to be concerned, but rest assured Graham and Trina will be all right."

Beth's shoulders sagged with relief. "Okay. Thanks. I realize I'm not Mennonite, but I do care a lot about Trina."

Deborah gave Beth's cheek a quick pat and turned back to the stove. Beth took that as her hint to leave. She returned to the dining area and sat down in a booth next to

Trina, joining in the conversation. But at the back of her mind, a question hovered: How would the community take care of Graham and Trina?

Something poked the sole of his left foot. Graham grunted in frustration. "Chuck," he rasped through a throat that felt as gritty as sandpaper, "quit it."

A low chuckle sounded, and then his right foot got the same treatment.

With a snort, Graham opened his eyes and focused blearily toward the end of the bed. "What're you —" Then he realized Chuck wasn't in the room. A tall man in a white shirt and rainbow-colored tie stood smiling down at him. "Who're you?"

The man moved closer. "I'm Dr. Howey. How are you feeling?"

"Like I got hit by a truck."

The doctor chuckled again. "Are you in pain?"

Graham considered the question. He wasn't comfortable — a pressure in his back made him wonder if someone had stuffed something under the mattress, and his head felt twice its normal size, but he couldn't honestly say he was hurting. "No. Not really."

The doctor moved back to the foot of the

bed and grasped Graham's feet, squeezing his toes. "Are you able to feel this?"

Graham scowled. "Yes. Never have cared much for people messing with my feet."

Dr. Howey let go and returned to the side of the bed to pinch Graham's wrist and frown at his own wristwatch for several seconds. While the doctor did his checking, Graham twisted his head and found a clock on the wall. Three fifteen. But morning or afternoon? With the window shades drawn and the lights in the room on low, he couldn't be sure. The uncertainty left him feeling unsettled.

And something else occurred to him. "What day is it?"

Dr. Howey released his wrist with a pat. "Friday."

The accident had been on a Friday. Had an entire week passed? Graham pressed his memory, trying to account for the time. He recalled riding in an ambulance, telling his folks to make sure Trina stayed home and studied, but after that . . . nothing.

"Have I really slept away an entire week?" It hurt his throat to talk.

The doctor put his hand on Graham's shoulder. "It was important for your body's recovery for you to remain perfectly still. So we used drugs to keep you in a coma, Graham. Keeping you still brought the inflammation down enough that we could do surgery. So early this morning, we replaced your crushed vertebrae. The fact that you can feel me touching your feet is a good sign, but I need you to try to do something for me." He moved back to the foot of the bed. "Can you wiggle your toes?"

It took great concentration, and sweat broke out across Graham's forehead, but he waggled the toes of both feet up and down.

"Wonderful!"

Graham closed his eyes, exhausted from the effort. Sleep claimed him. When he opened his eyes again, instead of the doctor, he found his parents and brother lounging in plastic chairs. The clock read seven forty-five. He swallowed against his sore throat and managed a weak greeting. "Have you been here the whole time?"

His parents leaped from the seats and rushed to the bed, leaning over him. His mother stroked his hair. "And where else would we be with you here?" Her scolding tone let Graham know the depth of her concern.

"But a whole week . . ." Guilt struck as Graham realized how worried his parents must have been. "I'm sorry."

"You don't have anything to apologize for,

son," his dad said. "You didn't do anything wrong."

Graham hoped that was true. The details of the accident were fuzzy, other than trying to get out of the way of the truck and praying Trina wouldn't be hurt. He hoped there wasn't something more he could have done. Fear made his heart pound, but he managed to ask, "Is Trina . . . ?"

His mother squeezed his shoulder. "Trina is right as rain. A sprained wrist, some bruises, but nothing serious."

"Thank the Lord." Graham released a heavy sigh. "She hasn't been here, has she?" He wasn't sure what answer he wanted.

"In and out a couple of times," Mom said. "She's been studying, just like you wanted her to."

Relief flooded Graham that the accident wasn't putting her behind on her course work, yet he admitted to a prick of disappointment that she wasn't here when he opened his eyes. "Good." The word grated out without much enthusiasm.

"Lots of people have been in and out," Dad reported, his hand on Graham's arm. "We kept a book and had them write their names down so you'd know. Your uncle John and cousins have kept the lumberyard going, and they said they'd work as long as we need them to. The doctor said we'll spend at least a couple of weeks in Nebraska at a rehabilitation clinic to help you get on your feet, but then your job will be waiting for you."

Graham processed everything his father had said. He focused in on one thing: rehabilitation clinic in Nebraska? He'd never been out of Kansas, and he wasn't sure he wanted to go. But if it meant walking again, he'd go. He had to walk. He had to work. He couldn't allow this accident to keep Trina from finishing college. She depended on him.

The pressure in his back increased, turning into a dull ache. He grimaced, squinting his eyes closed.

"Are you hurting, son?" His mother's anxious voice carried to his ear.

"A little."

"I'll get a nurse."

Graham decided he would avoid asking for painkillers as much as possible. The medication instantly put him to sleep, and he'd already lost too many days of his life. From this point on, he needed to be awake and alert. He had work to do.

The doctor came in Saturday morning with a chart of a spine to explain Graham's

injury. Graham found the terms *cervical,*
thoracic, and *lumbar* confusing, but he managed to comprehend that his injury —
which the doctor called a T-11 — affected
his legs but not his arms. The doctor explained that many people with lower thoracic injuries regained the full use of their
legs over time, and he encouraged Graham
to make walking his goal.

"Of course," Graham retorted with vehe-
mence.

But when the doctor indicated months of
therapy, Graham's resolve wavered.
Months? He didn't have months. He'd sold
his house — he would be living in Mom
and Dad's upstairs. He needed to work to
support Trina — how could he cut and haul
lumber from a wheelchair? And would it be
fair to Trina to saddle her with a husband
who couldn't take care of her? Of himself?
He didn't want *her* taking care of *him!*

After the doctor left, Graham closed his
eyes so his parents would think he was
sleeping, but inwardly he raged at the
unfairness of the situation. He might as well
be an invalid. He would only hold Trina
back. Her studies would be set aside so she
could see to his needs. Instead of caring for
animals, as she'd planned, she'd be stuck
caring for him — a grown man.

He stifled the anguished groan that longed for release. *Oh Lord, I don't understand. Why did You allow this to happen?* Graham had been taught that all things worked together for good for those who were called to God's purpose, but he couldn't see any good in being stuck in a wheelchair while Trina set aside her own dreams to wipe his chin and help him change his socks.

His back throbbed. His legs ached. Temptation to ask for more pain medication to give him blessed escape pressed hard. But he knew the moment he awakened from the drug-induced rest, the worst pain would still be with him. How could he set aside the sharp agony of disappointment?

TWENTY-EIGHT

"Here you are, Trina." Dr. Groening placed a paycheck into Trina's waiting hand. "It includes a small bonus."

Trina's eyes widened. "Oh, Dr. Groening, that isn't necessary!"

The older man smiled, his eyes crinkling. "You let me decide what is and isn't necessary. I appreciate your hard work, and I know you have a heavy load to carry between working here and keeping up with your studies." He frowned, crossing his arms. "When are finals?"

"Another four weeks," Trina said. She didn't know who would take her — Graham was still in Nebraska with his mother, although his dad was home running the lumberyard. No one seemed to know when Graham's time in rehabilitation would end. Her chest held a constant deep ache from missing him.

"Being able to use both hands must make

things easier," he said.

Trina rubbed her left wrist. The splint had come off only three days ago, and it felt odd not to have it there. A twinge reminded her not to overuse the wrist, but typing shouldn't tax it too much. "Yes. It will be better to send files by e-mail instead of cassette tapes through the mail." She released a light laugh. "Easier for me and for my instructors, I'm sure."

Dr. Groening chuckled. "Well, it's good you have this Thanksgiving break, then — a couple of free days to concentrate on studies, hmm?"

Trina managed a smile.

The doctor went on. "Has Marc talked to you at all about his plans?"

Trina shook her head. Even though she spent every day at the clinic, her path rarely crossed Dr. Royer's. He preferred to spend his time at farms, going to the animals rather than remaining at the clinic and letting the animals come to him. Trina admitted the arrangement suited her fine — something about the man continued to intimidate her.

"Well, I'm sure he will when the time is right. He has some ideas for expanding the clinic, and he indicated you would be instrumental in seeing those plans through."

Trina pinched her face into a puzzled scowl. "Expanding the clinic?"

Dr. Groening rubbed his finger over his lips, a grin hovering. "Well, not exactly making this one bigger, but having two clinics. This one and one in Hillsboro."

Trina shook her head. "That would be a lot to keep track of."

"Yes." Again a chuckle rumbled. "And even someone as tall as Marc can't be in two places at once. Actually, his ideas aren't bad. I think you'll find them interesting."

Trina offered a slight shrug. "I'll wait, then, for him to talk to me."

"Probably after the holidays," Dr. Groening said with a nod. He lifted his gaze toward the window when the sound of a truck's engine intruded. "There's your ride. Have a good Thanksgiving, Trina."

The holiday wouldn't feel right without Graham. Last year right before Thanksgiving, he'd made known his intentions to court her. Now they were miles apart. She swallowed. "I'll do my best, Dr. Groening. You have a good weekend, too."

She slipped her arms into her sweater and headed outside. Tony waited with the engine running. Climbing into the warm cab felt good after her brief time in the nippy November breeze. She sat quietly as Tony turned the pickup toward Sommerfeld, her heart pounding as they approached the spot where the man's pickup had crossed the line and hit Graham's car.

Each time she drove past the accident site, she looked around carefully. Over the past month, the place where the ground had been scuffed by the rolling car had smoothed out. Except for a few bare patches of missing grass and the occasional wink of broken glass, you could hardly tell something monumental had occurred there. But Trina still knew. She lived with the consequences.

She sighed, sending up another silent prayer for Graham's recovery. Although she wrote to him every day and called every Saturday, it wasn't the same as having him close enough to talk to or to touch. The telephone conversations were far from satisfying. She sensed Graham's impatience to be done, yet they wouldn't release him until he could pull himself into a standing position. *Hurry, Lord, and bring healing,* Trina's heart begged. She needed Graham home so things could return to normal.

Suddenly, from behind the steering wheel, Tony erupted in a hysterical giggle, which he quickly squelched.

Trina sent him a puzzled look. "What was

that all about?"

He pinched his lips together and didn't answer.

Trina stared at him for a few minutes, but when he kept his eyes on the road, humming to himself, she turned her gaze forward. Silence reigned until they reached the Sommerfeld turnoff. Then, as Tony made the curve, another snort of laughter burst out.

Trina bopped him on the arm. "Stop that!"

"Stop what?" He giggled nearly uncontrollably.

"What's so funny?"

"Nothing." Yet the giggles continued in spurts until he pulled up in front of their house. Then he cleared his throat several times, pasted on a serious face, and said, "Well, let's go in."

Awareness prickled down Trina's spine. "Tony?"

But he just hopped out and jogged up the sidewalk as if he hadn't heard her. She followed more slowly, holding her sweater closed against the bite of the wind. When she reached the front door, Tony was waiting, a goofy grin on his face. He swung the door open for her, and she cast a sidelong glance at him as she stepped over the threshold.

The moment she entered the room, an exultant shout rose: "Surprise!"

Trina staggered backward, connecting with the doorjamb, as dozens of people — family and friends — popped from various locations. She pressed her hands to her chest and stammered stupidly, "W–what?" And then a movement toward the back of the group captured her attention. The bright flash of light on steel forced her to blink, and when she opened her eyes again, her heart fired into her throat.

"Graham!" She raced across the short expanse of carpet and grabbed his hands, which were curled over the padded bar of a silver walker. "You're home!" Oh, how she longed to catapult into his arms, to press her lips to his, to feel his arms wrap around her and hold her close forever. But the frame of the walker created a barrier, so she had to be content to lean as close as possible and beam into his face. "Oh, it's so good to see you! When did you get back?"

"Late last night." He looked older, thinner, haggard. But his dear blue eyes were as warm as ever as he tipped his face toward hers and placed a kiss on her forehead. "Did we surprise you?"

"Yes!" She sent an accusatory look in

Tony's direction. "Although Tony tried to give it away by giggling."

Tony assumed an innocent expression, and Andrew gave him a teasing smack on the back of his head. Everyone laughed. Mama stepped forward and put her arm around Trina.

"It was Graham's idea not to tell you he was coming home so you could be surprised." Mama's smile bounced back and forth between Trina and Graham.

Mrs. Ortmann stepped beside Mama, her round face glowing. "And not to be outdone, *we* have surprises for both of you. Sit down."

Trina walked beside Graham as he made his painstaking way to the sofa. His steps were slow, measured, his feet scuffing against the floor. But Trina's heart pounded in happiness at the sight of her Graham on his feet, in her house back in Sommerfeld again. She held her breath as he maneuvered the walker in a small circle before lowering himself to the sofa. Once on the cushion, he released a huge breath, and Trina allowed her air to whoosh out, too. Then, with a smile, she snuggled as close to him as she could get without climbing into his lap.

The others gathered near, surrounding the sofa. Beth and Sean stepped forward, and

Sean held out a black leather case. "Trina," Beth said, "now that Graham is home, we know you won't want to spend your evenings at our place on the computer, so . . ."

Sean placed the case on the sofa cushion next to Trina and unzipped it, folding back the cover to reveal a slim, black laptop computer. Trina gasped.

"You can take this wherever Graham is and do your assignments. You'll need to establish Internet connection, but then you can send your assignments from home — wherever that may be." Beth's eyes twinkled. "We're so proud of your accomplishments, Trina, and we wish you much success as you finish your education."

Applause broke out from the group, and several people gave Sean pats on the shoulder as he stepped back. Beth leaned down to give first Trina then Graham a hug, and Trina was too stunned to even protest the extravagant gift.

Deacon Reiss pushed to the front. Mama, Dad, and Graham's parents flanked him, as if forming a wall of support. An air of expectancy filled the room, and Trina took Graham's hand, pressing it tightly between hers.

Deacon Reiss spoke. "Graham and Trina, over the past months, we've seen you exhibit great dedication: dedication to following God's will in your lives and dedication to one another. You have been an inspiration to all of us in facing difficulties with faith and fortitude." He linked his fingers together and pressed them to his middle, a prayerful stance. "We know this accident has created a hardship for you to see your plans through."

Graham flicked a glance at Trina, his brow furrowed. Trina looked back, as puzzled as he.

"There aren't any guarantees when Graham will be able to return to full-time work, yet Trina's college classes will go on. There will be costs involved to pay for school, maintain a home, and meet your daily needs. So . . ." The man drew in a great breath, sending his gaze around the circle of faces before looking at Graham and Trina again. "The deacons and minister met last Sunday afternoon; then they paid visits to every family in the fellowship, and we have gained commitments to contribute a small love token each month for your use. When these tokens are combined, it totals an amount that should meet your monthly needs until Graham is able to work full-time again."

"But we couldn't — ," Graham started.

"Oh, but — ," Trina started at the same time.

Deacon Reiss raised his hand. "No arguments. We're your family, we love you, and we want to help. Besides —" His lips curved into a smile. "When Trina comes back as a veterinarian, she'll be meeting our needs. You'll have the chance to repay us then."

Tears burned behind Trina's nose. She looked at Graham, and he blinked repeatedly, moisture glimmering in his eyes. She waited for him to decide whether or not to receive this gift. Finally, he swallowed, cleared his throat, and lifted his face to the waiting audience.

"Trina and I appreciate your love and support. Thank you."

Another cheer rose from the group; then everyone crowded close, offering hugs and words of encouragement. Slowly they drifted out the door, leaving Trina, Graham, and their parents. Mama crooked her finger, and the four adults moved to the back half of the house, leaving Trina and Graham alone.

The moment the room was vacated, Trina raised her arms to throw them around Graham's neck. She remembered in time the need to be gentle and cupped his cheeks instead. "I've missed you so much!"

"Me, too," Graham said, turning his face to kiss her palm. "I never want to leave you again. It felt like forever."

Trina pulled back, feigning shock. "You mean it *wasn't* forever?"

Graham laughed and shifted against the couch cushion. He sighed. "Oh, Trina, it's so good to be home."

Very slowly, Trina leaned sideways until her head rested lightly on his shoulder. He tipped his head, pressing his cheek to her cap. They sat for several long minutes, simply enjoying each other's nearness. But then Graham lifted his head and gave a gentle nudge with his shoulder, dislodging her. She sat up and faced him.

"There's much we need to talk about," he said, his expression serious. He took hold of her hands.

Trina nodded. "I've been so worried about finances — how we'd make it." A lump filled her throat. "But we'll be all right."

He sighed. "The financial support is a blessing. That's for sure." His thumbs traced lazy circles on the backs of her hands. "But I'm still not sure where we'll live. I — I can't climb stairs, so the upstairs rooms at Mom and Dad's won't work. On the way home, Mom suggested we take the back downstairs bedroom at their house, and we could, but it won't give us much privacy. It's right off the kitchen."

"It won't be for long, you know. And being right off the kitchen means it'll be easier for us to get midnight snacks."

Graham smirked. "Midnight snacks?"

"Studying makes me hungry," Trina said, grinning. "And besides, I need to fatten you up." She shook her head in mock dismay. "Didn't they feed you at all while you were gone? You're as skinny as a scarecrow."

Graham made a face. "Food never tastes good when you're far from home. Now that I'm here, I'll put the weight back on."

"I'll see to it." There was much Trina would see to — his therapy, his meals, his emotional needs. She squeezed his hand, sending a silent message.

"And I'll help you with your studies," he said. His fingers convulsed. "About our wedding . . ."

Trina sat bolt upright. "We aren't postponing it." Heat flooded her cheeks at her own audacity. Had she just told her future husband what to do?

Graham gave her hands a tug. "I'm not asking you to. Between the hospital and rehabilitation center, I've spent six weeks away from you. I'm as eager as ever to make you my wife." He lifted her hands to his lips and kissed her knuckles.

Trina nearly sagged with relief. "Then what?"

He patted the walker, which waited beside his legs. "I want to stand in front of the guests without leaning on this thing. It will take a lot of work to strengthen the muscles in my back and legs enough to make that possible, and we don't have many weeks to spare." He licked his lips, his fervent gaze pinned to hers. "Will you help me?"

"Of course I will! Whatever you need, I'll do it."

"But it takes time, Trina, and you spend your days at the clinic and your evenings studying. I don't want your other responsibilities to suffer."

Trina leaned forward and planted a quick kiss on his lips. Cupping his cheeks with her hands, she whispered, "Graham, there is nothing more important to me than you. You put aside your own wants and needs to help me achieve my goal. Well, I can set aside some of my activities to help you achieve yours."

Graham closed his eyes a moment. When he opened them, tears glittered in their deep blue depths. "Together, Trina, I think we can accomplish it."

"Together, with God's help," Trina agreed,

"we can change the world." She smiled, her lips trembling, as a burst of laughter came from the kitchen. "He's already made big changes in our small corner of it."

Twenty-Nine

Graham eased back on the pile of pillows propped against the headboard of his bed and released a sigh. The sliding glass door across from the bed allowed in a healthy dose of early afternoon sunshine, but he could see gray clouds building in the east. Would they have snow for Christmas? He hoped so.

The month between Thanksgiving and Christmas had disappeared in a rush of activity that often left Graham's head spinning. Thanks to the unusually mild winter weather, the men in town had been able to build an addition to the back of Graham's parents' house, doubling the size of the bedroom he and Trina would share after their marriage. The addition included the sliding glass door and a small deck with a ramp, making it easy for Graham to roll his wheelchair in and out of the house rather than struggling up the front porch stairs with his walker.

A week after coming home, he had returned to the lumberyard half days. He worked on the floor, serving customers, rather than out in the warehouse, but at least he felt as though he was earning his keep. He used his wheelchair part of the time and the walker part of the time, making himself walk until tiredness forced him back to the chair. But his walker time was gradually increasing, giving him hope that eventually he would be able to set aside the wheelchair for good.

He spent a couple of hours napping in the afternoon, something he despised, yet his body demanded the time of rest. Before falling asleep, he read passages from the Bible and prayed. He fingered the edges of the Bible, still open to Jeremiah 29, where only a few minutes earlier he had underlined the words, "For I know the thoughts that I think toward you, saith the LORD, thoughts of peace, and not of evil, to give you an expected end."

A smile found its way to his face as he reflected on that promise. The Bible-reading routine helped remove the impatience and frustration that often twisted through his belly. He missed the days of being whole and healthy, yet he'd never had such a large block of time to commit to Bible study and prayer. He discovered a true blessing in being able to rest in God's Word on a daily basis.

Each evening after supper, Trina came over and kept him company while he did his muscle-strengthening exercises. She brought her laptop, and it always made him smile to see her in her Mennonite cap, dress, and tennis shoes, carrying the leather briefcase — such an unusual picture, yet somehow fitting. He'd come to expect the unexpected when it applied to Trina, and he wouldn't have her any other way.

He looked ahead to this evening's visit. Andrew had driven her into El Dorado to take the first of her semester exams. When she returned, depending on how things went, she would be either in a celebratory mood or in need of comfort. Whatever she needed — whether cheering on or cheering up — he would provide it. Graham clamped his jaw, regret striking. How he'd wanted to take her, to offer encouragement and a kiss before sending her through the door to the classroom. But he wasn't allowed to drive yet. The money from insurance waited in an account at the bank for the day when he could drive again. Hopefully before their wedding, since Trina hadn't yet learned.

He emitted a soft chuckle, remembering the day he'd tried to teach Trina to drive. They'd try it again — probably in the spring — and this time he'd stick with it until she mastered it. She could master it, he had no doubt — his Trina could do anything she set her mind to.

A yawn stretched his face, and he settled a little lower on the bed. His back ached, but he'd grown accustomed to that and could block it out most of the time. Closing his eyes, he muttered, "Strengthening rest, Father. Give me strengthening rest."

"So how do you think you did?"

Trina smiled at Andrew's question. It was similar to the one Graham had asked after the midterm exams. She replied, "As well as I could."

Andrew nodded. "That's all anyone can do."

Trina leaned her head against the seat's headrest and sighed. "I'm glad the tests are over, though, and I'll enjoy these next weeks of no studying."

Andrew shot her a puzzled look. "No studying for weeks?"

"During January, they take special classes on the campus, but none are offered online. I wouldn't have signed up for one anyway.

My wedding is coming" — a jolt of eager anticipation doubled her pulse — "and I want to be able to focus on it."

"I understand." Andrew shifted his hands on the steering wheel, his lower lip poked out in thought. "How long before you'll need to start taking classes on campus rather than online?"

"At least two years, maybe three, depending on the course work," Trina said. "With veterinary science, there are a number of classes requiring laboratory assignments." She grinned. "I can't do those over the Internet."

"I imagine not."

"But for as long as I can, I'll do online classes and keep working at Dr. Groening's — oops! Dr. Royer's." She grimaced. "I'm not sure I'll ever get used to that change. It's been Dr. Groening's Clinic my whole life."

Andrew sent her a short, speculative look. "Are you getting along okay with the new vet? I've heard he's knowledgeable but not quite as personable as Dr. Groening."

Andrew had heard correctly as far as Trina was concerned. She toyed with the ribbons of her cap while she answered. "I admit it has been hard for me to warm up to him. He has a way of looking down his nose at me that sets my nerves on edge. But he knows what he's doing. I wish he were more like gentle Dr. Groening in the way he relates to me, but he is good with the animals. That's what matters most." She sighed, admitting, "And even though I still wish I could have taken over the clinic, this has worked out best for Dr. Groening. I'll just have to trust that God has something else planned for me."

Andrew nodded. "His plans are always best, even when we people try to mess them up." He offered a sheepish look. "I'm sorry I tried to mess yours up, Trina."

Trina gave his shoulder a brief squeeze. "It's okay. You had a heartache, and it colored your judgment." She paused then braved a question. "How is Livvy doing? She doesn't say much."

Andrew shrugged. "There isn't much to say. Wishing things were different won't change them. She can't have children, and that's all there is to it. But I haven't given up hope. We've looked into adoption, but it's pretty expensive, so I'm setting money aside each month. When the time is right, if we're meant to be parents, God will open the door."

Trina sat quietly, thinking about Andrew's statement about timing and God's doors.

She'd seen such evidence of God's hand at work in hers and Graham's lives over the past several months. Andrew's words had proven true for her; surely they would also prove true for him.

"I'll pray to that end, too," she said. "You and Livvy would make wonderful parents."

He smiled, giving her hand a pat. "Thanks, Trina. Just pray for God's will."

"I will." She yawned then giggled. "All that studying has worn me out."

"Well, close your eyes and take a little nap. Before you know it, we'll be home, and you can go over and tell Graham all about your examinations."

Trina settled more comfortably into the corner. "Sounds good." The hum of the tires on asphalt provided a lullaby, and sleep claimed her. In no time, someone shook her arm, bringing her to wakefulness. She sat up and peeked out the window, sighing in satisfaction when she realized they were home. Then she noticed a vehicle parked in front of her house, and her feeling of well-being fled.

Andrew pointed. "What's he doing here?"

Trina's mouth went dry. She licked her lips. "I'm not sure, but I hope I haven't done something wrong . . . again."

"Do you want me to stay?" Andrew's

concerned tone offered encouragement.

Trina, knowing neither of her parents was home, nodded. It wouldn't do for her to be alone in the house with Dr. Royer. "Please."

They opened their car doors in unison, and at the same time, Marc Royer swung his door open. He glanced at his wristwatch, a silent reprimand, then met Trina on the sidewalk.

"I've been waiting for you. Can we talk?"

"Of course. Come on in out of the cold." She scurried up the sidewalk, Andrew and Dr. Royer on her heels. Once inside, she gestured to the sofa. "Make yourself comfortable." She sat in Mama's overstuffed chair in the corner, and Andrew moved to Dad's chair.

Dr. Royer perched on the edge of the cushion, with his elbows on his knees, and fixed Trina with a serious look. "I need to visit with you about my plans for the clinic."

Suddenly Trina feared her job was in jeopardy, and she involuntarily sucked in a fortifying breath.

"I believe, to better serve the area communities, I need to expand to two locations — keeping the Lehigh clinic and opening a second one closer to Hillsboro." Dr. Royer plunged on, seemingly unaware of Trina's concerns. "Obviously, this involves quite a financial undertaking, and it isn't something that will occur overnight, so to speak, but it is my long-term goal. I have put together a strategy, based on Dr. Groening's past several years' records and a demography of the area, and I believe within the next five years, I will have the funds to establish the second clinic."

Trina blinked rapidly, absorbing the man's words. If he was preparing to fire her, he had chosen an odd way to do it.

He sat upright. "Of course, with two locations, hiring a second veterinarian becomes necessary. That's where you come in."

Pressing her hand to her throat, Trina gasped, "M–me?"

"If you're interested."

"If?" Trina curled her hands around the chair's armrest to keep from leaping out of her seat and hugging Marc Royer. His timing couldn't have been better if she had planned it! Five years down the line, she'd have her veterinary license in hand, and working at the clinic would let her stay right here in Sommerfeld, just as she and Graham wanted. Swallowing, she forced a calm tone. "Oh yes. I'm interested."

"Good. Then I will refrain from seeking prospects elsewhere. There will be other details to discuss, naturally, but we can cover those at another time." Dr. Royer slapped his knees and rose.

Trina bounced up. "Thank you, Dr. Royer, for giving me this opportunity. I appreciate your confidence in me."

He lifted his chin, peering down his nose in his normal manner, yet somehow it didn't seem condescending this time. "I know I can count on you, and the people of the community already have a relationship with you. So hiring you is in my best interest." He held out his hand, and Trina shook it. "After the first of the year, Groening Clinic will change to the Royer Clinic for the Treatment of Livestock and Domesticated Animals. When you have your degree in hand and our partnership is official, we'll add your name behind mine. Royer and Muller."

"Royer and Ortmann," Andrew corrected. Dr. Royer sent him a puzzled look. Andrew added, "She's getting married in February."

"Ah. Yes. Royer and Ortmann, then. Well." He crossed to the door then paused, his hand on the doorknob. "Keep up your studies, Trina. You'll make a fine veterinarian." He headed out the door.

Trina stared at Andrew in amazement.

"The Royer and Ortmann Clinic for the

Treatment of Livestock and Domesticated Animals." Andrew carefully enunciated each word of the clinic's future name and then whistled through his teeth. "Whew, that's a mouthful. I feel sorry for anyone who has to write all of that on a check."

Trina laughed. "I know. But Dr. Royer is a man of length . . . in all ways!" She spun a happy circle, her clasped hands beneath her chin. "Oh! I can't wait to tell Graham!"

Christmas morning, Trina awakened before the sun's rays slipped over the horizon. Her first thought was *"Happy birthday, Jesus,"* followed by, *"Merry Christmas, Graham."* She would miss him today after seeing him nearly every day since his return from Nebraska, but they had agreed they should spend this day with family. Their time for Christmases together was near — they could wait.

She slipped a robe over her nightgown and crept to the kitchen on tiptoe, intending to start breakfast. But the lights were already on, and a wonderful aroma greeted her. Mama straightened from checking something in the oven.

"What are you doing up?" they both asked at the same time.

Trina, laughing, gave her mother a hug.

"Merry Christmas. I was going to fix break-fast."

"Too late." Mama grinned. "I've got an egg casserole in the oven." Trina sniffed appreciatively, breathing in the scent of eggs, ham, peppers, and onions. Mama put her hands on her hips. "I whipped it up last night after you'd gone to bed so I could surprise everyone."

Trina selected a mug from the cupboard and poured a cup of coffee. "There have been a lot of surprises in Sommerfeld lately."

"Good ones and bad ones," Mama said on a sigh. She stirred cream into a cup of coffee then faced Trina. "But mostly good, I guess. It has been quite a year, hasn't it?"

"A year of change, that's for sure." Trina held the thick mug between both palms. Steam swirled beneath her nose, enticing her to take a sip.

"And more changes coming." Sorrow tinged Mama's voice.

Trina took another sip of the hot coffee and used a teasing tone. "Yes, just think — no more Trina underfoot in another few weeks."

"Well, now," Mama blustered, putting down her cup and swiping her apron across the clean countertop, "I don't think anyone's ever complained about having you underfoot."

Trina's heart turned over, recognizing her mother's penchant for covering deep feelings with brusqueness. "I'll miss you, too, Mama."

For a moment, her mother paused, peering across the kitchen at Trina with her chin quivering. Then she gave a nod and swished her hands together. "Yes, but it's the way of the seasons. Children grow up and move on. It wouldn't be natural any other way."

"I'll make some toast," Trina offered and, at her mother's nod of approval, set to work.

In time, the good smells drew Dad and Tony from their beds, and the family enjoyed a pleasant breakfast. When dishes had been washed, they carried coffee mugs to the front room, where, as had been the tradition for as long as Trina could remember, Dad read the Christmas story from the Bible. Then they prayed together and opened their gifts.

Always practical, Mama and Dad had purchased Trina a set of good cooking pans, and Mama had sewn a half dozen new aprons. Trina gasped when she opened her gift from Tony — a book on the anatomy of cats. He had ordered it online with help from Beth, and he blushed crimson when

Trina assured him it would be very helpful.

Afterward in her bedroom to change for the big family get-together at Grandpa Braun's farm, Trina reflected on the fact that this would be her very last Christmas living under Mama and Dad's roof. Sadness brought a quick sting of tears, but anticipation washed them away. She had a grand future awaiting — a future that included being Graham's wife and following her heart's call. A future designed by God's perfect hand.

Someone tapped on her door. "Trina?" Tony's voice. "Dad's got the car warmed up. Are you ready to go?"

Trina smiled. Oh yes. She was ready to go. With a song in her heart, she called, "I'm coming!"

THIRTY

The Friday evening before her wedding, Trina turned over the little sign on the café door to show CLOSED. She turned and sent her mother a huge smile. "Now the fun begins."

Mama laughed. She slung her arm around Trina's shoulders and led her to the storage room, where a box waited. "Let's get busy."

They spent an hour rearranging the tables to clear a wide aisle and leave a space at the far end of the dining room that would accommodate the minister and the wedding party. Trina scrubbed the tables and booths clean, and Mama draped every table with a white linen cloth. The café took on a festive air when Trina placed a glass bowl filled with colorful mints in the center of each table.

When the dining room was finished, they lined up Crock-Pots along the worktable in readiness for tomorrow's dinner. Although many Mennonite families chose to forgo the wedding dinner, Mama insisted that for her only daughter's wedding they would celebrate with fellowship *and* food. Trina didn't mind.

"I'm sorry you'll only have the weekend before you have to go back to your routine," Mama said as she and Trina walked home. "It would be nice if you and Graham could at least get away for a day or two."

Trina shrugged. She and Graham had discussed the situation, and neither resented returning to their routine, as Mama had put it. They felt fortunate that they were able to follow a normal routine considering how different things could be had the accident been more serious. "Graham and I will have our time away from everyone when we go to a campus. In the meantime, we enjoy being here with our families."

Mama released a sigh that hung heavy on the frosty evening air. "Ah, Trina, it will be strange not having you at home. But I couldn't be happier for you. Graham is a good man, and I believe God will bless your union."

Trina curled her arm around Mama's waist, and Mama pressed her cheek briefly to Trina's temple. Then, in typical Mama style, she tugged loose and scolded, "It's cold. Let's hurry."

Saturday dawned bright and cold. No clouds cluttered the crystal sky, and even the wind stayed calm, providing a wonderful day for Trina's wedding. She slipped the light blue dress over her head, smoothing the skirt over her hips. When she'd modeled the dress for Beth, her friend had snapped a photograph.

"Capturing a moment in time," Beth had said.

Remembering the comment, Trina wished she had a photograph of her with Graham — her in her wedding dress, he in his suit — just to know what they looked like side by side in their finest clothes. Then she closed her eyes and created her own image in her mind. She smiled. Perfect.

"Trina?" Dad stood outside the door. "If you want a ride, you'll need to hurry. Your mother is eager to get to the café and put the food in the Crock-Pots so everything will be hot by dinnertime."

Trina called, "Just let me get my shoes on!" Instead of her typical anklet socks and tennis shoes, today Trina wore flesh-toned tights and black satin slippers. Dad had insisted she remove the little ribbon bows that had decorated the shoes, saying they were too ostentatious for a good Mennonite girl, but even without the bows, Trina thought the slippers made her feet appear delicate and feminine.

"Trina!"

"I'm coming!" She snatched up her coat and dashed out the door.

When they reached the café, several cars and two buggies already waited on the street, and the people followed Trina's family inside.

"Just find a seat," Mama instructed, hurrying Trina into the kitchen away from the others. She whispered in Trina's ear, "Stay in here out of sight. I'll let you know when Graham arrives."

Trina perched on a stool in the corner and listened as more people filled the dining room, their voices cheerful and loud and full of celebration. She smiled to herself. Only a few months ago, she had felt as though the community would never accept her choice to break tradition and go to college. Now here they were, turning out by the dozens to wish her well not only on her wedding day but on her future.

"Thank You, Lord," she whispered with heartfelt gratitude.

A hush fell in the dining room, followed by a wave of excited babble, and instantly

Trina knew Graham had arrived. She jumped from the stool, her heart pounding, gaze glued to the doorway, awaiting his appearance.

Mama rushed over. "It isn't quite time, Trina. Another ten minutes. Sit back down."

Her limbs trembling, Trina climbed back onto the stool and twirled the ribbons on her cap around her finger repeatedly. It occurred to her that after today, she would snip away the white ribbons and replace them with black, a symbol of her new status of wife. *Wife.* A shiver shook her frame, but she knew the cause was excitement. Only a few more minutes, and she would be Graham's *wife!*

The last minutes passed so slowly Trina wondered if the clock had stopped ticking, but finally the voices from the dining room ceased. Mama stepped into the kitchen, her eyes sparkling with unshed tears, and crooked her finger at Trina. Trina skipped across the floor on black satin slippers and delivered a kiss to Mama's cheek.

Mama whispered, "Be happy, my daughter."

"Always," Trina whispered past the lump that suddenly filled her throat.

Mama placed a white Bible trailing with pink and blue ribbon into Trina's waiting hands. Then she took hold of Trina's shoulders and turned her toward the dining room.

Through the open doorway, Trina glimpsed Graham. Her groom. Seated in his wheelchair, attired in a black suit and white shirt, his hair neatly combed and face shining. His eyes met hers, and his lips tipped into a sweet smile of anticipation. She stared, mesmerized, almost neglecting to breathe, as he leaned forward and swiveled the footrests of his wheelchair out of the way.

The soles of his black lace-up shoes met the tiled floor, and he braced his hands on the armrests of the chair. Then his shoulder muscles bunched beneath the black wool fabric as he pushed, and Trina's breath released in a rush when he stood in front of the chair. His dad stepped into Trina's line of vision and offered Graham his walking aid — a cane carved from a length of sycamore, handcrafted by an Amish artisan to resemble a post wound with ivy.

One hand firmly grasping the cane, he held the other out to her, his smile triumphant. With a little cry of joy, she raced to his side. Tears distorted her vision as she slipped her hand through the bend of his elbow, but she blinked the moisture away, determined to memorize every sight and sound from this special day.

Graham pressed his elbow against his rib cage, giving her fingers a squeeze, and then — on two sturdy feet, with the assistance of the beautifully crafted walking stick — he escorted her slowly through the center of the café to the waiting minister. Trina felt the gazes of their gathered guests, but her eyes remained riveted on Graham's strong, proud profile until they reached the end of the aisle.

The minister cleared his throat, and Trina turned her gaze forward. She listened attentively, aware of Graham's pulse pounding through the sleeve of his jacket, surely matching the eager beat of her own. The familiar Bible passages from Ephesians and 1 Corinthians took on a greater meaning when read during her wedding ceremony and applied to her God-given duties as Graham's mate.

She prayed silently, *Let me honor You, Lord, by being obedient to my call as wife and, if You see fit, mother.* At one point, Graham's eyes slipped closed, and Trina sensed he, too, offered a silent prayer. Her heart seemed to double in size, unable to contain all of the joy and gratitude and anticipation of the moment.

At last, the minister asked them in solemn tones to repeat the selected vows. So many had already been put to the test — for richer, for poorer; in sickness and in health — and they had emerged triumphant. Trina's voice trembled with fervor as she vowed to love, honor, and obey Graham from this day until the day she died or Jesus returned. Listening to Graham's deep, tear-choked voice as he promised to love, honor, and cherish her filled her with such a tumble of joyous emotion that she could no longer control her tears. They spilled down her cheeks in warm rivulets.

But she smiled through the tears, laughing out loud when the minister announced to the waiting guests, "I present to you Mr. and Mrs. Graham Ortmann. What God hath brought together, let no man put asunder."

Trina tipped her face up to Graham and begged, "Kiss me, please."

And he did. Willingly.

Hours later, Graham's parents dropped him and Trina off at the house. His mother hugged Trina, kissed her cheek, then said, "Welcome home, my dear."

Tears appeared in Trina's dark eyes, but a smile lit her face. "Thank you. I'm so happy to be part of your family!"

Dad helped Graham into his wheelchair and started to wheel him to the house, but Trina rushed forward.

"No, no!" She laughingly pushed in front of Dad, taking control of the handles. "He's my husband — I'll do the honors."

Mom and Dad climbed back into the car with Chuck, and they pulled away with waves and smiles. When they'd first mentioned spending the night at Graham's grandparents to give him and Trina complete privacy their first night as husband and wife, Graham had protested. They shouldn't have to leave their own home. But when he'd mentioned it to Trina, she'd exclaimed, "Oh, that would be wonderful!" So he'd told his folks to go ahead and make the arrangements.

Now, as she pushed him around the back of the house and up the ramp to their own little deck, he was glad he'd told his family to go. Being alone with Trina — his wife — was a blessing beyond compare. They reached the glass doors, and Trina scampered around the wheelchair to slide the door open.

A pang of regret struck, and he sighed.

Trina paused, looking over her shoulder. "What is it?"

He pinched his lips into a brief scowl. "I wish I could carry you over the threshold."

Trina stared at him for a moment, her eyes wide. Then she hunched her shoulders and giggled. "Okay." With a graceful swirl, she seated herself in his lap and wrapped her arms around his neck. "Carry me in!"

Graham hooted with laugher. He grunted with the effort of pushing both of them over the slightly raised threshold, but he made it, and they celebrated his success with a kiss that lasted longer than Graham knew two people could kiss without losing consciousness.

Finally, the cool breeze through the open sliding door forced Trina off his lap. Once she'd closed it, however, she came right back and made herself at home again.

Graham curled his arms around her waist, relishing the feel of her cheek against his shoulder. They sat for long moments, their hearts beating in synchronization with each other, even their breathing finding a matching pattern that made Graham feel as though they truly had become one, just as the minister proclaimed them to be.

He whispered, his lips brushing the organdy cap of their faith, "I love you, Trina."

She released a breathy sigh, her lips curving upward in a sweet smile of contentment.

"Oh, I love you, too."

Then slowly, he lifted his hands and removed the pins that held her cap in place. Trina sat up, staring at him with her eyes wide and lips slightly parted, as he slipped the cap free and laid it on the end of the bed. Reverently, he smoothed the ribbons into a line over the edge of the coverlet. Raising his hands to her head, he went on a second pin hunt, popping them loose one by one until her hair fell in tumbling, walnut-colored waves across her shoulders.

He smiled, his heart catching at the sight of Trina with her hair down. "As beautiful as I always imagined it." To his ears, his voice sounded husky.

"Oh, Graham . . ." Trina leaned forward, meeting his lips with hers.

He crushed her close, breathing in her scent, twining his fingers through her silky hair. She shifted in his lap, and a shaft of pain shot through his lower back. Involuntarily he grimaced.

She pulled back in alarm. "What's wrong?"

"A pinch in my back, that's all."

She hopped off at once, slipping to her knees beside the chair. "I hurt you?"

The concern in her eyes brought tears to his. She was so sweet. He cupped her cheeks. "Not you. Never you. It comes and goes. But I don't want you to worry about it."

She remained beside the chair, clinging to his hands and peering up at him with love-filled eyes. "Of course I worry about it. I'm your wife. That's what wives do — worry about their husbands."

He grinned. "Is that right?"

She nodded, her hair bouncing. Her long lashes swept up and down in a beguiling blink. "Wives are very busy people. In addition to worrying, they also cook for their husbands, and clean, and mend socks, and do laundry, and —"

"That all sounds very monotonous," Graham said, pretending to yawn.

"Oh, not at all," Trina protested with an innocent expression. "It's pure joy when you love the person very, very much."

"The way you love me?"

"Of course."

Graham chuckled. "So what else do wives do?"

Slowly, Trina shook her head, her eyes twinkling with mischief. "Oh no. Now it's time for you to tell me what husbands do."

"Ah." He nodded, narrowing his eyes and trying to appear wise. "The husband's duties . . ." He stroked the length of her hair,

419

catching a silken strand and twisting it loosely around one finger as he recited, "Husbands provide for their wives and protect their wives and listen to their wives and —" He gently tugged Trina close and whispered a husbandly privilege in her ear.

She jerked back, her eyes wide, and gasped, "Graham!" But then she erupted into giggles.

His laughter rang, too, and when it died out, she rose and held out her hands.

"You said husbands listen to their wives, so . . . come out of that chair, Mr. Ortmann." The love light in her eyes sent a shaft of warmth through Graham's chest. He pushed himself free of the chair, and she tucked herself beneath his arm and walked him to the bed.

He sat on the edge of the mattress, and she curled next to him, nuzzling her face into his neck. All teasing left her voice as she murmured, "Of all the blessings of the past year, Graham, you are the one I treasure most."

Graham wrapped his arms around his wife — his greatest blessing. He searched for words to convey everything his heart felt, but in the end, the only thing that found its way from his lips was the simple statement, "How I love you, Trina."

And her smile told him those words were
enough.

ABOUT THE AUTHOR

Kim Vogel Sawyer is wife to Don, mother to three girls, grandmother to four boys, and a former elementary school teacher. A lifetime writer, Kim travels to women's groups to share her testimony and her love for writing, tying together the skill of writing a good story with the good plan God has for each life. She is very active in her church, where she serves as adult Sunday school teacher and participates in the music ministry in both vocal and bell choirs. Please learn more about Kim's writing and speaking ministries by visiting www.Kim VogelSawyer.com.

The employees of Thorndike Press hope you have enjoyed this Large Print book. All our Thorndike, Wheeler, and Kennebec Large Print titles are designed for easy reading, and all our books are made to last. Other Thorndike Press Large Print books are available at your library, through selected bookstores, or directly from us.

For information about titles, please call:
(800) 223-1244

or visit our Web site at:
http://gale.cengage.com/thorndike

To share your comments, please write:
Publisher
Thorndike Press
295 Kennedy Memorial Drive
Waterville, ME 04901